One Hell of an Actor

Lauren Bacall
(Beverly Hills
1977)

ALSO BY

GARSON KANIN

PLAYS

Born Yesterday   The Smile of the World
The Rat Race   The Live Wire
Come On Strong

Musicals

Fledermaus   Do Re Mi

Adaptations

The Amazing Adele   The Good Soup
A Gift of Time   Dreyfus in Rehearsal

NOVELS

Blow Up a Storm   Do Re Mi
The Rat Race   Where It's At
A Thousand Summers

SHORT FICTION

Cast of Characters

FILMS

With Ruth Gordon

A Double Life   Adam's Rib
Pat and Mike   The Marrying Kind

In Collaboration

From This Day Forward   The More the Merrier
The True Glory

Original Stories

High Time   The Right Approach
The Girl Can't Help It

Original Screenplays

It Should Happen to You   Where It's At
Some Kind of a Nut

NONFICTION

Remembering Mr. Maugham   Felix Frankfurter: A Tribute
Tracy and Hepburn   Hollywood

One Hell

of an Actor

A NOVEL BY

GARSON KANIN

HARPER & ROW, PUBLISHERS

NEW YORK

HAGERSTOWN

SAN FRANCISCO

LONDON

FIRST EDITION

Designed by Sidney Feinberg

Library of Congress Cataloging in Publication Data

Kanin, Garson, 1912-
  One hell of an actor.
  I. Title.
PZ3.K137On   [PS3521.A45]   813'.5'4   76-47252
ISBN 0-06-012249-8

77 78 79 80 10 9 8 7 6 5 4 3 2 1

To
THORNTON WILDER
(1897–1975)
GENEROUS MASTER
INCOMPARABLE FRIEND

One Hell of an Actor

16 January 1977

. . . and, further, I decided today to abandon, once and for all, the God-damned Tumulty project. The decision depresses me and leaves an inside void until I recall Thornton's saying, "Remember. A writer's best friend is his wastepaper basket." In any case, there is no alternative. I cannot come to grips with it in any form. Odd, though, that in giving it up, I am not certain what it is that I am giving up. A play, a movie, a history, a short story? What? Since the day I made the first note on him, Tumulty has been a figure in every sort of form and frame. A lusty, exciting, lovable, but maddeningly elusive character. I wonder if I know too much about him, or too little.

Will I ever know why I failed with Tumulty? There was no mistake, so far as I can see, in the beginning. All characters in fiction are modeled, to a greater or lesser degree, on persons whom the writer has known or observed or heard about. This is the raw material which, fed into the furnace of imagination, begins the creative process.

The first time I heard of Tumulty, I experienced the unmistakable tremor that invariably accompanies the recognition of a good subject. I determined to pursue it. The more I found, the better it felt. His story came to me in bits and

1

pieces, and, since my informants were many, had its share of contradictions. There were many missing links and compound mysteries, but the time came when, convinced that I had enough, I began to set it down in outline form. I invented material and incident to fill in what I had not been able to find out, but long before I had finished, I saw that it would not do. The joins were clumsy. Truth and fabrication were of different textures entirely. I have since done some rooting around, and have made several additional false starts.

Stuck in San Francisco for eleven weeks while Ruth was shooting *Harold and Maude,* the subject of Tumulty again possessed me—as it always did in San Francisco—and I began again, this time as a film. Streets and buildings, taxi drivers with earthquake memories, the superb newspaper files and morgues, excellent libraries and fascinating bookshops, the old theatres—all were grist to my mill. I enjoyed the work, and doing it in S.F. made it real to me—for a time. Then the contradictions surfaced once more, the unanswered, unanswerable questions came up and I went down. The drama turned into melodrama as I substituted fact for fancies. The good guys and the bad guys kept changing places. Moreover, I became increasingly apprehensive as I recalled the time when, pursuing the truth about Tumulty and his complex relationships, my life was threatened. In time, I saw that the story had run through my fingers again.

Now I mean to stop trying, once and for all. Just for the hell of it, though, I am going to go through the notebook and pick out all the entries labeled TMY, which have been for so many years the code letters by which I have identified notes on this man or ghost or memory or invention(?): John J. Tumulty.

2

5–15–40.   Hollywood.   RKO

Out to the valley on the weekly visit to the Motion Picture Home. Seven of us on the committee, and today only three turned up. I felt martyred and holier-than-thou all the way out.

But an odd thing happened, one that demonstrates the nonsense of planning and arranging too carefully. You never know where or when a subject or a character may turn up. An idea comes to me today by way of what began as a duty chat with—well, call him The Old Actor.

I am not yet sure how to use this. Only a part of the story came to me today, but I hope to get more next time. The main thing, though, is the character. Remember that all the hot works are hot because of their characters. Plots become outmoded, themes fade, but characters live always if they are great characters, such as the one I heard about today. Name: John J. Tumulty. (I will have to change it but doubt I can match it. It is perfect.)

The Old Actor came up to me right after lunch and said, "I should very much appreciate a word with you, sir."

I replied, "You bet!"

It came out far more cheerily and patronizingly than I meant it to, and his gray eyes did not take it well. Anyway, he walked me over to a trellised little summerhouse at the far end of the kitchen garden. Inside it was surprisingly cool and comfortable. The big, built-in chairs around the tree stump table reclined at just the right angle and were unusually comfortable. I mentioned this.

He bowed, slightly. "You are courteous. A great man once said, 'Courtesy is the lubricant of life.' "

I must have seemed puzzled, because he went on.

"You see, I built this structure. Yes. Every inch of it."

"You don't say!"

"I learned long ago that those who work in the realm of the imagination have need to cultivate some manual activity. A matter of balance, don't y'know?"

"Do you—?"

"However, that is *not* what I wish to discuss with you today, sir. There is something more pressing, and I am aware that your time is limited."

"Not at all. I'm here to—"

"I wish to ask you, sir, point-blank, if there is any truth in the so-called scuttlebutt that we are to have a blasted motion picture machine thrust upon us?"

I was amazed to hear him put it so. At the last meeting of the full committee, there had indeed been some discussion about providing a 16-mm. projector and getting the studios to lend prints for screenings; all this while planning the installation of a proper projection room. I did not anticipate that these plans would cause annoyance to anyone. I replied simply, "Yes."

"An outrage!" said The Old Actor. "I speak not only for myself, but for several of the guests here who have been— so to speak—retired from the legitimate stage."

"It was only that we thought," I began, "that it would—"

"Motion pictures, sir, and that even *more* artificial nuisance, radio, have been the death of every solitary . . ."

He went on. On and on. My hearing left him, but not my attention. I studied him, trying to place him in a convenient category. His body was old, although his face was young and always would be. Ten thousand applications of greasepaint

4

had left a glowing, iridescent patina. He was speaking angrily, blaming his inactivity and his failure on science. An old die-hard, I thought. Stubborn, immovable. I nodded politely, pretending to listen, but thought of asking him if he honestly believed that civilization would be better had movies and radio never come to be. Furthermore, what could be more appropriate than motion picture facilities at the Motion Picture Relief Fund Home? This guy, I guessed, must be one of those rare anachronisms: a West Coast stage veteran—and a trifle crazy, no doubt, if there is such a thing as being a *trifle* crazy. I wanted to leave, but reminded myself that this sort of listening was part of my responsibility. I turned my ears on again.

". . . to be a black day for drama, there in Edison's Black Maria," he was saying. "Needless to say, as soon as moving picture offers began coming in, they began to desert the stage in droves. And, mind, at that time it was not necessary to have a voice. They wanted models, not actors."

With his reference to voice, he dropped his own a tone or two and demonstrated its unmistakable richness.

"I chose to stand by him and his theatre," he continued. "I will say nothing of my own modest accomplishments, but it is a well-known fact that John J. Tumulty was the greatest actor produced by America up to that time, and has not been equaled or so much as approached since. I was a member of his company, don't y'know?"

That little laugh, which exaggeration invariably trips, came up in my throat, but I managed to turn it into a cough. Then I said, "Tumulty," being careful to make it a statement rather than a question.

"John J. Tumulty," he repeated, "of Oakland, California."

It seemed my turn to comment, but I could think of nothing to say except "Think of that."

He looked down at me from his sudden height, and said pityingly, "I don't suppose you have ever *heard* of John J. Tumulty."

"Well, I never *saw* him," I said, floundering.

"You are an Easterner, I presume?"

"Yes."

"I thought as much. That explains it. Mr. Tumulty never played in the East, although he was urged to do so time and again. He felt that his mission was here, up and down this great American coast, and he fulfilled it, by God! He gave them what they wanted to see, yes; but he also made them take what *he* wanted them to see. *Shore Acres* one night, and *Richard Three* the next. We were barnstorming in those days."

(Title: *The Barnstormer?*)

I asked The Old Actor when all this went on. He cleared his throat, and spoke impressively.

"John J. Tumulty was born in the year eighteen and forty-nine. He died in the year nineteen and thirty at the age of eighty. 'All this'—as you put it—happened in between."

"Did he leave anyone? Any children?" I asked.

He looked at me, carefully, sizing me up. He offered me a cigarette.

"One of these?" he asked. "Or would you rather your own? These are Turkish."

I took one, in the hope that doing so would help me get an answer. I was right.

"He left a son. Someone you know, perhaps."

He mentioned a prominent film director whom I have encountered a few times. His name, however, is not Tumulty. I inquired about this.

"His *real* name is John J. Tumulty, Junior," said The Old Actor. "He changed it, or had it changed *for* him, back in the silent days, when he made something of a splash as a leading man. He changed it then, and never changed it back." He looked at me, slyly. "Just as well, though, in view of the fact that he is *not*, in point of fact, John J. Tumulty's son."

"Sounds like quite a story," I said, hoping he would continue.

"It is. He *might* have been Mr. Tumulty's son. In fact, he *should* have been. But he was not and is not, although he insists he is. And I well remember the time he claimed he was not."

I was leaning forward, confused but interested. "When was that?" I asked.

There was a long pause. The Old Actor smoked, carefully, treating the cigarette as though it were his last for all time. Nearing the cork tip, he tamped it out, and turned to me.

"Will you be good enough, then, to inform your committee that some of us, many of us, take a dim view of this proposed motion picture intrusion?"

For a moment I wondered what the hell he was talking about. I had been back, way back, with the barnstormers. I had been thinking of roll-curtains and gaslit theatres and Adah Isaacs Menken and jugglers between the acts of *Hamlet;* of Lotta Crabtree, and of this Tumulty. Had he really been a great actor? Could he have been? Without meaning to do so, I was already filling in the bare outline. Hell of a period. Early California. Theatre stuff. Tour de force for an actor.

All this is only background, though. The main thing is the character. I must find out more about him. See old newspapers. They would not have this son story, though. I'll have to get that from this old guy if he'll give it.

"Let me assure you," I answered, "that nothing will be

7

done until every angle has been investigated."

"Thank you, young man," he said, and rose. I wanted to ask him to sit down, please, and go on about Tumulty, but chose patience instead. We parted friends.

That was this afternoon.

The more I think about it, the more I can see the beginnings of a something here, probably better for a film than for a play. We would want to see the company moving up and down the coast—different towns—snatches of different plays. They *did* have between-the-act numbers then, didn't they? Songs, dances, and so on? It feels like fruitful stuff. If I can pump this old guy at the Home enough, maybe I won't have to invent much, just edit and organize.

Do any others out there know of Tumulty? I'll ask around. How about his son, or his not-son? No. Surely nothing there, even if he could be questioned. For the moment, stick with The Old Actor. Caution: Grain of salt. Several grains. It is not a question of his lying or dissembling, it is simply that he seems to be the sort of man given to overdramatization. Also, considering his age, it would be imprudent to trust his memory.

5-17-40

I have been thinking about it a lot. Too much, in view of the fact that Ettinger is still beefing about the ending of TDH. What he wants is twenty great jokes one after another. I don't know twenty great jokes. And I keep wandering off into the Tumulty stuff. Watch it. It may well be that Tumulty is nothing, and in an effort to get away from this chore that I hate, I am building it into something important. It is too early to know, anyhow. The plain fact is that I know little about barnstorming, but hope to get more next weekend. Or should I bother? I could probably invent better incidents than I am going to get. I *would* like to know about the son, though. That was arresting. Oh, well. The facts will doubtless turn to dishwater, and John J. Tumulty will prove to have been just another old hambo.

(Title for this. *The Hambo? The Ham?*)

5-22-40   Beverly Hills.

Out at the Home all day today, ostensibly doing my duty, but actually trying to run down some more of the story. I ought to be ashamed of myself and I am, a little. I looked everywhere for The Old Actor, but he did not seem to be around. Finally I asked Miss Sillcox, who informed me that my friend was not feeling well. I thought, just my luck, something will happen to him before I hear the rest—but it turns out to be no more than a slight chest cold. I went up to his room to see him. He seemed glad to have a caller. I stayed almost three hours. My hunch about this material was right. There is something here, but I don't know what. He showed me through two of his scrapbooks, with a running commentary. Endless photographs of him with John J. Tumulty. I realize it is difficult to tell from photographs, but Tumulty certainly gives the impression of someone special.

For one thing, he does not look like an actor. He is big rather than tall; strong face, soft eyes. In the photographs, he seems to be acting with his whole body, not just his face.

Another thing. No matter how elaborate the makeup, there is never any question as to who is under it. No attempt at disguise, only a donning of character as though it were a costume.

More important than this, today I heard, from The Old Actor, the story of the son. At least, a version of it. He did not seem to mind my taking notes; in fact, it stimulated him. The sound of his voice is still in my ears:

"I trained for the ministry at one time, but abandoned it for personal reasons which I prefer not to discuss. One evening, I happened by a hall in the city of Bakersfield, and noted that Russell H. Conwell was to deliver his famous lecture entitled "Acres of Diamonds." The price of admission was twenty cents. I purchased a ticket and attended. Now all this is doubtless before your time, but Russell H. Conwell was a celebrated figure and it was said that this lecture of his had inspired more young men to do more great things and so on. Well, it inspired me, too, but not in the way he meant it to. I thought him an old windbag, and conceived the idea that I could deliver a better lecture than his with a minimum of effort. I have always had a fine, resonant voice. I am not boasting, merely stating a fact, and in any case, the voice, being God-given, is not a point of vanity. You understand, a voice was important in those days since there were none of your inhuman microphones and loudspeakers and what-have-you. I went to the public library the following morning and set to work. I sifted through material relating to several subjects of interest to me: Jesus Christ, the history of this state, the perils of alcohol. In one week's time, I had evolved a lecture which I entitled "The Conquest of California." I committed it to memory and went to San Francisco. There I called upon a Mr. Gillis, who was the representative of the James Redpath

Lecture Bureau. I spoke my lecture to him—one hour and ten minutes precisely—and was—no surprise to me—engaged at once. My fee was to be fifteen dollars per lecture and I was guaranteed a minimum of three lectures per week.

"Now, in Oakland one Sunday evening, some months following, I was preparing to begin my lecture and, waiting for the audience to assemble, I stood in the wings, chatting with the chairman. Suddenly, there was a great burst of applause in the auditorium. The chairman looked out and informed me that we were honored by the presence of none other than John J. Tumulty and several members of his company. I, quite naturally, affected the pose of being not at all disconcerted, but I was, and to a considerable degree. In those days, you follow, theatrical performances were not permitted on Sundays, although lectures were. I may say that I never delivered my lecture in more spirited fashion than I did that night. The presence of this great artist inspired me. He came back afterward, congratulated me, and invited me to supper with himself and members of his company. I accepted, it goes without saying. Oh, I liked them at once. All of them. As for Mr. Tumulty, he became my idol that night and has remained so to this day. You can imagine my surprise when he asked me whether or not I might be interested in joining his company. I protested that I knew nothing of the theatre nor of the art of acting, but when Mr. Tumulty looked at me and assured me that he would teach me as much as I needed to know, I agreed. This was in the year eighteen and eighty-seven. I was twenty-four years of age, he was all of thirty-eight.

"His leading lady at this time was a part-Mexican girl named Juanita Perez. [Note: This name n.g.] A fine actress she was. *Beautiful* voice. They were very, very close. Ex-

11

tremely so. You understand that in those days, there was precious little of your loose living around a theatrical company of that caliber. Mr. Tumulty was bent on setting a high standard and he put up with no excessive drinking or roistering or fornication. Within the company, I say. But it was no secret about him and Juanita. They scarcely ever took their eyes from each other and their scenes together were truly wondrous to behold. We did a beautiful piece called *The Captain and the Princess.* He played Captain John Smith, and Juanita depicted Pocahontas. I cannot say, for certain, how many times we performed this piece, but I *can* say that its climax never failed to bring tears to the eyes of every member of the company onstage.

"On the night they announced their engagement, we were every one delighted, but not in the least surprised. This was in late January. Our tour was to close in mid-June. That was when the wedding was going to take place, and there was talk of a honeymoon in Mexico, where her people still lived. It brought a jubilant spirit into the company. I daresay there has never been a happier group living together, working together. Then, in March—alas—Mr. Tumulty brought Clay Bannister into the company.

"This Bannister presented himself one afternoon, and asked to be heard. He was, I will say, as handsome a figure of a young man as I have ever seen. A poor voice, but Mr. Tumulty liked him and took him on. That was his way of building the company, don't y'know. He preferred to train his own in his own way, rather than take on experienced players who might have trouble changing their ways to fit in. He used to say, 'I don't want actors who've had years to perfect their mistakes!' A witty man, withal. That explained my presence in the company, and Bannister, and Juanita, who had been a singer and dancer in a cabaret in San Diego.

But the color of the company changed almost at once. Bannister fixed his sights on Juanita and kept them there. Before long, he had his way. We all saw it, except Mr. Tumulty. It's often so, I find. It led to some harrowing moments, I can tell you.

"Rehearsing *The Country Wife,* there was a scene where Mr. Horner kisses Mrs. Pinchwife. That is to say, this Bannister and Juanita. We all stood about, watching. Juanita, with everyone around her knowing, could not perform. He was even worse. Now, Mr. Tumulty was one of the rare stage directors at that time who endorsed realism. He insisted that a kiss be a kiss and not merely a fake. So he showed the boy and then he showed her and he kept putting their faces together and holding them there and making them do it over and over, until not one of us had the heart to look.

"So it went for a time, miserably. Finally, they got too careless; and one day, caught. It was in Bannister's dressing room just before a matinee. Mr. Tumulty behaved differently from what you might expect. No noise, he merely told them both to see him after the performance, that it seemed as though they all three had a common problem to talk out. The boy wouldn't have it and went rushing out of the theatre. For a while, it looked as though we might have to cancel. At curtain time, Mr. Tumulty said he would go on and play the boy's part if I would play his. That was a bad afternoon, I can report. In the face of everything, the poor man had to go through all the love scenes and although I've forgotten the words by now, I recall that every line seemed to cut deeper and deeper. The boy never came back, and by night, Juanita was gone, too.

"There was some talk of closing down, but not from Mr. Tumulty. We kept playing, night after night. His comedy was never more sparkling, the tragedies were never so fierce. The worst times were when *The Captain and the Princess* was on. We were all relieved when that awful season came to a close.

"We reopened four months later. As the holiday season approached, we went to San Francisco with the full rep. The day we arrived, I walked to the theatre with Mr. Tumulty. When we got there, she was waiting for us, Juanita. She looked bad. He went right up and touched her, and he said, 'Just in time, Nita, we open with *The Cap and the Prin.*' She said, 'I can't. I'm sick. I've got to get to the hospital. I need some money.' Mr. Tumulty sent me out to the box office, and the doorman for a hack. And somebody to call a doctor about the hospital. We got her in all right, but she never got out. A few weeks later she had a baby, a boy. This Bannister had diseased her, though, and she went right under, pretty fast. Just eaten away. It was frightful to see."

(I am putting this down as well as I can, far from word for word, but close enough for my purpose, since I don't see that much of this can be used. Some of it might be effective, the theatre stuff especially. Two good scenes there. TMY directing their love scene. Him playing it with her. The syphilis business, of course, hopeless. Maybe could be suggested? No. Doesn't have to be that, of course. But a big worry here is the character of the girl. The fact that it happened so in life —assuming that the story is true thus far—does not make it acceptable for any fictional form. *Why* does the girl walk out on Tumulty with the punk? Because he is younger? Handsomer? Evil eye? Whatever the reason, the moment she does, everything that has gone before fades into a meaningless jumble. Also, the fact that Tumulty is going to assume the care of the child makes it absolutely necessary that the audience share his compassion, and believe in his love for her. This they will not do unless the girl is a completely sympathetic character. Maybe there *is* no long romance involving her and Bannister. Maybe it is just one great explosion. One mad mistake. Does he get her drunk? Does he rape her? No. Too sordid. On the other hand, as the old boy told it, I must say I did feel sorry for her. Why? How can this be translated into dramatic terms that will make the audience go along? The truth, in this instance, simply isn't quite good enough, or full enough. Either she was in love with Tumulty or she wasn't. If she wasn't, there is no situation. If she was, then how explain this thing with the Bannister character? In life, nothing has to be explained. In a story, everything. Well, set down the rest of The Old Actor.)

"Of course, Mr. Tumulty hung onto the boy and reared him. In some ways, we all had a hand in it. That child was a part of the company from his first day. He wasn't a year old when he was carried on in *East Lynne*, and by the time he was four, he was going on in the olio with Mr. Tumulty. You know, those divertissements between the acts. Along about then, we put *Little Lord Fauntleroy* into the rep, and the boy played in that. Oh, he got to be in them more and more—*Mrs. Wiggs of the Cabbage Patch* and *Oliver Twist* and *Peck's Bad Boy*. People got to know him and he became a fine novelty attraction.

"Mr. Tumulty was all the time teaching him and showing him how to do this and that and after a time, had him playing all sorts of things. He did his share of beards, too. It was funny, sometimes. There they'd be: Mr. Tumulty playing the lead and the boy, all made up, impersonating Mr. Tumulty's father."

(Potential comedy scene here. Also, if a film, I can see a series of scenes of the boy growing up via scenes from plays with Tumulty. The curtain going up and down, maybe? See him do a little song and dance with Tumulty first. Then a scene. A number alone. Another scene. And so on. Huckleberry Finn? This section not bad. Did Tumulty adopt the kid legally? Whether he did or not, should he do so in the story? Schooling? What about this? Ask next time.)

"There was something developed later and no one mentioned it. The few of us left in the company who were there in the Juanita time began to notice how much the boy looked like his father. His real father, that is. Clay Bannister. It was enough to give you a turn now and then. One time in *Under Two Flags,* he was no more than seventeen, he put on a dark base and a mustache to give him age, and when he walked on for the dress rehearsal, I looked at Mr. Tumulty and saw him go dead white. None of us ever mentioned any of this, though.

"When the war came, Johnny went into the Navy, and when he came back, he was not the same. Mr. Tumulty wanted him to play *Hamlet,* always a safe bill, but he balked. He referred to it as 'gobbledygook' and that was the first time they clashed. Before he'd gone away, he'd looked up to Mr. Tumulty. Now he looked down. Where he'd once thought of the Tumulty company as big-time, he now considered us provincial nobodies. I suppose if Rose Adriance hadn't been with us at the time, the boy would've left. Rose would have kept anyone anywhere, she was that lovely. The entire company was in love with her, from Mr. Tumulty right down to the bill-poster. But the match was with young Johnny. Mr. Tumulty produced them in *The Taming of the*

16

Shrew. Delightful. And somehow, Johnny didn't think of Shakespeare as 'gobbledygook' any longer. Young John had been a considerable tomcat up to this time. We none of us knew how much Mr. Tumulty knew about his activities and we none of us ever told him. But this thing with Rose slowed him down. Stopped him, almost. Note I say 'almost.' Rose was not the kind you could loose around with. Maude Adriance was in the company—her mother—and kept a sharp eye. A strait-laced old party, *she* was.

"Johnny started playing a fairly mean game, carrying on with this one and that one, for no other reason than to devil poor Rose, and it worked. Mr. Tumulty was troubled and he talked it over with me, among others. By then, I believe I was the only one of the old company left. He wondered whether or not to tell the boy who he was. I advised in the affirmative. My point was that he would find out sooner or later in any case, and it was best coming from Mr. Tumulty. So Mr. Tumulty took him down to the Monterey Peninsula one Sunday and spent the night at The Mission Inn, and told him the whole story, omitting not a jot or tittle. It shocked young John. He seemed dazed by it and thrown off his balance. It even showed in his playing for a time.

"Then we did a Los Angeles week, at The Mason Opera House, and when we left, Johnny stayed behind with one of your moving picture contracts. He went big from the start, though from what I saw of his work, I couldn't see why. I resented his success, but in some curious way, Mr. Tumulty considered it a matter of pride. Young John had about ten years of going up, up, up. They were the same ten years of Mr. Tumulty going in the other direction. I speak of the commercial aspect. He was acting better than ever before, but business fell away steadily. More and more of your blasted leaping tintypes took the theatres, and traveling—

17

trouping, I should say—became impracticable.

"It was during the war that Mr. Tumulty decided to establish in San Francisco, and stay. There was one small theatre available, The Grand Opera House. Why it was called that, I have never guessed to this day. It was not a house, did not play opera, and certainly was not grand. He asked me what I thought of the idea and I said I thought it was splendid. He then confessed he was out of funds and that his credit was exhausted. I inquired as to the needed amount and he said that seven thousand dollars would get things under way. My savings amounted to eleven thousand. I offered the seven, and to my surprise he *took* it! That was the beginning of Tumulty's Grand, as it came to be popularly known. I was paid back in time, every cent. And paid back even more by those years up there. In spite of adversities, Tumulty's Grand lasted almost as long as he did.

"I attended the showings of each of the new moving pictures young John appeared in, but never saw him again in the flesh. Mr. Tumulty did, though, from time to time. He would go down to visit him. Never the other way about. We laid off one Holy Week, and Mr. Tumulty went down to Los Angeles. When he came back, he was suddenly old. Something had happened. I don't know what, but he was changed, from that day."

Big help, this, I thought. "Something had happened." What? And clearly no way of finding out. Also, as the narrative built, I found it full of holes. The Old Actor was speaking with such authority that he gave the impression of knowing the whole story. But I suspected he did not. For example, how to explain the petering out of the

Johnny-Rose relationship. The OA tells me that they were apparently stuck on each other, that had it not been for her, Johnny would have left long before. What keeps all this from resolving itself then? What is the barrier? Age? No. Religion? No. Family? No. What? On this particular point, I interrupted and inquired. He obviously did not know, so pretended it was something he did not want to talk about, but I think he simply does not know. (I realize that a piece will have to be invented here if this episode is to be used.) But he went on.

"After a time, Mr. Tumulty began to behave strangely. He talked of marrying Rose. Imagine it! She was easily thirty years his junior. But then, praise be, before anything so foolish could happen, she and young John got together."

"Married, you mean?" I asked.

"Oh, yes. Indeed."

"What happened, then? Because they're not married now, are they?"

"No, no, he's married to that Italian woman used to be a movie star."

"And Rose Adriance?"

He thought hard for a time, apparently blowing on the embers of his memory. Finally he spoke, slowly. "I—don't—know. She died, I believe. Anyway, she had left him just before it all went smash. Saw it coming, probably. They'd made several movies together."

"I thought you said she was so nice."

"Did I? Well, people change. At any rate, I lost track of her."

(No matter. All this is outside the realm of the story. The thing to do is to focus on Tumulty.)

"When your talkies came, young John suddenly failed, along with some of the other big guns. You remember I told you about his father's poor voice? Nasal and all? Well, Johnny had inherited it, along with the good looks. While he was with us, Mr. Tumulty had him working and practicing daily, but in the silent moving pictures there was no need, so Johnny let it slide. He was one of those whose natural voice did not match his physique. The effect was laughable, and he was washed up almost overnight. But then he did a surprising thing. He took a trip around the world, stayed away a year or more, and when he came back he'd bought several European plays and movies and had signed up this Italian girl. He went straight into the movie business as a director and producer, made a go of it, and, of course, there he is to this day."

I said, "He sounds as though he was a better businessman than his father—than Mr. Tumulty."

"He most certainly was. Mr. Tumulty had no head for figures at any time. He was generally broke, and if he ever had any extra money, he'd put it into a new production. Yes, that was Tumulty."

(What was? So far, there is a great deal of incident, but it doesn't tie together. And the whole thing is oddly lacking in climax. Maybe something can be built out of that last cock-eyed triangle. Young John walks out on Rose, finally Tumulty says he is going to marry her, and this somehow swings young John back into the picture. Somehow. Was it a stratagem of Tumulty's? And what about her? Did *she* ever know about Tumulty's plan or desire? Long way to go on this, but it is still interesting.)

20

2–3–41   Beverly Hills.

A long time since I have added anything to the Tumulty saga, mainly because I have had nothing to add. I have seen The Old Actor several times, but he talks of other things. I think he feels I am pumping him about Tumulty. So he clams. On any detail, that is. He keeps saying, "I don't know" or "I don't remember." Maybe he doesn't. In any case, that well seems to have run dry. I suppose what will happen is that someday I'll come across a story or incident or character that will match up with this material and act as a sudden catalytic agent. I have often noticed that most workable ideas are really two ideas. Male and female? One lies there until fertilized by the other. Sometimes you get a locale, then comes a story to fit it. Neither one good without the other. Together, yes. Sometimes, two characters match up. Or two incidents. Or a theme and an incident. Or a character and a place. With all the Tumulty stuff I have, it still needs that other dimension, that second sex.

June 1, 1941   San Francisco   The Mark Hopkins

My first leave from Fort MacArthur and I head for San Francisco. Walking around, I begin to think of Tumulty. I am grateful to anything that will take my mind off the barracks life, a truly dehumanizing experience. I ask two

21

cops in turn if Tumulty's Grand is still standing. Neither one knows. I go around to The Geary Theatre and ask the box-office man. He says it was torn down years ago, but tells me exactly where it was. I go over there. A garage.

At the first-rate San Francisco Public Library, I look through some old newspapers. There is only material published since the earthquake, or—as they touchily prefer to call it here—the fire. There is a lot about Tumulty. The Old Actor may not have been exaggerating as much as I thought. Tumulty is not only brilliantly reviewed again and again, but *seriously* reviewed. Moreover, he is often panned in a way that leads one to believe he set a standard so high they would not permit any letdown. Many references to his power, which appears to have been generated without rant. He was, undoubtedly, one hell of an actor.

6–3–41

Still in San Francisco. I should have gone to L.A. yesterday but got held up on Tumulty business. No matter. Right now, I'd rather be up here anyway. The climate is less enervating, personal problems not present, also plenty of places to stay up late, consequently sleep better.

My friend John Hobart is the drama critic here on the *Chronicle.* I ask him if there are any very old men at the paper who have been there for a long time. He says he will find out. This morning he calls and says there are two and do I want them sent C.O.D. or what. I ask him to set one up for lunch and one for a drink later.

He says, "The sooner the better, boy, I can't guarantee these lads are going to last. They are really what I call *ancients!*"

>>> <<<

Just back from lunch at the Salmagundi Club with the first. Amos Craley (or is it Kraley?). Venerable, indeed. He is an editorial writer, and has been for years. He knew Mark Twain when Twain sailed to New York from S.F. and wrote a series of "letters" back to the San Francisco *Herald*.

After two drinks (he ordered "bourbon and branch") and a pleasant warmup, I began: Did he ever know John J. Tumulty? The old gentleman looked startled, put down his fork, and stared out the window.

"Good living Lord," he said, "I haven't heard that name articulated in a hundred years." Then he said it himself, seeming to taste it, almost, "J. J. Tumulty. Best damn actor I ever saw in all my life."

"Do you really think that, or was it that you were more impressionable in those days?"

"Who knows?" he answered. "You know who his son is?"

"Yes," I blurted out, like a goddamn fool. Kraley picked up his fork and went on with his lunch. How could I have made such an amateurish blunder? Obviously, the way to find out anything is to seem to know nothing. I thought I had put a cork in this guy for sure. Luckily, he went on.

"There used to be some scam around about how he was not really Tumulty's own son." (Odd to hear this sort of new slang coming out from above the stiff, starched collar. Newspaper office, I suppose.) "Some ten-twent-thirt bunk about the kid having been dropped by some poor little ingénue in his company, and adopted by him. Nothing to it, of course. I knew them both, father and son. Hell, they looked alike.

23

Even acted alike, there for a time."

"I understood Mr. Tumulty had never married," I said.

He looked at me, with a pleasant little leer, and said, "I didn't say he had!"

(The confusion depressed me and I wondered if I was not wasting time. Wasn't all this effort of mine an evasion of the creative job of work to be done? After all, I am not thinking of a definitive biography or a piece of straight reportage, so what does it matter which version is true? Use the one that best suits the story or invent a third, if need be. Or can it be, I begin to wonder, that I am just plain nosy? Still, I pressed on.)

"Well, it's pretty generally agreed, anyway, that he was a good actor. What else was he?"

"In the truest sense of either word," replied Kraley, "he was a gentleman and a scholar. That was a day, remember, when actors were considered faintly immoral and indeed some were. Tumulty dressed well, spoke well, and could have coached a diplomat. He drank, yes, but seldom in public. The lady-folk of the town were gone on him, and without knowing it, I suppose a good many of us used to imitate him, or try to. He set the fashion, if you gather my meaning. He read everything, knew Spanish and French, talked brilliantly, and listened even better than he talked—now, *there's* a rare talent. He was strong, too. We came through the great fire together, and his behavior was exemplary— physically and spiritually heroic."

He stopped, fork poised, looked off into distant recollection, and began to describe what he saw there. "Then there was the occasion he and his son had the fist-fight. I was on the sports desk then and was supposed to be an expert in the field of prize fighting. He came to me—Tumulty did—and announced there was to be a match between him and his youngster. I told him not to be a damned fool, that men got hurt swinging on each other. He said he knew it and asked me if I could give him a few pointers. I said I certainly could and that the first pointer was to call it off. He said, no, it had to be. That he and the boy had had a roaring set-to and that the boy had said if he wasn't his father he'd paste him. That was when JJ said, 'Well, I'm *not* your father, so let's step over to the Athletic Society in the morning and see what happens.' This may have been how the rumor got started about JJ not being his father, but it was no more than a crack, as I see it.

"The next morning—it was a cold Sunday, as I remember —we turned up at the Athletic Society. There was the boy, looking as though he knew he was up to something wrong, and six or seven men who happened to be in the gym. JJ and the boy took off their shirts and put on the gloves. It was agreed to fight three rounds. In those days, rounds were five minutes long. They went to it. The young one was faster, of course, but wild. JJ stood his ground well, and kept cool. Each time the young one rushed in, and he did so often, JJ would paste him, hard. The old boy seemed able to handle just about everything the young one was throwing. I'd have called the first round a draw, with maybe the young one having an edge. The second round, the boy came in slowly and led right off with a fine cross. At this, old JJ sang out, 'A hit! A hit! A palpable hit!' This was only the beginning. He began clowning and saying some line out of a play for anything that happened. If he hit the young one or if one of them missed; and when he slipped, he stayed on his knee and did several appropriate lines from *Richard the Second* about—oh, you know:

'Dear earth, I do salute thee with my hand,
Though rebels wound thee with their horses' hoofs:
As a long-parted mother with her child
Plays . . .' something something—then:
'So, weeping, smiling, greet I thee, my earth,
And do thee favours with my royal hands.' "

(I am impressed. The damnedest people know the damnedest things.)

"Well, pretty soon, the young one couldn't help smiling, then they both got to laughing, and it was a mad thing to see, these two laughing but still going at it hammer and tongs. Then the young one got a bloody nose, some of it got onto JJ's gloves and he started on that 'Lady Macbeth' stuff, I forget the words, but all about the perfumes of Araby—that one. And it wound up that way. The bell rang and they threw their arms around each other and we all went up and had a second breakfast with beer. Lord, I haven't thought about that mad morning for years, but it's not the sort of thing one would forget, would you say?"

(Thank you Mr. Kraley! Craley? This is more like it.)

June 4, 1941   Fort MacArthur   The PX

The second old guy turned out to be empty. Hobie brought him over to the St. Francis for a drink. He was lean and nattily dressed and even older than Craley. His name is Fritz Immerman. I asked him if he knew John J. Tumulty. He said of course, and launched into a wandering reminis-

26

cence that had me winging until I realized he was talking about the wrong man. When I straightened him out, he seemed to remember, but only vaguely. He said the doorman at The Alcazar Theatre had once been an actor in Tumulty's company. He thought so, anyway. I hoped a few extra drinks would jog his memory, but they only stewed him and it wound up Hobie and I had to take him home. (I told Hobie I was scratching around for some background on Tumulty and his times. Hobie said he would keep an eye out.) I had to call Abe to tell him I might not get down to L.A. this leave, and then there were a lot of other distractions (best left unrecorded).

By the time I got to The Alcazar Theatre, the day doorman had left. Since he is the one I am looking for, it had to wait until today. I would have done well to skip it, because I am now more bewildered than ever.

I got to the Alcazar around noon. The doorman was a small man and, I felt certain, not my party; there are few small actors. I chatted with him for a few minutes, faking, then asked if he had ever heard of T. He looked at me, turned away, and spat.

"*Heard* of him! I was in his goddamn *company* for six years."

"I suppose you remember him well, then?"

"It would be pretty hard to forget as big a son of a bitch as *he* was!"

"John J. Tumulty?" I asked, amazed.

"John J. for Jesus—*he* thought—*Tumulty!*"

I sat down. He went on, as sore at me as at the memory of Tumulty.

"I come down from Seattle to join him," he said. "Comedy and second business. Them days it was well known in the profession, there was two sure spots for short men. Mansfield

27

in the East, Tumulty in the West!"

He stood up. About five-five, I would judge.

"Why was that?"

"Because they were runts themselves, the two of them, and they wanted runtier ones around to make themselves look tall."

"I had the impression Tumulty was rather tall."

"You did, huh? Well, if you know so goddamn much about it, what're you asking *me* for?"

I shrugged. He went on.

"He was no more than a half a head taller than me. He was a runt! And a heart to match, what's more!"

This was a hell of a note. I thought back to The Old Actor for a moment and realized that he, too, was short. Could there be any truth in what this bird was saying? If so, where am I? I mentioned The Old Actor's name.

"*That* horsecock! He still kicking? I'm sorry to hear it. He was Tumulty's spy. We all knew it. He couldn't act his way out of a wet paper bag, but he got kept around to do odd jobs and spying and lying. *Another* runt. There was this one time Tumulty—that's right, the great JJ himself—went and got this Mexican ingénue in the family way. So what does he do? You want to know, I'll tell you. Blames it on some dumb juvenile and throws him out of the company. And what does the ingénue do but kill herself. Then he gets this kiss-ass to spread around how he's going to take care of the poor little bastard anyway. Because of his big heart."

"Were you with the company when Juanita was?"

"Who's that?"

"The boy's mother."

"No, I wasn't. Anyway, that wasn't her name. It was something else. I forget."

"I see."

28

"The kid was wise to him, though. His own kid. He took no guff from him and made off first chance he got. He's a big Hollywood shot now. I done some bits for him before I retired. He hated the old man's guts. Go down and ask *him*, why don't you? And the old scrounger coming around regular for a touch. Everybody knew it. He sponged right and left to the bitter end! Especially off his kid. It was like a blackmail, practically. And all that cowflop about no drinking in the company. Why, the old pirate had a trunkful of bottles right in his own damn dressing room all the damn time I ever knew him!"

(He continued the tirade, but I only half-listened. What is it about the quality of some testimony that makes it unbelievable? Two witnesses under oath tell conflicting stories. You believe one, you disbelieve the other. Is it in the matter itself? Or in the personality of the teller? Surely, the latter is unfair. An unattractive, arrogant fool might be telling the truth. For all I knew, this man was. But I didn't believe him, that's all. So Tumulty hired short actors. What about it? That might have been no more than intelligent stagecraft. Bottles in his dressing room? Probably true, but no matter. Juanita killed herself? I assume this could be checked. Are there hospital records? Hell, too late. They would be gone in the earthquake—sorry, fire. As to the little doorman, I tipped him a dollar and had better forget him. He'll cloud the image if I take him seriously. He probably had some private feud with T and has never forgiven him. Come right down to it, everyone is a son of a bitch to someone. True. Ask around. It would be hard to get a one hundred percent report on *anyone*. The most celebrated actors have their detractors. Frequently honest. I have heard it said that Tos-

canini is a bum and that Renoir was a fraud. There is no
Supreme Court of judgment and taste, and a good thing,
too.)

3 June 43   Washington.

TMY. Tonight, a cool evening at last and we are able
to walk. These wartime Washington dinners at 5:30 provide
long evenings, if nothing else. Ruth and I get to talking
about styles in acting. How do they come about? How and
why do they change? We have been married for six months
and she amazes me daily. Among other things, she knows
more theatrical history than anyone I have ever encountered, and so I suppose I should not have been surprised
when she mentioned John J. Tumulty. I stopped and looked
at her.

"What is it?" she asked.

"How do you know about *him?*"

"I don't much, but Laurette Taylor once said he was the
most original actor she ever saw."

"Did she ever work with him?"

"I think not. She and Charles Taylor had their own company then, but she used to see Tumulty a good deal. He
may have influenced her in some way, maybe without her
even knowing. That's what I mean about style, that it isn't
always—"

"Wait a second. Let's stay on Tumulty."

"Why?"

I told her. It took hours. She asked questions, to some of

which I had answers. (Could Laurette help? Not much if she knew him only as a spectator. Still, I must get with her someday soon and ask.)

Later, sleepless, I try to use the perspective given me by intervening time to see the shape of the Tumulty story. Beginning, middle, end. Or is that, in itself, out of fashion? Does a portrait need a beginning, middle, end? TW says, "The business of literature is to describe human beings."

Maybe I should dig no more but simply attempt to lay out a scenario with JJT and Big Director (hereafter known as BD) as the leading characters; Juanita, Clay Bannister, Rose Adriance, and the others as the supporting cast. Of course, it's a story. A California company of traveling players. (Tumulty: Spencer Tracy?) A romance with Juanita, CB hired, he and Juanita, the child, the adoption. The boy becomes, to all intents and purposes, Tumulty's son. Now what? Where does it lead? All the real stuff from there on in is not good. Why not? Unhappy. What's wrong with that? Muddy. That *is* bad.

There are a couple of valuable elements. One: the boy succeeding by imitating the old man. Two: Wait. How would this be? Hollywood, early days, an estrangement of some sort. (Over the girl?) The boy stays in Hollywood. Makes good. T struggles. Later, the boy, in professional trouble, remembers a sure-fire play and performance—brings T down to make a picture. Late-life recognition. Like Marie Dressler. Frank Bacon. Always moving, this notion. The End. Anything? Who knows? These days, with everything that is going on, all this spellbinding and yarnspinning seems pretty damned hollow. Some other time, if there is to be some other time.

31

4–3–50   New York.

TMY. Damnedest thing. Last Tuesday, a call from Larry at Metro. They are putting my screenplay, OMT, into production. I had pretty much written it off after all these years. Larry asks about my availability for the polish job. I told him if it got polished any more, the plating would come off. I reminded him that it was not, after all, pure gold. Or even pure pewter. He made a big thing about the necessity of three or four weeks with the director (when they got one) so I told him to call Abe and fix it up.

This morning—and here comes the aforementioned damnedest thing—I hear that the picture is going to be directed by none other than BD, who is, of course, John J. Tumulty, Jr.!

There seems to be an odd fate pressing me toward the TMY story. Or can it be that *I* pressed *fate?* True, I brought up his name in a talk with Larry, who said, "No, he's an old warhorse, and I'd like to get a *young* warhorse." But maybe that planted seed . . . ? In any case, I will now get to know the man. Here I want to warn myself about being too eager. So far as he is concerned, I have never heard of T. I must remember not to ask questions or so much as bring up the subject. If he ever brings it up, I must remember not to pounce. And try to avoid cleverness and hinting and all that. I am no good at it, even if I think I am.

32

May 12, 1950   M-G-M.

TMY. First meeting with BD. He is an hour and a half late. I had to go over to Twentieth to see him since he does not report here until next week. He has an elaborate bungalow there. I am told to go into his office and wait. The place is full of Tumultyana. There is an oil of John J. Tumulty, Sr., done from a photograph I have seen. Red hair. Blue eyes. Square jaw. Striking. T as Richard III. On the wall, a framed photograph of Edwin Booth and a letter. I copy it, fast.

THE BAY HOTEL
113 SUTTER STREET
SAN FRANCISCO

18 August '86

My dear Tumulty,

Allow me to commend your spirited depiction of Don Quixote last evening. It is a role I have studied, although never played, thus am familiar with its [word I could not make out] pitfalls.

I regret that I shall not have the pleasure of seeing you in any of your other roles this week, as I must begin the [another scrawl] journey instanter.

Believe me, sir, to be

Yours respectfully,

Edwin Booth.

33

The great man turns up at 11:20 for our 10 o'clock meeting and starts with a simple "Hello, there." No apology for being so late, no explanation, nothing. I dislike him at once. He orders coffee (for himself), invites me to tell him the story, says he has only glanced through the script. My impulse is to tell him off, and I believe that were it not for the fact I want to mine him, I would have. I tell the story, badly. When I finish, I say, "I haven't told it well, but that's the general idea."

"No," he says, "you haven't told it well, but I will. That's my business."

With this for openers, I find it hard to explain how I wind up a couple of hours later, stuck on the bastard. For one thing, he is a relaxed man. Well, I would be, too, in his position. More than that, he is sensitive to the right things. He asks questions, listens to the answers. His casting ideas are original, inspired. Above all, he has charm—that most valuable, ineffable quality—and what's more, he knows how to use it. (I kept thinking he looked like T, but this may have been eager imagination at work.)

He doesn't like the airport scene, and he doesn't like the ending.

"Maybe if you read it a little more carefully," I suggest.

"Or maybe if you *write* it a little more carefully," he says.

He gets up and begins pacing about slowly.

"It's the same thing wrong in both spots," he says. "Conventional. It always surprises me when you young punks are conventional. That ought to be left to us, the rutted ones. You pick up everything so fast, but all the *wrong* things. The lingo, the switcheroo, the trick finish, the punch line, the sock in the jaw. It's all been done before, hasn't it? You've picked the easy way out here, in two key places. A fight scene to make the hero a hero, and a death

34

scene to make the tragedy a tragedy."

"It *is* a tragedy," I insist.

"The hell you say. The tragedy for this character is not to die, but to go on living. He's no romantic figure, he's a twentieth-century man."

I knew he was wrong, but did not want to say so at once. He kept on talking.

"Now this dim-witted fight scene. That's just an out, so you wouldn't have to write the scene that belongs there. Life's full of scenes, but damned few fist-fights. How many have *you* had? I've had one."

I almost said, "I know."

He stopped pacing. "You'll be surprised when I tell you who my opponent was. My father. That's him, up there." He pointed to the portrait. "I was full of resentments. He was so important and I was so not. We scrapped a lot. He was constantly pushing me to do things—professional things—I didn't want to do. One night, he got so mad he swung on me —and missed. Then he said, 'God damn it, defend yourself!' Well, I didn't want to, but he took me down to the cellar and we squared off. He was a powerful man, knocked me over twice. Finally, I'd had enough and said so. Later, he came to my room and told me he was sorry. I remember saying, 'I respected you till you apologized. Now, I don't.' That hurt him more than any blow I could have struck.

"Anyway, the point is damn few people go around belting each other these days, and the ones who do aren't respected. I know the leading men love it. It makes them seem manly, even to themselves, but it's bunk. And I know it and you know it. What's more, and more important, the audience knows it—or senses it. The audience—that idiot genius."

(Well, now. What the hell was all this? In the San Francisco version, the fight wound up with them friends. In this tell-

35

ing, the opposite. The detail of it, I don't care about. Craley probably had it right. This could be nothing more than a movie director's notion of a better setting. Anyway, he does *talk* about his father. That ought to lead somewhere.)

5–17–50   Metro.

TMY. An incident today, but not sure yet what it means. BD is on the lot now, and except for our continuing dispute re the ending, all is going well. Lunch in the commissary with him today, and on the way back to the office, we run into Frank Whitman. We stop and talk.

Well, it was not as simple as that. We were coming toward him and the minute BD laid eyes on him, he began talking to me and quickened the pace. Frank slowed down. Then he stopped, right in front of us. I feel sure BD would have passed him by.

Whitman is one of my favorite characters around here. A huge old man, tart and sharp. He is something in the exploitation department, I don't know what. The most outspoken man on the lot. When ML, who had been running the studio, died, there was the usual overblown funeral. During the fulsome eulogy, Frank turned to Spence and muttered, "There must be two MLs in that box, boyo, because he sure in hell ain't talking about the son-of-a-bitch *I* knew!" This is typical Whitman. Anyway, the three of us stopped. They shook hands.

Frank: Welcome to our city, sire.

BD: Thanks.

Frank: I've read your script. When do you start?

36

BD: Any year now. As soon as I can get young stubborn here to see the light.

Frank: Well, hurry up and get it in the can. I've got a hell of a tie-up with Gillette for you.

BD: That so?

Frank: Yuh, a free razor blade with every ticket so the customers can cut their throats on their way out.

He laughed and so did I, but BD just said, "Let's have lunch some day."

Frank said, "Sure thing."

That was all. We went back to the office and continued with the cutting, a thing BD does supremely well. After about an hour he stopped to go into his private john. He came out a few minutes later and stood there thoughtfully, buttoning his fly.

"Whitman," he said. "Friend of yours?"

"Just around here a little."

"He hates me."

"Why?"

"He enjoys it."

"I'm surprised. He seems such an amiable old cuss."

"I knew him when he wasn't old, and wasn't amiable. Funny. You think of me as a veteran, but to Whitman, I'm still an upstart."

"I don't know what makes you think—"

"He was a great friend of my father's."

"Tumulty?" I asked, stupidly.

"Yes. As it happens, he's the only father I ever had. How many have *you* had?"

"I meant—" I began lamely. "Well, I don't know *what* I meant."

"You sound like some of your dialogue, boy."

"Because he was a friend of your father's? You think that's why he hates you?"

I dove in without meaning to, without planning it, without thinking.

"Yes," he said, sitting down at the desk. He put on his glasses and added, "Where were we?"

A bonehead play on my part, since it gave the impression of prying. I'll bet it's going to be hard to get him back on the subject. However, the day did turn up a new clue. Whitman.

27 May 50   Beverly Hills Hotel.

TMY. I was right. BD has clammed up. I have tried a few delicate gambits, but no go. However, last night I went out with Whitman, and it was worthwhile. I saw him standing in the lobby after the preview of Arthur's picture—*Annie Get Your Gun*—and invited him out for a drink.

He said, "Sure. Where would you like to start?"

I didn't understand at first, but soon got the idea. His way is to go from place to place, having one drink in each. He says it keeps you from getting stewed too fast, avoids table-hoppers, and is more interesting. I have never had such an evening. Nine places, nine Scotches, and I wound up feeling fine. I suppose the walking in the fresh air in between, or whatever. We started at Musso-Frank's, sitting up at the bar.

As soon as we had ordered, he turned to me and said, "You want to talk to me about your boss. Right?"

"Not particularly."

"You're a liar. Just for that, you can pay all night."

"I'm more interested in his father."

Whitman was astounded. "Why?" he asked.

"I've heard a lot about him and he sounds like an interesting character."

"He was not a character," said Whitman tightly. "He was a man."

"I didn't mean it that way. I didn't mean character that way."

"Look here!" he said with considerable heat. "If what you know about him you know from that clown you work for, you don't know a goddamn thing."

"Other places, too," I mumbled.

"Such as?"

I mentioned The Old Actor's name.

"Holy Christ," said Whitman softly. "Is *he* still breathing?"

"I believe so. We exchanged Christmas cards last year."

Whitman slid off the bar stool. I paid the check, and we began the long pub crawl.

Whitman may turn out to be the best source yet. For one thing, he has an astonishing memory. He recites conversations from years ago in a way that carries conviction. His quotes of various people are repeated in language styled entirely unlike his own and unlike one another. He has not yet been wrong about a date, or a name, or the title of a play or film. He dazzles me.

He loved Tumulty and insists that if he were alive today, he'd still be the best actor going.

"He'd be pretty old, though, wouldn't he?" I ask.

"He'd be about a hundred. You call that old?"

"Yes, I do."

"Balls. I'm damn near that myself."

"No!"

"Eighty-four."

"Well, that's not a hundred."

"They go a lot faster when you get up around here. Furthermore, I have every intention of making it, so don't look at me like that."

"Like what?"

"I'll make it to the century, but I'll take a bet *you* won't! I call a hundred old. Anything under that, no. Charles Macklin was still acting at the age of one hundred and that was in the 1790s, when the average life span was about thirty-five. Acting is healthy, like any other profession where a man can express himself—blow off steam—answer his anxieties—beat his frustrations. I got laid last night—that surprise you? Not only laid but congratulated. This is the middle of the twentieth century, boy. Get with it. . . . I like order. Rules, definitions. Rich is a million bucks. Under that is only well-to-do. Summer is June, July, August. Autumn: September, October, November. Winter: December, January, February. Spring: March, April, May. I pay no mind to weather. I dress and behave for the seasons the way I arrange them. Order. Important."

Was he rambling, or conveying something? Was he getting plastered so early on? In an attempt to get him back onto the track, I asked, "Why won't *I* make it to a hundred?"

"Because the people who live the longest are the ones who mind their own business."

"Right now, my business doesn't seem as interesting to me as John J. Tumulty's."

He laughed. "Go ahead."

"What did he die of?" I asked.

"He died of living."

We went to another place. Ciro's this time. We were both hungry by now, so sat at a table and ate. Trying to soften the

40

impression that I had only invited him out to dig him about T, I asked, "How'd you like the picture tonight?"

"It was a picture. What's the difference? Some people will enjoy seeing it and some won't. Too damn much opinion around, anyway. Used to be, people went to a show or a movie to have an experience, now they go to have an opinion."

Pretty soon we were back on Tumulty. Whitman was drinking more than I was. His pink face became pinker. He talked easily now, enjoying it. It turns out he used to work for T, as business manager—mostly toward the end, in the days of Tumulty's Grand. There were times when they couldn't pay off at the end of the week; Whitman borrowing from banks and sometimes from moneyed people who were glad to kick in something to keep the theatre going. T was not aware of this. Obviously, he had no business sense at all. A few times, the spot gets really tough. Whitman suggests T tap his son. T flatly refuses, although, according to Whitman, BD at this time rolling in it. He tells of the time when it looked as though they were absolutely finished and could not go on. He took a long chance and went down to Los Angeles himself to see BD.

"He was living out on Los Feliz, in one of those mansions, right next door to Wally Reid's place. In San Francisco, old John was living in one bum room. I waited all afternoon—outside, by the way—for him to come home from the studio. God, I wish he'd stayed an actor."

"Good?"

"Worst I ever saw anywhere. That's my point. If only he'd stayed an actor, he'd be on his keister today. No, he had to go and become a director, for which the heel has terrific talent. Well, he got home and the minute he saw me there he was upset. He claimed he thought maybe something had

41

happened to John, but he wasn't pulling any over *my* eyes. I told him we were in bad shape up there and that if John knew I'd come down to ask him for help, it would be the end of me, but that I just didn't know where else to turn and could he help us out.

"What do you suppose he hands me? Naturally, he was in no position to go poor-mouth on me, sitting there in all that luxe. So he puts on a surprise act and tells me he doesn't understand what I'm talking about in view of the fact he had just that week sent John a substantial amount of money! How's that for gall? He knew I'd never be able to check this, so that's how he fobbed me off. Not bad, eh? 'I can't do any more than I can do,' he said. Then he asked me if John knew about the squeeze, and I said no, I tried to keep as much as possible from him so as not to affect his work. Then he said he thought I ought to tell John and he was sure John was in a position to handle it. That settled me. I remember as I was leaving, he says to me, 'Let me ask you something. Do you think he's serious about this mad plan of his to marry Rose?' Rose Adriance was our leading lady at the time. Lovely girl, but as John was sleeping with Maude, her mother, our comedy lead, I didn't think it was likely. But I could see the idea was troubling this prick, so I said, 'Yes, I think he *is* serious. *Very* serious.' 'Couldn't you talk him out of it?' 'Why should I?' I said, and left."

"Where do you suppose he'd heard this?"

"God knows. Made it up for all I know, to make the old boy look nutty. Anyway, I brooded about all this for a time, then went to John and put the whole thing up to him. I told him we needed four thousand and if we didn't get it, we'd have to close. John said, 'Well, we close, then, because I don't own four *hundred* let alone four thousand.' And that was the end of Tumulty's Grand."

"What'd he do *then?*"

"Oh, he worked. Jobbed around. Put on something now and then. Went into some of the road shows. He was still popular. I don't know for sure what he did, day to day, because the company disbanded. I saw the handwriting, so I went to work for the Vitagraph Exchange in Denver and lost touch for a while. Rose Adriance, by the way, a short time after, went down and married our friend. I never understood her doing that. What I *did* understand was when she left him."

"She's dead now, isn't she?"

"Is she? I'm not sure. No, I heard she lives in Europe somewhere. Maybe not. I don't know. Want to stop in at a nice gentle little cathouse I know? Right above the Strip. You don't have to exert yourself unless you want to. Just sit around a while. They're fine company."

"Some other time. I'd rather talk tonight."

He laughed and said, "Well, damn my eyes! You're the first lad I've ever run into who'd rather talk *than.* Say, how old are you, anyway?"

>>> <<<

It is now a quarter to four, but I don't want to go to bed until I have noted all the important TMY references. If I remember any others, I'll lard them in later.

I'm glad this is only background I'm looking for. If I had to get this story and get it straight, I can see it would be a lost cause. The versions won't fuse. How the hell does anyone ever write a biography? How do they find the truth? It must be guesswork, a lot of it. Remind me never to try.

Some of it hooks up, though. The Rose Adriance story. But how? The Old Actor says that T talked of marrying Rose. Down in Los Angeles the son knew it, probably from T himself. Yet Whitman, though obviously close to T, thought it a lie. And if he is right about the relationship between T and Rose's mother, it gives the whole thing a sort of not-for-children color, all right. I doubt that it is possible to find the true happening here, ever. Probably the only one who could tell it would be T himself. Rose? BD must know where she is, *if* she is.

This hole in the narrative could doubtless be plugged with invention. The angle of father and son competing for the same woman is stale. A switch might be if each of them did not know of the other's intention. Thus the audience would know that T is planning to marry her, or would like to, but before he can get to it, she is off with the son. No, no good.

What if T thinks she and young John belong together, and uses this means of waking young John into action? What the hell, for all I know, this may be the *true* version.

4 June 50   Beverly Hills

TMY. The picture is shooting. I have not seen any of the dailies (haven't been invited), but the reports are good. BD calls me now and then and asks me to drop over to his place in Bel Air to talk about the stuff he is going to shoot the following day. This is unusual for a big-shot director, and I appreciate it.

Beautiful house. Beautiful wife, Rosella. She is serene and warm, not at all like those passionate, predatory witches she used to play in the early days of the talkies.

Their home is beautifully organized and appears to be in the hands of a remarkable Englishwoman, Ena Drysdale.

She is a stolid, strong, efficient take-charge. One of those treasures. I envy her employers.

BD is a thorough worker and absolutely concentrated. It is hard to get him to talk of anything but the picture now that he is shooting. Had it not been for the gaffe I made last night, I'm sure the subject would not have come up. It was terribly late, and I was tired. He asked me where I live. I told him, and he started telling about the time when The Beverly Hills Hotel was a country boardinghouse, about weekends there, and how he and Douglas Fairbanks (Sr.) once walked from his house to the hotel.

"All the way from Los Feliz?" I heard myself asking.

"That's right." There was a long pause—too long—during which he studied me. Then he said, "How'd you know that?"

"Know what?"

"Where I lived twenty-five years ago."

"I *don't* know."

"Yes, you do! Don't give me that!" He was angry.

"I think Whitman must have mentioned it."

"How'd he happen to do that?"

"We were just talking."

"About me?"

"No, more about your father, really."

He went over and got a bottle of beer. My glass was empty, but he didn't offer to refill it. I could have used a drop.

"What else did he mention?" he asked.

"He admired your father a lot."

"Everybody did. Including me. My father was easy to admire, and hard to like. He gave a lot of people the impression that they were, somehow, closest to him. Fact is, he was never all-the-way intimate with anyone, with the possible exception of himself. At his funeral, Lionel Barrymore did

45

the spiel. And he started in by saying, 'I was John Tumulty's best friend.' Long silence, you could feel the resentful tension. Then he said, 'And so was each one of you.' It was one hell of an opening, even though it did have an uneasy moment in the middle there. The thing that made it effective was the amount of truth in it. All actors are narcissistic to some degree. My father was a great one, so the quality was more pronounced. He always had trouble keeping the real and the unreal separated in his mind. He was an exceptional man, though. See you tomorrow."

(Damn. The more I find out about T, the less I seem to know. There is probably some truth—or do I mean "fact"? —in every single report. How to sift it out, though? Even that mean little doorman in S.F. couldn't have been *all* wrong. If only there were some way of finding out for certain if BD is his son or not. That would be a key. Maybe someday I'll know him well enough to ask him. I doubt it.)

June 8, 1950   Beverly Hills.

TMY. A shock this morning, as a result of which this may be the last entry with those code letters.
Let me try to recall it exactly. No mail with breakfast today. Too early. At about 10:15, a sharp knock at the door. It startled me, as I was blinders-on concentrated on the new screenplay. The first draft of anything always holds me harder than the next fifteen. Figures. The first is discovery, all the rest self-castigation.
Ruth was out walking, so I went to the door. A bellboy

with the mail. I took it, tipped him, and closed the door. I dropped the mail on the coffee table and was on the verge of going back to work when, oddly, I decided to look through it.

There was not much. The usual fourth-class junk. Some Academy stuff. Bills. And one small, *unusually* small envelope. Pink. A bit larger than calling-card size. Someone announcing the birth of a baby, I thought. Addressed to me in perfect italic handwriting. No return address. I opened it, took out a tiny pink folded card, and read:

> Curiosity killed the cat. Are you a cat? A man? Or a mouse? Or a rat?

That is all. The same perfect hand as on the envelope. So standard that any penmanship teacher could forge it easily. Impossible to identify.

I decided not to show it to Ruth. Not yet, anyway.

I admit at once to being apprehensive. No. That is not the word. "Scared" is.

There is always the possibility that this is a joke. Some joke. The notepaper, the hand, and especially the wording of the message convey to me the unmistakable impression that this is the work of someone not all there. Kooks terrify me.

I must stop rooting around in the Tumulty history. There must be something there—buried there—that someone does not want unearthed. Who?

47

My first guess is BD. But would he employ this bizarre method of threat? I doubt it. He is hard and straightforward and would have no hesitation in telling me to lay off. But would he threaten me? Probably not.

It must be BD. Who else *could* it be? Who would care? Should I face him with it? Certainly. But what if I'm wrong?

For the moment, three things: don't discuss it with anyone; lay off Tumulty; wait till the picture is finished, then have it out with BD.

12 Aug 50   Beverly Hills.

TMY. The picture was sneak-previewed last night in Pasadena. I have high hopes for it. BD has done a sensitive and imaginative job. He was right about my ending. I fought him on it all the way, but it is no good. It may be because of the way he shot everything leading up to it. (Am I making excuses? Looking for an out?) In any case, it is going to have to be reshot. We drove home together and discussed it. (Me with the question of the pink letter on the tip of my tongue the whole time. Even the suspicion colors him in my eyes. What about innocent till proven guilty? Sure, but what if you know it but can't prove it?) As to the ending, I can write it this afternoon. It is not really writing. He has more or less dictated the scene he wants, and that is all right with me. I have no proprietary feeling about the damned thing. You never do, with a picture. You do with a play. I wonder why that is so. I stopped in at his house for a drink, told him how much I thought of his work. He seemed pleased.

48

"How'd old Whitman like it? I saw you talking to him."

"Crazy about it."

"Is that so?"

"All but the ending. I told him you never *had* liked it and would probably reshoot it."

"Why didn't he say anything to *me*, do you suppose?"

"He will, I'm sure."

"No, he won't. The hell with him. One more?"

"Just a weak one. I've got a day's work tomorrow, looks like."

"What's Whitman got against me?" he asked, as he poured. "Do you know?"

"No, I don't."

"You must have *some* idea."

"Why don't you ask *him*?"

"Yes, I suppose I should. I would if I cared enough."

"The older I grow, the more respect I've got for—what's the word?—candor."

"Tell me what *you* think is eating him."

He handed me my refilled glass. The drink was not weak.

"Well, this is none of my affair," I said, "but it looks to me like an old feud and—what the hell?—I suppose it has something to do with what we talked about a couple of months ago—about when he was working for your father."

"Go ahead."

"Whitman's like anyone else. He thinks of Number One, too. He had a good job, a congenial situation, and then, all of a sudden, it was over, and he blames *you* for it. I'm sure he wouldn't put it as crudely as that, but that's how it looks to me."

"What in the name of Christ am *I* supposed to have had to do with *his* job?"

"I guess he thinks you could have kept Tumulty's Grand going, if you'd wanted to."

He looked at me for a long time. A great many years seemed to pass across his face. He couldn't have been acting, he was truly stunned.

"Well, as you say," he began, finally, "it's none of your business. Just the same . . ." He stopped, and seemed to be thinking something out. I recognized the expression. It was one I had seen many times during these last weeks, whenever he was trying to invent an approach to a scene, or solve a problem in staging. After a while, he went on. "When do you think you can give me the new windup?"

"Tomorrow."

"Don't do that. Take your time. The thing about a retake, you're pretty sure it's going to be in the final picture. Let's see, this is Friday—well, Saturday, really. Take the weekend. How about Tuesday?"

"Thanks."

"Bring it over around five, say—and stay to dinner. Then, in case it wants some tidging we can do it in the evening. You realize it has to play—the whole thing—in the attic set?"

"Oh, sure. That's all right."

"Fine."

I said good night, and thanked him again. When I got back to the hotel, I went out for a long walk. I should have been thinking about the scene, but I got all wound up in the Tumulty stuff. There is a story there, but too much of it on the melo side. What does that mean? A heightened, surface unreality. Effect for the sake of effect. False emotion. What Thornton calls "kitsch." But if I can get at the true happening, there is no reason why it *should* have this flavor. What if I told BD I would like to do a picture based on a character

50

like his father? Maybe do it with him? No. Then the whole thing would be seen through a cockeyed prism. It is better to get more of the facts, think them out, then discard them, and do an outline based on the elements but inventing all the way. I still don't get T, though. Is he a hero? A villain? Is he a unique father or an ordinary one? We react one way or another to people we meet; like them or not, in varying degrees; or remain indifferent. Then there are those we do not know personally: figures in political life, or science, or in the arts. We read about them, hear about them, see their photographs and react. In still another, more remote category are the figures in history. I like Molière, adore Ben Franklin, admire Jefferson (but cannot warm up to him), dislike Dreyfus (even though he is a martyr), revel in Mark Twain, disapprove of Thoreau and Marie Antoinette, and so on. Why is it that even after all this time, I have no fixed feeling about John J. Tumulty? And no more than ambivalent reactions? I simply do not know him, although I do know a great deal about him. It goes without saying that until I do have a definite feeling and point of view about him (or the character I mean to base upon him) it would be folly to attempt to write him.

16 Aug 50   Beverly Hills Hotel.

TMY. Last night with BD. Trouble. He read my new finish and did not go for it at all, said it was flat. I suppose it was. He suggested that rather than rewrite, it would be better to start again from scratch. After dinner, I typed and he paced. Jesus, how I hate collaborating! However, we finally came up with something he believes in. I don't know what I think of it, but in the circumstances, that doesn't seem to matter.

It was a little after 2:00 A.M. when we wound it up. He said he would get it to Stenographic first thing in the morning, and that was that.

As I got ready to leave, he said, "Don't go yet. Do you have to?"

"No."

"I want to show you something I dug out for you."

He took a large manila envelope out of a locked desk drawer, came over and sat beside me on the leather sofa. He began taking papers out of the envelope, and as he arranged them, talked.

"Funny thing, reputation," he said. "If somebody'd come to me recently and whispered that you're a fairy, you'd be confirming it to me ten times a day. I'd be considering you from that point of view, don't you see? So every time you put your hand on your hip, or brushed back your hair, or did that shrug of yours, it would be corroborative evidence. Now Mr. Whitman thinks I'm no good, so anything I do is colored by his prejudice."

"He told me he thought you were one of the four best directors around."

"Four? That means I'm fourth, doesn't it? Some compliment. A horse comes in fourth pays nothing. Anyhow, I'm talking about personal stuff. This sort of stuff."

He waved the papers he was holding, and went on.

"My first job down here was in nineteen twenty-one. Right?"

"How should *I* know?"

"Because you know all about it, for some reason. At least, you *think* you do."

He had gone pale, and his hands were trembling.

"One twenty-five a week. That was my first salary. I didn't get into the real money for quite a while, no matter what he tells you!"

"We've never discussed anything like—"

"Let me talk! All right. So I had a job, one twenty-five. Nineteen twenty-one. March. Here's the contract. Want to look it over?"

He put it on my lap. I did not touch it.

"I believe you," I protested. "What *is* all this?"

"The accused is acting as his own attorney. Situation. Use it sometime. All right, now look at this."

He handed me a canceled check dated April something, 1921. Made out to 'John J. Tumulty, Sr.' in the amount of seventy-five dollars. I studied it, longer than necessary.

"Turn it over," he said.

I did so. It was endorsed with the unmistakable flourish that was T's signature. It reminded me of something, I couldn't remember what, but I've thought of it since: the famous John Hancock signature that is the trademark of the insurance company. He handed me another check. Then another and another and another. I got the idea, and said so, but he wouldn't stop. He handed me check after check, in varying amounts, ranging from twenty-five dollars to— there were a good many, I think, for ten thousand. There must have been over a hundred checks, and he made me look at every single one. He saw that I was embarrassed, but it didn't matter. He seemed to be getting a tremendous release out of the demonstration. Finally, the last check. This one was dated some time in 1930, the year of T's death. It was for thirteen thousand dollars. I longed to get out of the house and try to put this jigsaw together.

Now he handed me a letter from his accountant with

53

the checks listed and totaled. It came to something over $647,000. I don't see numbers like that often and it gave me a turn.

"See that?" he asked.

"Sure."

"How much?"

"A lot."

There was a sudden note of irritation in his command, "Read it out!"

"Six hundred and forty-seven thousand dollars."

His voice turned mellow. "Correct," he said.

He got up and fixed two drinks. He was sweating.

"Tumulty's Grand," he said. "When did it close?"

"I don't know."

"Come *on,* boy."

"Nineteen twenty-eight, wasn't it?"

"That's right. October sixteenth, nineteen twenty-eight. A week or so before, that was when the great Whitman came down to see me, so that would make it about October ninth."

"Yes."

"Now look through the pile there and see if you can find anything for October, nineteen twenty-eight."

I knew there was no point in demurring, so I did as I was told. There turned out to be several checks in that month. One was dated October 2. It was for seventy-five hundred dollars!

"See it?" he asked.

"The big one. Yes."

"Let me explain that," he said, bringing me the drink.

"Why should you? Thanks."

"Because I'm going to!"

I took a huge, welcome slug of the drink, and settled back to listen.

"He turned up this day, my father, and said, 'It's something important, laddie.' This was the cue he had developed. 'It's something important, laddie.' Every one of those checks is the end of a conversation that began with 'It's something important, laddie.' But this time it really was. Here he was, in his seventies, and he tells me he's thinking of getting married. I thought of Maude Adriance. I'd heard they were around together. But he said, 'No, it's Rose I have in mind!' I told him he must be off his head."

At this point, BD went into an automatic imitation of John J. Tumulty. I have no way of knowing how accurate it was, but it was complete: posture, voice, speech, age. He turned into another being before my eyes. I wonder if Whitman is right about BD having been a terrible actor.

"He said to me, 'Well, now, laddie. Well, now. You disappoint me. I'd hoped for your blessing, and a bit of a bundle for the young people, just to set them on their way. Now you seem to be forcing me to do it with neither.' " BD laughed, remembering. "Oh, he had charm, all right. The thing that complicated the situation was that Rose had been coming down to L.A. more and more and I had only been waiting for *me* to get a better footing before carrying out a plan of our own. I thought he knew about it. I asked him and he said, 'Oh, we gathered you'd long since changed your mind. Of course, in the end, it'll be up to the child, and poor thing, she's so young and addled she might choose you, at that. Anyway, how about the loan, laddie?' He always called it a loan, and always insisted on an exact figure, and never took less. Or more, I must say. This time he sort of shamed me into it. A few months later we got together, Rose and I. Half-kidding, I wrote him a letter and said that things having

55

turned out as they did, how about returning the seventy-five hundred? He wrote back and said he meant to go ahead with his plan anyway, and marry Maude. I remember a line in his letter that struck me. He wrote: 'The difficulty is, how does one make an honest woman out of an honest woman?' He said he'd rather have a bad part than no part, something like that. He never did, though. Get married, I mean. At any rate, you see how responsible *I* was for the end of Tumulty's Grand."

"I certainly do. Is it all right to mention any of this to Whitman? Just for the record?"

"Suit yourself. He won't believe you, but I don't give a good goddamn."

He gathered up the checks and the papers, carefully, and put them back into the envelope. I got ready to leave.

"See if you can think up something more original for the cop to say, will you?"

"Sure," I replied, although at that moment I had no idea what he was talking about.

I drove back to the hotel, but when I got there, decided to drive around a little. A little turned out to be all the way to Malibu. I stopped at a place there and drank coffee and bought cigarettes and drove some more. I have never been less sure of what I think. On the basis of last night's evidence, Tumulty is certainly a sponge and a liar and a thoroughly reprehensible old reprobate. Not only does it appear that he lied, but he lied to those closest to him. (Remember BD saying that no one ever did get really close to him.)

When I got home, I looked back through some of the notes, a hell of a job since they are scattered all through the notebooks. I ought to cull them one day. When? No time. Never time. Maybe Miss Schiller could do it. No. Too much stuff in the notebooks not meant for anyone to see ever.

The thing that bothers me most is Tumulty taking The Old Actor's seven thousand and risking it in the theatre, when he obviously had dough of his own stashed away. Or did he? What the hell *did* he do with it? It was supposed to be for the theatre, for his living expenses. But how much could they have been? Illness? No. Nothing serious has ever been mentioned by anyone. Once or twice, according to BD, he spoke of personal obligations. What could they have been? Gambling? Horse races? Dames? Whatever it was would certainly pull the plug out of this. After all, there is no point in telling the story of a crafty old scrounger. For any line-up I can visualize now, that batch of checks will have to be forgotten. I have to keep reminding myself that I have no intention of setting down The Life and Times of John J. Tumulty. What I want is accurate atmosphere and character ingredients.

The surprise is that BD can feel as kindly toward the memory of T as he does. T seems to have bled him unmercifully across the many years. Certainly BD owed him something which cannot be calculated in dollars; nevertheless, that was one impressive total, all right.

About the Rose thing. Something tells me the old boy was larking. I don't believe he ever had any intention of going through with it.

He is damned hard to figure, after last night. So much double-dealing and dissembling that to plot it out along lines of reasonable motivation seems hopeless. A thought. Why does there have to be reasonable motivation, that thing we are always belting at? Is there always motivation in life? No, but there has to be in fiction or the audience won't believe it. They believe anything in real life, but in the theatre or in films they want it all proved. It has to come out even.

18 August 50   Hwood.

I run into Whitman at the Vine Street Brown Derby. BD was right. What a die-hard! He has some people with him. When they leave, I tell him what I have found out.

"I don't believe it," he says, "and you can't make me. Go ahead and try, though, if you want to. It might be enjoyable."

I tell him I have seen the checks myself.

"Probably out of the prop department," he says.

"Oh, come now."

He sticks his right forefinger into my face and says, heatedly, "Look here, friend, if you want to take a little trip tomorrow and travel as King Farouk, I can arrange it for you out at the plant. That's right. Complete with passport and harem. Don't kid me. I got to this town with the celluloid. What'll you bet I can have forty men with broken noses, all pointing east, in your office tomorrow morning? You forget something, buster. This is Hollywood, where we invent magic and manufacture dreams, and sell 'em."

"These were no props, Frank. Believe me."

"Why should I? You been pasteurized?"

"Maybe I haven't got the whole story yet—I don't claim to—but you've got this guy wrong."

58

"Wrong is right. And that's the way I want to keep him. Don't look for my soft spot. I had it filled with gravel last week. Let's go over the Beachcomber's and see if they ever heard of rum."

Home late. The idea that those checks are false is out of the question. Whitman makes the mistake of coming to a conclusion before acquiring the evidence. The fact is that little documentation has turned up. A few scrapbooks and clippings, that letter from Edwin Booth, these checks. Everything else is talk and memory. Well, talk is cheap and memory is elusive, and so where does that leave us?

But I still feel (stubbornly?) that there is a story in an actor at the turn of the century on the West Coast. Snatches of various parts in various plays and a personal story as the spine. But what personal story? He gets the girl onstage, but loses her off. Not as bald as that, but along those lines. Maybe simply the one situation of Juanita. She dies. He brings up the kid. Then what? The kid turns out good? Bad? When the kid comes of age, he tells him. Big shock, and the kid takes off. The old boy keeps going, finally is almost through—the kid does something great for him, they are reunited. Two strangers whose lives become intermingled by circumstance. No. Maybe. In this sort of setup, the boy could go into silent pictures, further interesting background and color. Maybe what happens is that the old boy gets recognition late in life, through the faith of the young man. (Those two phrases—old boy, young man. Interesting.)

(Title: *Man and Boy? The Old Boy?*)

2 Sept. 50   Beverly Hills.

I leave here tomorrow morning, so today I phoned BD and went over to his house to see him, ostensibly to say goodbye.

We talked about the picture. He is still deep in it and worried about some of the sound. He plans to do a new dubbing on the last two reels.

Finally, my heart pounding, I said, "Well, thanks for everything. Except *one* thing."

"Oh?" he said. "And what's *that?*"

"This," I said, and took the pink letter out of my breast pocket and handed it to him. I hoped he would not notice that my hand was trembling.

He looked it over carefully, but not as carefully as I looked *him* over as he did so.

He gave no sign of anything. I reminded myself that he is an actor. He handed the letter back and lit a cigarette at once. Significant.

"What's it all about?" he asked.

"About Tumulty," I said. He stood up, too quickly. So did I, adding, "I think you sent it to me."

He moved to me and I sensed I was about to be slugged. He glared at me, clenching and unclenching his fists, then turned and left the room. I started out. He came back.

"All right," he said. "Listen. I don't owe you any explanations. I don't owe you anything. Not a God-damned thing. But for the record, let me put it this way. I had nothing to do with that message. *Nothing,* you understand? And I'm

60

good and offended you should think I did."

I said nothing. He went on.

"On the other hand, I can understand your worry and even how you could think of pinning it on me."

"O.K."

"Anybody second on your list?"

"No. Do you have any ideas?"

"No. Let me see it again."

I gave it to him. He studied it.

Without taking his eyes from it, he said, "Why does this refer to Tumulty, necessarily? It could be something else. You've probably got that long nose of yours in other places it doesn't belong."

"No," I said. "Not that I know of."

"You've got a reputation for digging and delving, did you know that? All over town."

"No."

"Well, you have. People talk about it all the time."

He's trying to get you off the track, I thought. He sent it or had it sent.

He handed back the letter and said, "Let me know if you get killed."

He laughed, and like an idiot so did I.

We shook hands. I left.

Should I take this up with a lawyer? The police? No, nothing. See what happens and maybe use a little more discretion in the future.

All at once I remember the time I asked René Clair for an exact definition of farce. "Farce," he said, "is when you get a group of characters into a situation where somebody should call the police—but nobody calls the police." According to this rule, I am involved in a farce. As soon as the police are involved, it may become a drama.

I do not seem to be thinking clearly. Certainly not sensibly —but we never do when we are rattled. I am rattled.

Could that be true? What he said about my reputation? Of course not. He is one of those Machiavellian shits who knows instinctively what an adversary's vulnerable points are, and attacks them.

5 Feb 51   Beverly Hills Hotel.

TMY. Odd to write those three letters again. I have not thought of Tumulty for months. Too much going on in New York, completely unrelated. Also that last crack at fusing the stuff into an outline was too discouraging. The whole thing is probably nothing. So I was surprised to get a call from Whitman last night. He saw in the Hwood *Reporter* that I was back.

"Welcome to our city," he began. (It always sounds fakey on stage or screen when a character uses a single characteristic expression, but how often they do so in life.)

"Thanks," I replied. "I'm going to be here for three or four weeks. Maybe we can get together."

"You don't love *me*," he said. "You just love John J. Tumulty."

"That's all over," I said. "Didn't you see it in Louella's?"

"I've been holding a surprise for you. When do you want to see it?"

"What is it?"

"If I tell you, you lunkhead, where's the surprise?"

"Tomorrow morning?" I suggested. "Ten o'clock?"

"Deal. My office. See you."

I tried to figure out what it might be, but I was all wrong. My guesses were far off the mark. I had been thinking in terms of letters, clippings, photographs, memorabilia, perhaps financial records to refute BD's checks. But no. Whitman had dug out, somehow, two old silents, starring BD. We went down to a projection room to see them. They had some trouble getting the old reels on the machines, and then, because they are nitrate, had to get special permission to run them, so there was a delay, during which we talked.

"You think I'm against the guy for no reason," said Whitman. "Wait till you see his performance in this. That's something *no* one could ever forgive."

"Well, all silents look a little ridiculous if you look at them from today's point of view."

The projectionist squawked through that he was ready, and on came the first—a college picture. BD (my God, he was handsome!) played the part of a young Frenchman in an American college. It was pretty bad, and so was he, even by silent standards. After about four reels of it (it was a six-reeler, I believe), I turned to Whitman, who sat there, giggling.

"All right," I said. "I get the general idea."

He signaled the booth and the next one came on. This one was the story of Captain John Smith and Pocahontas. BD as Smith, Rose as Pocahontas. Rose! There she was. I began to understand—if not everything—at least more than I had before. Even with the heavy overlay of silent movie makeup and the harsh effect of the klieg lighting, she was clearly the essence of desirable femininity. For God's sake. Rose.

Whitman giggled even more noisily for a while, then stopped. We sat watching, quietly, and soon could not hear even the whir of the machine—because not only was it one hell of a picture, but BD was *superb* in it. An astonishing sense of period style. Relaxed, yet passionate. Immense realistic business. More John Smith than himself, although a minimum of makeup. Altogether tremendous. It ended. Whitman was the first to speak.

"Well, I'll be God-damned! How do you figure it?"

"Actors improve," I ventured.

"They sure do. Only the John Smith one was made three years *before* the other one! Your move."

It was not until late this afternoon that it hit me. The difference in BD's performances can be explained by the fact that the *second* one was a copy of John J. Tumulty, Sr. in *The Captain and the Princess*—maybe even that actual play filmed.

BD must have seen that performance many, many times. So what we saw was the John J. Tumulty, *Sr.* performance, or a reasonable facsimile. In a way, I have seen Tumulty act at last! My interest in this is rekindled.

Might there not be someone else out at the Home who knew him? Or is there an old actors' place in San Francisco? Find out. There is definitely a useful situation in a young actor making good by giving an imitation of an obscure old actor. Especially if the latter is his father, or if there is some emotional tangle involving them. The young one only good, only successful, only accepted when he imitates his father. A germ here. Maybe this is true, and why BD finally gave up acting altogether.

February 15, 1951   Beverly Hills.

TMY. There is no such place in San Francisco. The one down here handles them all. I went out there yesterday, having written beforehand to The Old Actor, to tell him I was coming. I asked him to find out about possible others. If any, I would give a little tea party at the Inn.

I arrive early. OA is confined to his room. He has been well, but is now sick again. (Eleven years since I first met him. He was about seventy-six then. Eighty-seven now. I see no change.) His new complaint is that there are too few television sets in the place! An outrage. He has put six old Tumulty production stills into an envelope, wants to give them to me. I decline.

He says, "You're going to have them sooner or later, why not now?"

I offer to pay something.

He says, "No, no." Before I leave, though, he indicates he would not object to receiving a few cigars.

He tells me that of the ones who are up and around, only the ancient Mrs. M knew Tumulty. She will be glad to see me at tea. The prospect does not appeal to me. It might be different with a group, but there is no turning back now.

"How well did she know him?" I ask.

"I don't know how *well*. But *long*, I'm sure of that."

"Is she pleasant?"

"That is something you must decide for yourself. I am biased. We have not spoken all week."

"Why not?"

"She took offense. A result of your letter and my inquiries. She heard of them and wanted to know why I hadn't asked her. 'Because I know about *you*, dear,' I said. 'I'm trying to find others.' This led us into a long remember about Mr. Tumulty. After a time, she turned coy, and said, 'He *could* be a devil, you know! He tried with me, you know. Several times.' And I said, 'If he tried with you even once, let alone several, he succeeded, because Mr. Tumulty never failed!' That was when she took offense, and we have not spoken all week. Oh, she's an affable enough old biddy, but may I warn you of one thing? Don't—under any circumstances—believe a word she says!"

A fine beginning. Still, I had to go through with it and am glad I did. Mrs. M may not be truthful, but she is colorful, which is often more important. She treated our meeting as though it were an assignation. She must have spent all day getting ready. She is a standard type: leading lady grown old. I have the impression that I have seen her before, but this is only because I have seen so many like her. Her hair is light blond, her eyes deep blue and, from tip to toe, there is plenty of leftover beauty. Her outfit is jaunty, and she is made up skillfully, professionally. She must have rested, too, because I was amazed at her youthfulness when we met, then saw it leave her in two hours. When I brought her back to the Home, she had scarcely the strength to say goodbye. I suppose that is what age is, mainly—fatigue.

"So you were a friend of Jack Tumulty's," she said, as we drove toward the Inn.

"In a way, yes."

"You're a young thing to have known him."

"I never did."

"Oh," she said. "I see." But she didn't.

Out came the familiar stuff. How fine he was in this part, how even better in that. A great deal about Juanita, but nothing new. At the Inn, I asked her how she wanted her tea, cream or lemon.

"Neither," she said. "Rye."

I wondered if I should.

"And leave out the tea," she said.

Then I remembered something from my research on *A Man to Remember*. Dr. William Osler, who is said to have said, "Whiskey is the milk of old age." With Osler behind me, I said to the waitress, "One rye and one double rye."

The waitress left.

"Who's the double for?" asked Mrs. M. "You or me?"

"You."

"Good!"

When she had downed the drink and I had ordered another, she looked at me, smiled teasingly, and asked, "All right, what do you want to know about Jack Tumulty?"

"Well, for one thing, did many people call him 'Jack'?"

I had wondered about this when she first said it. "Mr. Tumulty" to the OA, "JJ" to Whitman, "John" to Craley, "Tumulty" to somebody, and Lord knows what to that vituperative doorman.

"I don't know about many," she said. "I know *I* did."

"And what did he call you?"

"Oh, different things," she said coquettishly. "Depending on his mood. Different things."

"Moody, was he?"

"Well, he was more—full of a lot of things he never got out. Do I make myself clear? A lot of things."

"Yes, ma'am."

"And that boy was a trouble to him, too. There was some-

67

thing wrong with that boy. He never did get straightened out, I understand. Something wrong."

"You say Tumulty worried about the boy. Funny thing, and all the time the boy was worrying about him."

"The hell you say. Pardon my French."

"No, that's the truth." I decided to dig a little deeper. Easy, now. "The boy worried about Tumulty's spending."

"Spending what?"

"Money. Too much money. I happen to know."

"You don't *sound* as if you know. Listen, Jack Tumulty'd have died owin' a fortune in this town, except everybody was so *for* him they just tore up the bills. Never mentioned them, and neither did he. Tore 'em up."

("—this town," she says. She thinks she's in San Francisco.)

"They say he used to gamble quite a lot."

"They're a liar! He didn't know how, and that's the fact. Fact."

"People have little secret vices, you know."

"Don't tell *me,* young man. I *knew* Jack Tumulty. Why, we were engaged at one time. Engaged."

"For long?"

"For too long. That's why we never finished it up, I suppose. Too long."

"That and Maude Adriance," I needled.

She flushed, and her old eyes blazed, or at least smoldered. "What do you know about Maude Adriance?"

"Just that she was another friend of his, that's all."

"So *she* said, I suppose."

I ordered another round. Both singles, this time.

"What would *you* say?"

She took a deep breath and put a considerable amount of force into a single "Ha! That's what I'd say." She did it again, "Ha!"

"Nothing else?"

"Maude Adriance—her real name was Grogan—had the soul of a Chinatown madam, young man. She kept throwing that girl of hers at his head till it made us all laugh. First, of course, she tried to get him herself, but when she saw that was out, she tried to keep the boss in the family, so to speak, using the daughter, don't y'see? Using the daughter."

"It almost worked, didn't it?"

"Almost, my eye. He used to kid with me about it, sometimes. He used to say, 'Watch your step, ladybug, and watch *my* step, too. I've used up all my mistakes, and I'm not entitled to but four more and I want to use those for emergencies!' Oh, that Jack, what a kidder." Tears came to her eyes. She blinked them out, in the manner of one accustomed to frequent tears, and went on. "Then he'd tell me about what old Adriance was up to. Grogan. There she was, matchmakin' away. He didn't want it, and Rose didn't want it. The only one wanted it was the old girl. Matchmakin' away."

(But what about Whitman's account of T and Mrs. Adriance?)

"You know what I think?" I teased. "I think you were jealous of Mrs. Adriance."

"I wouldn't say that. *Miss.* She was never married. I don't give a snap *what* she said."

"Don't get sore, but I once heard *she* was his lady for a while."

Mrs. M looked into her glass, almost empty now, and spoke ever so softly.

"She may have been. May have been. He was full of girls, ol' Jack, but nobody minded. He had enough love in him for a worldful."

"But that gets to be expensive, doesn't it?"

69

"He never paid for it, if that's what you're sayin'."

She was slightly spiffed now, and I suggested food. We ordered hamburgers.

"In fact," she continued, "sometimes it was the other way round. Not with me. Poor ol' Maude one time got hit." She laughed wildly. "Not with me."

"What do you mean?"

"She gave him her money, that's how I mean!"

"How'd she happen to do that?"

"Let me tell you. We'd had a rehearsal one night. Puttin' on this thing *The Scheming Lieutenant* that it turned out later nobody wanted to see. Restoration or somesuch. Lord, it was worse than Shakespeare! This thing."

"Don't you like Shakespeare?"

"We don't like each *other!* And, Christ! You never get to sit down unless you play a queen. But about that night. Maude was there, and the girl, of course, and Jack, myself, a fellow named Whitman used to be his manager—he's dead now, Whitman. Nice bloke, he was. Tough, but nice. Anyway, Jack was blue. Way down in his dumps. Blue. And he says how if he only had a few thousand dollars he'd show the town something. What this thing needed was production, costumes, and a few new lights. And he went on about it, and next thing you know, he was crying. I mean *crying!* All right. What happened. Maude went out next morning and sold every damned piece of jewelry she owned and brought the money to him and he certainly put on a great production and we all wore the prettiest costumes and the only thing was, it turned out nobody happened to want to see us do it much. Nobody."

"And he never paid her back?"

"He would've if he could've. But no matter. Her girl got

the young one, so they all did fine for themselves."

"Where's Mrs. Adriance now, do you know?"

"No, and neither does she, poor thing. I attended her funeral, years ago. Beautiful, it was. Years ago."

"And Rose?"

"Now who was it told me?—somebody—saw her a while back. She lives in Paris, France. She has for years. Married to a doctor of some sort. French, I suppose."

"Did you ever know Juanita?" I asked.

"I did."

Some time passed before she continued. She seemed to be remembering, considering. All the while, she ate. After a long silence, she began, slowly.

"I knew Juanita, sure. And here's the truth. You didn't believe me when I told you I was once engaged to Jack—"

"Of course I did."

"Of course you didn't, but what's the difference? It was all in another world. Who cares? Why, by now, even *I* don't care. I'm mostly dead myself, don't y'know, like most of us out there in the jolly graveyard. Mostly dead. We just float around waiting for somebody to come and bury us. 'Did you know Juanita?' Listen, he was engaged to me and that's the God's truth, and I couldn't tell you to how many others, too. He went through his life getting engaged. Did I know Juanita? He meant well every time, and he'd try hard, but he never got to it with any of us. Sure I knew Juanita. That was the trouble. *She* was. He never got over her. You know what I used to do? I used to get myself up like her. You may laugh now, but back then I could almost do it. Almost do it. Our coloring was a little different, but I used to put on quite an impression. It was no good, though. And neither were any of the other tricks any of the other ones tried. He just stayed stuck. Right there on Juanita, damn her eyes. Just stayed stuck."

(This was touching as she told it, but I know that it is useless insofar as the story is concerned. The time has passed when an audience can be engaged successfully by the ideal love story based on the one-woman-for-one-man principle. Most men and women in the middle of the twentieth century believe it possible to love truly and deeply more than once in life. Thus this whole element in the Tumulty story —faithful to the dead Juanita—would make him seem foolish. Worse, it would make *me* seem foolish! Suppose he had been *married* to Juanita when she tangled with whatever-the-hell the guy's name was? Where would that lead? Nowhere.)

"Do you have any idea what made her go off with that fellow?" I asked.
"Does anybody?"
"What sort of a man was he, do you remember?"
"He was nothing. Good-looking. Nothing!"
"He must have been something to Juanita."
"Nothing."
"Why did she do it, then?"
"I don't know. I've done some damn crazy things in my own time I couldn't explain, so how do you expect me to explain somebody *else's* craziness? Can you explain everything *you've* ever done? Damn crazy things?"
"No."
"Well, then, there you are!"
She conveyed triumph, but I realized this sort of answer

would not serve my purpose. I tried a new lead.

"Somebody told me Juanita was always playing around, but that this happened to be the first time she got caught."

"Who gave you that?"

"I forget. I've talked to so many people about it."

She bristled. "Whoever told you that was making mischief. I got no cause to defend her, but she was no playaround, I can vouch that. She was the most religious girl I ever encountered. Vouch that."

"When she joined the company, was she a virgin, do you think?"

Mrs. M looked at me and blushed. She regarded me primly for a time before she spoke.

"Well, I must say, young man—this is all getting rather— well, rather *randy!*"

"Was she?"

"I'm sure I don't know."

She seemed ready to close the subject for good. We had coffee, and did not speak for a time. In my part of the silence, I tried to construct a line that would stand up. I began with Juanita as an innocent, religious virgin. Could she have been as innocent as all that? Even ignorant? On the stage, this guy—wait till I look up his name. Clay Bannister. Remember it. Clay Bannister Clay Bannister Clay Bannister. Now. Onstage he touches her. He kisses her, perhaps in a way she has never known. She does not understand her own response. T has always been gentle with her, kind, adoring. Paternal? Her feeling for him is deep, but thus far, on another plane. Bannister is rough, primitive, basic. Sacred and profane love. She is confused. She gives in to this, feeling it is wrong, yet unable to control it. Bannister is the cruel one. Perhaps nothing climactic has actually happened at the time of discovery. This might help to explain her following him. I don't know. All this is getting pretty damned clinical now. Of course, the whole situation must be thought of in terms of the mores of its time. This would have happened somewhere around 1888. Not the Dark Ages, after all. And yet . . .

I took Mrs. M back to the Home and thanked her. As I left, she seemed to be in tears, but she smiled and waved as I drove off, and the last thing I saw her do was blow me a kiss.

Feb. 22, '51   Beverly Hills

Yesterday, walking up to see Cukor, a car nearly ran me down. All at once, on the big Doheny Drive curve, a Rolls came into view heading for me. I jumped away and ended up, shaken, lying on someone's lawn.

Well, here it is, I thought. At last the threat had become a reality. I stood up and tried to pull myself together.

To my astonishment, the Rolls came backing up with tremendous speed. It stopped. A gray-haired, mustached man in wild sports clothes spoke. He seemed even more terrified than I was.

"Are you all right?" he asked. British.

"Yes. I think so."

"I'm frightfully sorry," he said. "My fault entirely. Please forgive me."

"Sure."

He roared off.

Later, walking home, I reviewed it all. Is this connected with last June's threat? I think so. I think not.

If it were, would the guy have returned with all that solicitude? Of course. Having missed me, that is precisely what he would do. Find out more about him? No. Hell with it. Forget it. Can I?

10 July 51   New York.

Reading some Walpole letters the other night (at Ruth's insistence), I began to wonder if I might have overlooked an important source of information with regard to the Tumulty story. There must be some letters around. How to get hold of them is another thing. Still, not impossible. In those days people wrote letters a hell of a lot more than they do now, and they also held on to things more. Doubtless, BD has some, but I cannot imagine asking him to let me see them. Who? Whitman? The Old Actor? Mrs. M? Could Hobie try to track some down?

Second thought. There might be a discreet sort of letter I *could* write to BD, telling him that I am doing or thinking of doing a story in that period with a theatrical background and so on and so on, and if he would let me see any photographs or letters or prompt scripts—something like that. What the hell, the worst he can say is no. I am going to write them all.

2 Aug. 51   New York.

The first reply to my letters comes today from Whitman. I told him expressly that all I wanted was *copies* of the texts of any letters he might have and that he would not mind letting me see. Instead, he sends me the originals of four. In his note, he says he has more if I find these of interest:

Dear Pinkerton:
   Out of my musty memory box, here are a few letters from J.J. What sort of detectiving are you up to, anyway? Your idea that I can send text copies is putrid. In the case of these letters, it isn't so much the what as the how. I could have them photostated, but do not want to go to the expense (I guess you've heard how business has been this last quarter). Anyhow, there is a certain difference between these scrawls and the original copy of the Bill of Rights. By the way, has that ever been paid? Come back. All is forgiven. Of course, you'll have to take the cut same as everyone else. Re the slashing going on around here like a Tong War: current studio scuttlebutt has it that when L.B. asked Arthur (his present favorite) to take a cut, Arthur laughed right in his ass.
   You're welcome.

                                             Thine, FBWhitman

I see what he means. The texts are not so much, but the manner is something. It is a large hand, and apparently T wrote rapidly. The words are almost connected, and there is a great deal of underlining— one line, two, even three. Some words are printed. I get an impression of J. J. Tumulty directing me as to the reading of each of his sentences. The letters have a sound. The first one is dated May 22, 1908; written from The Summit Hotel, San Francisco:

FRANK!

Let me not invade your realm, but merely whisper my objection to paying Miss Heath <u>one hundred</u>! No one—I say <u>NO ONE</u> can act one hundred dollars worth in a week; therefore the sum must involve what is vulgarly known as <u>draw</u> (flypaper to flies!) and this the young person does not possess in any measure. Further, I believe it to be bad for troupe morale to create so large a discrepancy. I saw an exceedingly <u>CLEVER</u> girl in Seattle two weeks ago, <u>Laurette Taylor</u> by name. Shall I inquire as to her availability?? Or am I locking this barn door too LATE?

Last night 733. Tonight 539 (rain). Rain last night, too! Ah, well, "Tell me not in mournful numbers——"

Yrs,
John

Another is on extraordinary stationery, a sort of parchment. A crest. The address, embossed: 15208 Los Feliz Boulevard, Los Angeles, California. No doubt that place of BD's. The date: June 28, 1922.

Dear Frank,

I pity the cinema players with a compassion I did not know I possessed! The reason—what a lamentable comedown <u>Paradise</u> will be for them! Johnny took me with him to the STUDIO (as it is called) to watch him "work" (as it is called). One man dresses him, another stands for him while the Kliegs are arranged. The director then metes out the bit, it is played, photographed, and so on. I said to Johnny that all he needed was someone to <u>act</u> for him and we could go home. The remark did not go down well.

Frank, you will think me poisoned by the rich food and the richer climate when I tell you that, in my opinion, <u>great</u> things might come out of this when they learn to use the toy. Even now there are some at work here to whom I doff my hat. Yet I long to be at my own again. Any word from Daly? Did you make it <u>CLEAR</u> I want "Beau Brummel" for San Francisco <u>ONLY</u>? We MUST find a farce for the first week. Is "Tons of Money" free?? Inform. "Le Dindon" by Feydeau would be <u>ideal</u> but, alas, I have been unable to find the necessary time to complete my translation. It is <u>LABORIOUS</u> work and even when put into English is not yet suitable. We shall doubtless do it one day, but, as I say, it is not ready at this time. We could do "Wild Horses," I expect, but I <u>GREATLY</u> prefer something <u>new</u>, and so, I have no doubt, would our loyal but long-suffering patrons. Please do <u>NOT</u> suggest "School for Scandal." I assure you I have left that School for <u>GOOD</u> and <u>all</u>! If you hunger for it, I shall take you with me one night to my beloved <u>El Borracho</u> and read it aloud to you against guitar and castanets. Write at once if you think the <u>cyc</u> will hold, else it might be possible to find a secondhand one here.

What should it cost?

I feel your hand in mine, old Frank.

Yrs,

John

A clue. El Borracho. It sounds like a nightclub or cabaret. His hangout? Is it still there? I must ask Hobie to look into this.

Then there is one from St. Vincent's Hospital, San Francisco. Date: January 2, 1929.

By golly Frank,

You <u>never</u> forget, do you? It was a <u>joy</u> to have your prosperous looking card. Did I not tell you once—<u>long ago</u> (Lord, <u>everything</u> is long ago!)—that there was gold in that there <u>CELLULOID?</u> Although now that it has begun to talk I ha' me doots. I beg you to write and tell me <u>candidly</u> what you think of Johnny's situation. I MUST know. He reassures me that all is well, that it is only a matter of time and a period of readjustment, but I <u>WORRY</u> about him, as I always have. He is a good lad, but with <u>WEAKNESSES</u>—"even as you and I." I am in the ward now—not a financial question but a matter of company. The private room was pleasant but equipped with a fifty-hour day, something for which I have little use now. We could have used a few in the old days, do you not agree? I am told, on <u>highest</u> medical authority, that this long run I have had here at St. Vincent's is coming to a <u>close</u>. The notice is up and it is only a matter of weeks now, perhaps even <u>DAYS</u>.

Let me hear from you—<u>especially</u> on the subject mentioned above. I shall be greatly indebted to you—even more than I am already.

Believe me to be,

Yrs,
John

Another chore for Hobie. When did T enter the hospital? What for? When did he leave? He was, at this time, about eighty. His handwriting is exactly as it was. No change, no effect of age or illness. Frank told me once that T was never ill. He obviously forgot this occasion.

The last of the letters is baffling. Irritating. It is from 18 Hobhill Road, San Francisco, c/o Jorgenson. What was this? Friend? Boardinghouse? Rooming house? Still there? Who is or was Jorgenson? The letter is dated March 8, 1930. T died in May.

Dear Frank,

You have often admired my watch, of solid gold, presented to me by Madame Helena Modjeska after our West Coast tour. I now offer it for sale at the price of $300. I have had it appraised and it is worth more, MUCH more. Do you wish to buy it? I suppose it is only fair to tell you that you are supposed to get the blasted thing, anyhow, according to a provision in my WILL. However, that WILL will not be executed until the customary time, and if signs can be believed, it is a long way off. I have had offers of employment, some interesting in the extreme. In fact, I may be seeing you soon in your vicinity. For the moment, however, I would like to know your disposition regarding the watch. If you do not buy it, someone else will have a devil of a job finding it for you when the time comes! As I see it, you have only one course open to you to protect the generous bequest! I would appreciate your reply by telegraph. Top o' the mornin' to you!

Yrs,
John

To this letter, Whitman has clipped a slip. It reads:

The dead man's reply to those phony prop checks. Next time you are out

here, I will show you the watch.
Maybe you would like to buy it from
me to give as a Christmas present
to BD, your hero.

                                    FBW

With the facts at hand, there is no way to tell the Tumulty story without making someone a villain or a liar or, worse (for my purposes), someone who behaves in an unbelievable way. I long to be back in Calif to get with Whitman and by now, what the hell, I might even go and talk to BD. I am obsessed by this material beyond its possible use in a story.

7 August 51   New York.

A reply from The Old Actor:

Dear Sir,
Yes I do possess a number of letters written to me by the late John J. Tumulty. Several of them are of a personal nature and cannot be revealed. Others, I shall be pleased to allow you to examine on your next visit, should you desire to do so. I have no facilities for making copies and do not wish to entrust them to the mails.
As to your other enquiries, I shall deal with them now. Death came to Mr. Tumulty in the ambulance on the way to St. Vincent's Hospital on May 8, 1930. Your information as to his residence at that time is quite correct. 18 Hobhill Road. This was a rooming house, owned and operated by Mrs. Tecla Jorgenson, a Swedish widow and fine woman. The establishment is no longer in existence.
As to his illness in 1929, I am indeed familiar with this.

Mr. Tumulty caught cold while performing the part of "Joaquin Miller" in the open air pageant entitled "The Golden State" given for one week at Gate Isle. Completing the week, this common cold developed into severe bronchitis and finally into pneumonia. A long siege, during which all his financial resources were exhausted (those were the days before your penicillin, and pneumonia was a lengthy affliction). He was compelled to be moved to the ward. My efforts to raise funds on his behalf were unsuccessful. I myself was not in a position to assist him. I visited him many times. His spirits were unfailingly cheerful and he would not permit the subject of conversation to be himself or his condition. He was ever interested in his visitor. I would say that this was a characteristic of Mr. Tumulty.

His last public performance took place during the period December 10, 1929–January 2, 1930. At that time, he produced a repertory of programs for children. I was honored to be a member of his company. The plays produced were as follows: "Rip Van Winkle" (the Joseph Jefferson version) in which he played "Rip"; "Peter Pan" (Captain Hook); his own adaptation of "A Christmas Carol" (Old Scrooge); "A Midsummer Night's Dream" (Bottom, the Weaver); and "Huckleberry Finn" (Jim). This last, of course, a blackface portrayal. These performances met with great success, and oddly, found favor with adults as well as children. I well remember a pertinent remark passed by Mr. Tumulty at the time, in reference to this fact. "Grownups," he said, "are all children pretending not to be."

The effort of producing these works, in addition to performing the various roles, proved a great strain. Toward the end of the engagement, Mr. Tumulty experienced several fainting spells. At the end of the engagement, he took to his bed, and as you know, left us in May of that year. I think it can be properly observed that he died "in harness."

His son John never visited him in San Francisco, to my knowledge.

I beg to remain,

Respectfully yours,
(signature)

19 Aug 51   New York.

I hear today from Hobie. He writes:

Operative XXYYZZ2 reporting. Sidelights on the manhunt. The only El Borracho here is a high-class supper club. The only other one in the memory of living man is a terrible Spanish bin that burned down years ago. This cannot be the place you have in mind as apparently it was a real dive and even the two who remember its existence do not admit ever having been in the place. There is talk of dope, drink, and dames. Your kind of place. There is a Chicano chick here in the office (Secy to Mng Ed) who claims to have a grandfather who would know such things. (Actually she is after my body.)

Later. FLASH. The girl's grandfather claims to have a friend who used to be a guitar player there. He is still playing!—but in a different joint. I will go there tonight with the kid herself, as the fellow's English may not be the same type as mine. By the way, this doll is not bad, thanks for the assignment.

JH

Later today, I got this wire from Hobie:

GUITAR PLAYER REMEMBERS TUMULTY COME HOME AT
ONCE YOU ARE A FATHER REGARDS
                                    HOBART CHRONICLE

Aug 22–51   New York.

Two final responses today, both unsatisfactory. I am
beginning to think I ought to get off this Tumulty kick. A
note from Mrs. M saying she has no letters, said in a way
calculated to make me think that of course she has but that
they are too hot to touch. I doubt it.

BD writes as follows:

> My dear Maigret,
>   Don't let anyone tell you that you lack gall! You have
> it in full, impertinent measure. I can think of no reason
> to let you go rooting around in my personal papers.
> Would you let me root around in yours?
>   Kindest regards,
>
>   (signature)

So much for that. I see his point. I had asked him about
Rose Adriance and her whereabouts if she is alive, but he
ignored this question. However, that should not be hard to
find out. Whitman?

7 Oct 51   New York.

I thought I was through with the Tumulty matter for good, but something happened on Wednesday night that got it all going again. I was walking down Madison Avenue, trying to think of a new opening for Act III (the present one is hopeless) and saw that at The Plaza Theatre, they were showing my BD picture again. Walked over to see if my name was on the credit thing outside. It was, in slightly smaller letters than the name of the guy who lettered the show-card. I stood there watching a few people going in and decided to go in myself. After all, I had only seen the picture twice, and that was months ago. It was about half over. People wandering in and wandering out all through it. Provoking. No one would think of reading a book starting with page 150, reading to the end and then starting from the beginning, but they seem perfectly content to take movies in this form. What is annoying is the thought of the immense trouble taken with construction and exposition, the introduction of various characters, the unfolding of the plot, the details so carefully and laboriously planted—and to at least half the movie audience none of it seems to matter.

A terrible sinking feeling came over me as the picture moved into the last scene. I felt all over again that maybe I had been right to start with and that this ending seemed a cheap cop-out. Too late now. Anyway, it got to the end, and I sat there staring at the screen. A cast of characters came on with the end-title music, and as it did, the curtains closed. Why they do that, I can't imagine. In any case, down at the bottom of the cast sheet a name hit me, at least I thought it did. I couldn't be certain, since the curtain was falling in folds and made the names almost impossible to read. I thought I saw the name "Clay Bannister."

I walked into the lobby and thought about this for a minute, examined the billing there, but it was incomplete. I left. At first, the name was only vaguely familiar, then I realized whose it was. Which one was he in the picture? Could it be the old Clay Bannister's son? Relative? Coincidence? It is not too unusual a name, after all. For some reason, I was getting sort of jumpy. I walked to Grand Central, then walked back to the Plaza and sought out the manager. I asked him how come they pull the curtain over the cast list when some people are interested in looking at it. He was surprisingly polite and said he'd look into it. I went in again. (I sure am adding to the gross of this picture —wish I were on a percentage.) I hung around at the side until it was almost over, then went and sat down. I watched carefully as the end-title cast sheet came on, and there it was, unmistakably. "Hotel Manager . . . . . Clay Bannister."

I can hardly believe what I did next. I sat through the whole bloody picture again watching for the Hotel Manager. He appears several times and has four little scenes. He is an old man, and now that I was looking carefully, there is no doubt in my mind that this is the fellow. BD's father. Does BD know? Does *he* know? Intentional nepotistic casting or accidental? Holy Smoke, I am off again. I am really busting to get back there now, but it seems unlikely for some time. I thought of writing Whitman, but what's the sense? I'll wait.

86

January 3, 1952   New York.

TMY. Dinner at The Lambs. I must do this more often. It is a warm, pleasant place and for me, there is nothing more entertaining than actor talk. Richard Sterling was there. I had not seen him since Ruth had to write his part out of *The Leading Lady* in rehearsal. I invited him to have a drink, and soon we were on to Tumulty. Sterling never knew him, but saw him in many things and says he was great. Well, I know that. Why did T never appear in New York? No explanation. I said I understood he was colorful offstage. Sterling didn't remember. Extravagant?

"Well," said Sterling, "everybody was extravagant in those days."

I said I had heard he had a number of illegitimate children.

"Really?" said Sterling. "There's only *one I* ever heard of. That motion picture director. I don't recall his name."

"Neither do I," I said. "But I understood *he* was adopted."

"Yes," said Sterling, "I heard that, too."

"Did you ever know an actor named Clay Bannister?" I asked.

"No, I never did."

So that was not much of a lead.

Things picked up later. Tom Powers came in. I remembered he had been out in Calif in the silent days, so I had a long talk with him. He knows BD well, says he was never much of an actor, except for sudden spurts in certain parts. All this fits. Did Tom know Rose Adriance? Yes, intimately(!).

He used to correspond with her before the war, but during the occupation of France, she and her husband disappeared.

"I knew BD before I knew *her*," says Tom. "We all used to hang around his place, wondering how he did it."

"Did what?"

"Lived on that scale. Hell, people have forgotten how to luxe it up. But in those days, it was something. A sort of second gold rush. Everyone was making dough and spending it, but there's a knack to profligacy. Not everyone has it and it's hard to acquire. He had it. Dance orchestras. Great food. Stag parties they talk about yet. And out in the main entry hall, on a low table—a great copper bowl full of money. Fives, tens, twenties, fifties. The idea was, help yourself if you need to. He was a great guy."

"Did you ever know his father?"

"That's a funny question."

"How?"

"I mean funny you should ask it, because it's not the kind I can give you a yes or a no to."

"Go ahead."

"Well, there's always been a lot of talk about BD, all sorts of fantastic yarns. I thought he probably wove some of them around himself, to give himself color. There were people around who knew him as John J. Tumulty, Jr. The people who'd signed him originally. In fact, he made his first picture under that name. He didn't change it until later. Say, *there's* an idea. If you have a flop, change your name. Why isn't *that* a good idea?"

"So?"

"I remember I was at his house this one Sunday—big crowd—nobody got introduced to anybody much, but somebody pointed out this man on the fringe of things and Mabel Normand told me it was Tumulty, BD's father. I'd heard of him, of course—he had a great West Coast reputation—so I went over and talked to him. A grand old guy. Then, that night at dinner—everybody dressed to the nines—God, we were handsome!—it was a sitdown for about sixty at least. Those were the speechmaking and toast days. Every so often somebody got up and talked—great fun it was, too. Toward the end of the evening, BD got up—he was a little fried— but nobody much noticed because *everybody* was, and he made a longish speech. It was frightfully sentimental. All about how nobody ever got anywhere on their own and about how every successful career had plenty of help from lots of people and how he was no exception. Then he went into one of those 'Everything I am or was or ever hope to be, I owe to a man who honors me and our ancient profession by his presence here tonight—my great teacher and dearest friend, John J. Tumulty, of San Francisco!' Well, everybody stood up and drank and then sat down to listen to the reply—all toasts were responded to. But the old man sat there, stunned, looking at BD. And BD was trying to get him to his feet, but Tumulty just sat. I thought to myself he was overdoing it a little. Finally, he did get up and then he delivered like a real old pro. He had that way of connecting with an audience, you know. And no mistake. I remember his speech about how disappointed we were all going to be when we got to Paradise, because it couldn't compare with the way we were living now—and then some stories about BD and what a terrible actor he'd been and how the most *he* had ever learned about acting he learned trying to teach BD."

"What else?"

"Holy Smoke, man, this only happened about twenty-five years ago, you want it word for word?"

"No, but didn't you think it was odd, right after you'd

been told this was his father?"

"Well, as I say, there was all kinds of gossip around in those days, that he was and wasn't and was adopted and so on, so it didn't seem to matter much. But a few minutes later, the old man disappeared. I never saw him again, except once on the stage. I remember looking around for him, but the butler told me he'd left—that he had to get back to San Francisco. But you know, talk about orgies—BD had a pool built in a glen, and there was a maze of hedges around, and usually, along about two in the morning . . ."

Somewhere, someone had told about a time T came back from a visit to Johnny and had turned old. Who was it? No matter, I can look it up another time. But this must have been the incident. Of course. I feel as though I've got a whole corner finished in a big crossword puzzle. This night was the big letdown. When, after all those years, BD turned him, in one minute, from a father into a friend.

I wonder if Whitman knows all this. Surely not. If he did, he would have told it to me by this time.

7 April 52   The Beverly Hills Hotel.

TMY. I am back here for a short stretch. Calif always revives my excitement about the Tumulty story.

Whitman has promised to let me have more Tumulty letters.

I ran into BD in Romanoff's at lunch yesterday. He was cordial, so maybe he was not as offended as I gathered.

I wonder if this isn't a simple father-son story, maybe with the added fillip of their not being physically related. Should

90

the real father come into it somehow? On that, I have looked through the Academy Players Directory but CB is not in it. No problem. He should be easy to locate. Bobby Webb in Casting? BD must have *some* relationship with Bannister; his presence in the cast of the picture cannot be coincidental. If I contact him, he may say something to BD and God knows what *that* might brew. (I am still convinced that BD was behind that pink letter. Or *am* I?) Pattern: a man with two fathers—the man who sired him and the man who brought him up. Is there a heredity-environment angle here?

4/10/52   Columbia Studios.

TMY. I have something to add to this, at last.

This morning I phoned BD at his house and asked him to have a drink someday. I said I had a script he might like.

He asked, "How about today?"

"Sure," I answered. "What time? And where?"

"Any time after six. Here."

"No, I'd like to buy *you* a drink."

"Here. If you insist on paying, I'll take your money."

I got there at twenty after six.

"Come out to the hideout," he said, and led me across the back terrace, over the lawn, past the swimming pool, and around the back of the bathhouse to a tiny, two-room cottage. There is nothing in it, much. No decoration, no pictures. Just a few large chairs. A long work table. A couch. The room is one of the pleasantest I have seen out here. No ego supports, no affectation, none of the Hollywood work-props, although I'll bet more work has been done in this room than in most of the "studies" I've seen.

He got a bottle of that great Berry Brothers All-Malt Scotch out of a cabinet, took it into the bathroom, and came back with two drinks in nonmatching glasses.

"Scotch and tap," he said. "Best thing in the world for you."

"I'm sure," I said.

"How've you been?"

"All right. Working on a play. Hard work."

"So they say."

"And then, of course, when you get it written, if you ever do, who do you get to play it? Actors for the stage get rarer all the time."

BD laughed, then laughed some more. Finally he looked at me and shook his head, pityingly.

"Fella, you're about as transparent as a Marilyn Monroe nightgown. Is that honestly the best curve-in you could think of to get on your subject?"

He had caught me flat-footed, but I tried to brazen it out. "What subject?"

"Oh, brother! You must think I'm good and thick. If you want to talk about Tumulty, why the hell don't you say so?"

I finished the drink. He had made it stronger than the ones I am accustomed to. That, and the fact that I had not eaten all day, made me lightheaded and reckless.

"I don't want to talk about Tumulty," I said.

"Yes, you do."

"No, I don't," I heard myself saying. Some small power of judgment tried to intervene, but was not strong enough to stem the boldness. "I want to talk about Clay Bannister."

"Go ahead."

His cool threw me. I recovered and said, "I didn't realize

he was in the picture—not until the other day. I happened to notice his name on the cast sheet."

" 'What sharp eyes you have,' said Little Red Riding Hood."

"He looks exactly like you."

"You mean *I* look exactly like *him*. What's so odd about that?"

"Nothing."

"He's a hopelessly incompetent actor—and gets worse and worse. By now he's had time to perfect his mistakes."

The echo of Tumulty in that remark did not escape me.

"I thought he was all right," I said.

"You have to be better than all right to be any good. No, he's a bum, but I always have him in my pictures."

"How do you mean, 'always'?"

"I'll tell you how I mean 'always.' I've made fifty-six pictures and he's been in fifty-six of them."

"A luck piece?"

"No, it's just that I want to do something for him, but the only thing he'll take from me is a job."

"Not like *some* people we know, huh?"

The wrong thing to say. He looked at me, long and hard.

"O.K. if I pour one more?" I asked. "Remember I'm paying."

He said nothing. I poured a drink, went into the bathroom, got some water out of the basin tap. When I returned, he had stretched out on the couch.

"Sit down," he said.

I did so.

"What is all this?" he asked.

I said nothing for a full minute, trying to organize my thoughts. I decided to follow Mark Twain's advice: "When in doubt, tell the truth." I told BD of meeting The Old Actor back in 1940, of getting interested in the subject, tracking down all the clues. I left out nothing, not even the doorman at the Alcazar.

When I had finished, he said, "Well, I'll be God-damned."

"Why?"

"I don't know. It sounds interesting, but you never think of yourself as a story, or part of a story. Why didn't you tell me all this long ago? You may be on the track of something, but your approach is cockeyed. Cradle-to-the-grave stuff always flops—there isn't room in a picture for the whole story. Then there's the *Citizen Kane* search-for-a-character gambit, but that's a tough one to handle. What you ought to do is pick one situation, then you might get someplace. Your best bet—if you've got a bet at all—is to choose a representative episode and use that as a reflecting glass for the whole story. What would you rather see? The story of Abe Lincoln from birth to death—told in two or three chopped-up hours? Or the full, well-organized story of the last day of his life? *Distill* your subject, boy, don't *spill* it. And don't try to make Tumulty the lead because you'll never do it. Find yourself a boy-girl story or—if you think you're up to it—a man-woman. And let old Tumulty be—whatever. Greek chorus, catalyst, matchmaker—a good minor part aimed for a supporting player's Oscar. But not—for God's sake—the lead. He was a peculiar and that gets to be dull."

"Why a peculiar?"

"Well, an eccentric, anyway. An audience wants to *understand* a leading character and they can't do that if *you* don't understand him and you never will. I knew him most of my life and *I* never understood him. He didn't understand *himself*."

I said nothing, but BD is one of those with an extra length

94

to his antenna. He spoke sharply and suddenly, in reply to my unspoken words.

"Listen, you didn't know him! I did! Do *you* like anybody who doesn't like *you?*"

"No."

"Was it *my* fault he ran into a bad piece of lady-work? No. But I was always the symbol of that to him."

"I wonder why he hung on to you, then."

"Who knows?"

"What did he ever do—or say—that gave you the impression—"

"Look, sonny, you're not my for Christ's sake *analyst,* after all. Lay off."

"Sorry."

We drank in silence.

"He was colorful, though," said BD with a hacking laugh. "As I say, be a great character for a number three spot. You know, two young people and then however he relates to them."

"Who are the young people?"

"How the hell do I know? What do you want me to do? Hand you a story so that you can sell it to me tomorrow morning? Don't try to make a middle-aged loser the central figure in a story. You'll go on your ass."

He went on talking, but it was rule-book stuff I had heard a thousand times before, not only from him, but from many others, including myself.

What he had said earlier, however, impressed me. I've thought of it all evening, right through dinner at Bill and Edie's and *High Noon,* which they ran afterward. Damn. I should have started something the day after I got the bare bones of the story from The Old Actor. Now I'm involved with the mystery of the *real* story. After all, my business is fancy, not fact. Supposed to be.

(Title: *Fact and Fancy*. If not for this, for something.)

BD and I sat for a while in charged silence. It started to get dark, but he turned on no lights. I had another angle I wanted to pursue. Should I? Why not? The ice was now broken. Moreover, I saw he was pleasantly plastered and have observed that this condition makes him less sensitive and more talkative.

"How did he and Rose get along?" I asked.

He sat up sharply. "Who?"

"Rose Adriance."

"Do you know her?"

"No."

"Then where the hell do you come off calling her *Rose*, you punk?"

"Sorry. I think of her as a character in the story."

"She's a character, all right."

He got up and started his slow pace-around.

"Really?" I prompted. "In what way?"

He laughed.

"If we're going to get onto the subject of Miss Rose Adriance, my boy, I'll have to go up to the house and find another bottle."

"Do you ever hear from her?"

I was surprised at my shameless insistence.

"No. And she never hears from me, either. We had it while we had it and then we were both glad to get rid of it. How the hell we ever got pasted together, neither of us ever knew. She was a superior proposition, though not as superior as she *thought* she was. She never said it, but there was always something faintly disapproving about her attitude. She never got the hang of this town. Or of me. She didn't like bad language. *That* kind. The whole thing was his idea.

96

He wanted it, believed in it, so he engineered it."

He started building a fire in the fireplace, and laughed.

"*There's* a story for you. Along the lines I threw you a while ago. Girl, boy, and charming old buttinski—maybe better if the boy isn't his son. Just a guy. Keep all your old theatre background. He thinks the boy and girl are right for each other—see?—so he plots and plans and gets her going, then the boy going. Finally has his way. The marriage turns out an absolute disaster. And whereas they begin by simply disliking one another, they wind up loathing one another—and him, too. How's that? Maybe do it with a few songs."

"Might be a notion at that."

"You sell that one, boyo, and I'll call you good. Maybe you could do it as a Swedish picture."

Now that he had begun kidding it, I knew that further talk was hopeless. I started to leave, but he kept talking and wouldn't let me go. After a while, there was a buzz. He picked up the house phone.

"Yes? . . . No, *cara mia,* I'm working. . . . Fine, he's fine. He's got an interesting new idea. . . . I don't know, an hour or so. . . . All right, dear."

He hung up. "My wife sends you *molte congratulazioni,*" he said, overdoing the Italian accent.

"Thank you. I like your wife."

"Make me an offer," he shot back.

What is it about certain remarks that gives them the power to shock?

"I wish she'd act again," I said. "She was great."

"She acts. Every day. She's given some of the greatest performances ever seen right up there in the big house."

I saw this was no subject to pursue, changed it.

"I'd like to meet Clay Bannister. Would you mind?"

"Why should I?"

There was a soft knock at the door and a moment later a maid came in, carrying towels. She was young (24?), not unattractive (Scandinavian? German? Swiss?), becomingly overweight, no makeup, hair in a bun.

"Good evening, sir," she said, almost inaudibly.

"Go ahead, Greta. It's all right."

"Thank you, sir."

She moved about the room with dispatch, emptying ashtrays and drawing the blinds. BD poured another drink and took it straight. A few seconds later the maid went into the bathroom. As she did so, he moved to me and said, "You can go now, if you have to. And I think you have to."

He smiled. We shook hands and I left. We had both forgotten that I had come, ostensibly, to give him a script.

4/12/52   Bev Hills Hotel.

TMY. What a day. BD asked me to lunch in his bungalow at Twentieth. He wanted a report on the Broadway season. While we were having coffee, the phone beside his plate rang. He picked it up.

"Fine," he said. "Wheel him in!" He hung up and turned to me. "Mr. Bannister," he said.

I gave a little jump. He laughed.

"What's the matter? I thought you wanted to meet him."

The door opened and Bannister came in. Tall, paunchy, beautifully dressed.

"Come in, Clay, sit down."

He introduced me. Bannister and I shook hands. BD said, "Be impressive. This guy's a writer."

"I can play *anything!*" shouted Bannister. He laughed a hollow laugh, which sounded exactly like BD's.

Now that they sat there together, the resemblance disappeared. I studied Bannister. How old would he be? At least eighty. His hair is white. Not gray, *white.* Complexion, pink. Eyes, blue. His mouth is slightly open at all times. How did Cecil Beaton describe that male model we once tested? "All those teeth and a mouth that won't shut!"

"Coffee?" BD was asking.

"If it's strong and hot, yes," replied Clay. "I'm on a hangover you could photograph." He laughed again.

"Take a Dexedrine," said BD.

"What's *that?*"

"Like Benzedrine, only kills you slower."

"No, thanks," said Bannister. "I'm so full of stuff now—no. Thanks though."

BD pointed to me with his cup. "This guy's interested in Tumulty."

"Who?"

"John J. Tumulty."

Bannister looked at me, vacantly. "He's dead," he said.

"I know," I replied.

"He wants to write a movie about him," said BD.

"No, I don't."

"Sure you do."

"Not about *him.* Just about those days, those times."

"Why?" asked Bannister.

BD looked at me. "There's one for you. Let's see you get out of *that.*"

They both laughed, and it was as though only one of them was laughing.

"Interesting," I muttered lamely.

"They were rip-roaring days, all right," said Bannister.

99

"Maybe we can get together and talk about them some-time."

"Sure thing," said Bannister. "But hell, I don't know how much I'd remember. I can't even remember what happened *last night!*"

"Maybe that's all to the good," said BD.

"Too true, too true," intoned Bannister.

Ellie stuck her head in the door. "Himself can work you in if you get right on up, she says."

"On the way," said BD. "See you later, men."

He was gone. Bannister and I sat there with nothing to say. Had I known I was going to meet him, I'd have worked out a plan. As it was, I was off balance, as though I had been suddenly introduced to a character in a novel I happened to be reading.

"I suppose you knew Tumulty pretty well?" I began.

"No, not well. But I knew him. He hired me fast and he fired me fast. I was just starting out in those days. A kid. Frankly, I wasn't much of an actor back then."

"What sort of fellow was he?"

"Jolly old cuss. Full of jokes and quips—but he could be tough, too, you know. I tell you frankly, we ran into a bit of a ruckus, he and I, over a female, see? I mean—Jesus. I didn't know. I was just a pipsqueak starting out—know what I mean?—and she was a hell of a handsome piece of ass, and nobody in the damn troupe tipped me, see, to the fact that she was *his* number. That was how we happened to blow up —not because of my acting. I mean to say, I'm not saying I was Booth in those days, but hell, none of us were."

"I understand Tumulty was, damn near."

"Oh, well, I suppose, for those days. I think he'd have trouble getting booked nowadays. He was what we used to call an over-*feeler*. He could get worked up over any old

100

part at all. Good director, though. I think Johnny here learned a lot from him along those lines—a few of the tricks of the trade—although he wouldn't admit it, the bastard—and by the way, don't ever tell him I said that."

"No, no," I said.

I saw at once that the way to dig out this part of the story was to get pally enough with him so that we could sit around panning BD. This might lead to other things.

I got up. "Well, I'm awfully sorry, Mr. Bannister, but I've got to get back to Columbia. It was nice meeting you."

"The pleasure was mine."

"May I call you?"

"Do that. Here's my card. I'll stick around. Maybe Johnny wants to see me about something."

2 May 52   Beverly Hills.

TMY. Dinner at Cukor's last night. Great luck, I get to sit next to Ethel Barrymore. It doesn't take me long to get onto the subject. I connect at least a part of her life with San Francisco. EB's memory is one of the wonders of the world. Also, I remember it was Lionel Barrymore who spoke at T's funeral.

"Miss B, how well did you know John J. Tumulty?"

"Are you being personal?" she answered, in that voice of voices, pretending to be shocked. "My Uncle John used to discharge members of his company for 'presuming.' "

"He's an interest of mine," I said.

"Well," she said, "I never knew him as intimately—shall we say—as most of the rest of the female population of San

Francisco, but I did know him. And, of course, he and Lionel were chums. He was a beautiful actor."

"Was he a beautiful *man,* too?"

"Physi*cule* or spiri*tule?*" she replied.

"And/or," I said.

"He wasn't handsome, at least not conventionally. But he was attractive in a way that the Arrow Collar types never got to be. He never shouted onstage, or even gave the impression of speaking up, but no one ever missed a word. I adored him. Off, he was as convivial as only an Irish actor can be. He never stopped acting, but it wasn't a matter of showing off—" she dropped her voice as she interpolated "—the sort we'll see around here tonight. It was simply that he couldn't possibly *not* act, heighten the effect of every moment, dramatize a ride in an elevator, and reproduce every person he so much as mentioned. Sometimes with a gesture or a word, sometimes with a full-length portrait. He could do anything." She laughed her famous laugh, and added, "What's more, he *did!*"

"What's the inside on the BD story?"

"Oh, dear, is *that* around again? I thought we'd disposed of it in seventeen seventy-six. Or was that another story? I hate gossip, anyway; it's usually so incomplete."

"Do you know Clay Bannister?"

"No."

"An actor out here?"

"No. Should I?"

"No."

"What about him?"

"If you didn't hate gossip, I'd give you a guess or two."

"And what has all this to do with Tumulty? Or am I in the right conversation?"

"Clay Bannister, some say, is BD's father. Do you think that's possible?"

"Well, *someone* had to be!"

"You don't think it was Tumulty himself?"

"Lord, no. As I remember the account, a girl in his company got into what used to be called 'trouble' and died of it. And John, as a lark, decided to keep the baby, and did. If you'd known him, you'd understand how he would think this a wildly amusing proposition. Then, of course, the fantasies began. That John was really the baby's father, that someone else was but that John had been in love with the mother, that the girl had committed suicide, that the girl was really Lillian Russell, Lord knows what else."

"What do you think was the nearest to the truth?"

"What I've said. This girl in his company left the baby and he took it on, that's all."

"Her name was Juanita."

"Whose?"

"The girl's."

"Was it really?"

At this point, Orry Kelly, on EB's right, took her attention, and though I tried all evening, I never got back onto Tumulty with EB. Her version certainly would not do. Some lark! No, it is clear that if T keeps the kid he has to do it for some reason other than a whimsical one. Sentimental or emotional or guilt. Something.

Maybe I could get a grip on all this if I dug deeper into its *meaning.* Thornton says the French stand in a false relation to women, which is why 90 percent (his figure) of French drama is about adultery; a woman is only interesting when she can be stolen, clandestinely. They are afraid to take the responsibility of the totality of her. He quotes Stendhal as saying that the man's vanity plays the major role. "Go to

Italy," said Stendhal, "where love is *total.*" (Maybe B should be a Frenchman?) How to relate the above to the new notion? I have a feeling I am on the wrong road.

6–7–52   Malibu.

TMY. The Ziffrens went to New York last week and said I could use their beautiful place here. I find it too far for daily commuting, but fine for weekends, so resolve to come out here whenever I can and try once and for all to organize the Tumulty story. After five days of studio superstenography, it is healthy to spend a couple of days writing something that does not need to please anyone but me.

I got here last night—brought no books, no magazines, no newspapers. Early this morning, I looked over a lot of the Tumulty notes. They are scattered all through the notebooks and my eye kept hitting other notes on other unfinished notions. Depressing. Who was it said, a writer must be sure to keep a notebook and must take care never to refer to it?

So I sat on the terrace and looked at the sea most of the day and thought over what do I know about Tumulty? Late in the afternoon, I begin to set it down in narrative form. It does not go well. Where it is real, or what I believe to be real, it smells of life. Where I invent or fill in or attempt to explain, it just smells. I could have written an essay on the ocean and what it looks like all day and how it moves and changes color and sound and rhythm—but nothing good came out on T. Tomorrow, no looking at the ocean.

6–16–52   Malibu.

TMY. I did a stupid thing—asked Bannister to come out here and spend the weekend. The whole thing was a total loss. I will return to Beverly Hills tonight after two of the most irritating days in my memory. He is upstairs now, sleeping it off. As soon as he wakes or if he doesn't, I mean to wake him and give him some cock-and-bull about having to go back into town. He is awful. A meaningless nothing. A bore. A fool. A completely feckless jerk.

Nothing is added to the story, except what is almost a final discouragement. This guy is without principle, without feeling, without intelligence of any kind. How the hell he could have been attractive to anyone ever is beyond my understanding. He is the complete voluptuary and nothing more. He talks of his sexual activities in the most disgusting way. He claims to be at it still, which I don't doubt. He takes shots, he says, and they work. Apparently that is all there is in life for him. To think that this louse and his appetites could have in any way touched Tumulty's life is dispiriting. And why the hell I am so for Tumulty is hard to understand. There are too many unanswered questions about him. The whole pack of them begin to give me a pain.

(To make it easier on myself, I set up the Butoba in the closet, hid the mike in the clutter on the coffee table, and recorded his spills.)

At first, he only faintly remembered Juanita. In fact, he did not recall her last name at all until I supplied it.

"Juanita Perez!" he exclaimed. "By Jesus, that's right.

105

That was her name, all right."

In view of the fact that she was BD's mother, and that this heel still lives off BD, it seems odd I should have to tell him her name. And he *does* live off BD. BD said Bannister never takes anything from him except a job. Well, BD is a liar or this guy is or they both are. Because according to this crumb, BD has looked after him for years. Pays his rent, restaurant bills, clothing bills, and every other damned thing. I see no reason why he would lie about this. On the other hand, there is every reason why BD would, particularly since he feels so bitterly about T and those checks.

More from Bannister on the subject of Juanita:

"She had some Spanish blood in her, I believe. Or Mexican. Man, she could go! I never got my fill of her, not by a long shot."

"How did it all start?"

"Well, see, I commenced lovin' her up on the stage, right there when we'd be playin' our parts. And she went right along with it. At first, I couldn't tell if she was acting or if it was the come-on, but I soon found out. It was there all right! The question was how to get at it. She and old Tumulty were hooked up in some way, and I didn't want to lose the job. Well, before we could get to it, he walks in on us one day. She'd been cryin' and kept sayin' no all the time I was hottin' 'er up. She *said* one thing, but she *did* another. You ever get any of those? Well, in he came and there was nothing for it, so I blew. I was packin' when in she came. Now what I *should've* done was put the boots to her then and there and let it go at that, but she said she was comin' with me. I asked her if she had any dough and she said no but she could get some. So I tell her do that and she does—and where do you think she got it?—from *him,* by God. And we headed for Mexico. Everything fine and dandy for a month or so and

106

then—got a match? Thanks—then she took to hysterics every hour on the hour. I couldn't make her out. And she'd be in the church all the time, and I mean *all*. I couldn't get her out. Then one morning I got home, and she was gone."

I made a careful note of "one morning I got home." There was much more along these lines.

He has gone, thank God. A couple of hours ago, I heard him stirring upstairs. When he started down, I turned on the recorder. He suggested he get on the phone and "line something up for later." I told him I had to work. He started hinting around about going back to town and I told him I'd get him a taxi right after dinner. He was pleased and relieved, but no more than I was. Meanwhile, I tried to get whatever else he had. I asked him about later meetings with Tumulty. There were four. Here they are, slightly edited.

One: "Somebody told me about this kid actor in the Tumulty troupe. Now, I'd heard Juanita'd had this boy and died, so naturally I was, y'know, curious to know if this was the one or not. I was shacked up with this husky old money bag in Santa Barbara at the time. So I got her to take a trip to San Francisco. The first night we went to see. The kid was cute, all right, but hell, I didn't know. I wanted to, though. I mean to say, that was only human, wasn't it? My own flesh and blood. Then after, I wrote this letter to Tumulty and had it dropped around to the theatre by our chauffeur. Oh, sure, we were the class. But I wanted to bust out because, to tell you true, the situation was gettin' to be too much for me. And the ol' girl, she was supposed to be a little off, at least that's what the rest of her family was all the time tryin' to prove to one court of law or another—and maybe she *was*

107

off in some ways, but she sure in hell never let *me* get two dollars ahead of her. She'd pay any damn bill of mine I had sent in, but she fixed it so I could never lay my hands on more than a couple hundred at a time. She figured if I ever loaded up, I'd blow, and how right she was. But she never gave me the chance.

"Well, the same day—I'm talkin' about the same day I dropped the note—I hear from Tumulty and he says, sure, meet him over at the Crystal, that was the place in those days. I got there first and waited for him. He came in, finally, after the show. I got up and waved to him and he came over and we shook hands and sat down. We ordered drinks and talked about this and that and it was all right. The only thing bothered me, though, was him lookin' at me the whole time and never takin' his eyes off my face. It's the kind of thing can make you nervous as all hell, know what I mean? I don't mean he looked at me hard or mad or even annoyed—but more like he was studyin' me, like he was lookin' for somethin' he couldn't find.

"He wanted to know all about it—where we went that time and where we stayed and for how long and what she said. I tried to make up some stuff—what I usually do—I tell people what they want to hear—that's why they love me. But it didn't work too well with Tumulty. I told him how a few days after we got to Mexico we had a fight and she said she was sorry she ever left him—that is, Tumulty. And he said, 'Don't give me that, mister. I want facts or nothing.' So I insisted that's what he was gettin'—how did he know it wasn't? And he said, 'Because you're as lamentable an actor off as you are on.' That's the way he talked—words like that. I tried to tell him I was sorry and all, but he wouldn't have that, either. After a while, my curiosity got the better of me and I said, 'That kid in your show. Is he mine?' Tumulty says,

108

'No, mine. *You're* his father, but he's *my son.*' I tell you, he was *some* dodo. I never knew what the hell he was talkin' about half the time. Then he asked me would I like to see the boy, and I said, no not just then."

Two: "Later on I went East and more or less lost touch. I'd see some little thing now and then in the *Mirror,* but that's about all. You realize the coasts were farther apart in those days. I had a pretty good streak there—in New York, I mean—for a while, but what the hell, I won't deny it, I've always been an easy-come, easy-go kind of a bloke—only way to be—so then I got sick. An old clap of mine kicked up and by the time I was better, I was right down to leather. New York was full of fair-weather pals, so I headed back West. A bad trip it was, too.

"By the time I got to San Francisco, I was close to shot. I looked up Tumulty—I didn't know anyone else there by then—and I told him the truth. I mean I put it right on the line and said I needed work. He hemmed and hawed, and finally he gave me a straight no. I said to him, 'Why die hard? What's gone is gone.' And he said, 'Sure, that's right,' but he didn't see how I would fit into his company. I said to him, 'You mean you don't like my acting?' And he said, 'No, I don't.'

"He was lying, of course. The thing he didn't want was havin' me around the company with the boy, and the way things were, I can't say I blame him all the way for that. But it wasn't helpin' me out of my tough spot. I said to him I *had* to have a hand and would he mind I talked to the boy. Now, naturally, I was only teasing along here askin' him, because I didn't need his permission, now did I? But I thought puttin' it that way, he'd get the idea of what I was talkin' about. So he tells me, no, he doesn't think I ought to do that, and about how the boy's just come out of the Navy and was havin' a time gettin' into things again and he thought it might be better if I didn't upset him and more along those lines, and he says, why don't I go down to Los Angeles where there's a lot of work for actors who're willin' to stay around the moving picture thing? And I said, yes, I'd been thinkin' about that, but a man needed a stake for something like that. I had to have a wardrobe and enough to get a bit of a front, and he said, 'What do you think it would take?' and I told him two or three thousand. Now, mind you, I didn't think it *would* take that, but I figured I better get the number up there because even if he came through, which I didn't expect he would, he'd be sure to cut me down. They always do.

"Well, imagine my surprise when he said, 'All right, come around tomorrow afternoon. I'll have three thousand for you.' I had an idea he was goin' to pull something, but I wasn't scared of him and I turned up and he handed me this envelope and in it there sure in hell was three thousand in cash. Nothin' but hundred-dollar bills. I said, 'Give me a piece of paper and I'll give you my I.O.U.' He says, 'I don't want your I.O.U.' All right, now you may think I'm touchy, but this hurt my God-damned feelings. I mean, what the hell, if you're goin' to make a loan to a guy, make it, and don't throw in an insult. I put the money back on the table and I said, 'I don't want any presents from you, Tumulty, I asked for a loan. You may have to ask for a loan yourself someday.' He says to me, '*Some*day! Where the hell do you think I got *this* three?' And I said, 'Wherever it was I guess they took your I.O.U., didn't they?' And he says, 'They sure in hell did.' 'Then, by God,' I said, 'you'll take mine.' And he did, too. I knew I had him in a corner. That was when I first came down to L.A. What a place in those days! More damn beaver around. And it's a real antsy climate if you don't stay in it too long at a time."

Three: "Down in Los Angeles, maybe three-four years later, I got a few letters from Tumulty, figured he was beginnin' to dun me for the dough, so I dodged him a while. Finally, I get this letter and he says not to worry about the money, that's *not* what he wants to see me about and we fix a date and I go on over. He's got a little inside single at The Hollywood Hotel, that was about the only place back then, and we sit around and talk a while. Finally, he gets to the point. The point is, he thinks the boy and I ought to get together. To this end he's come down, he says, and he's had a session with the boy and told him. Well, it turned out it was no surprise to the boy, though I suppose Tumulty thought it was goin' to be. The boy said, yes, he knew all about it. Of course, he didn't know me, or who I was, but he knew Tumulty wasn't his father, that was all. I didn't see the point of it, but he was a man so used to havin' his own way it was no use arguin' with him.

"We sat there and pretty soon there was a knock on the door and in came Johnny, or, that is, BD as he'd begun to call himself. Tumulty introduced us and we shook hands. We were both feelin' sort of funny, but Tumulty took the whole thing in stride. We all had a drink, then we got to talkin' about his new name and he said these people he was under contract to were the ones insisted. I said, 'Well, so long's you had to change it, too bad you don't use your real name.' He says, 'How do you mean, real?' And I said, 'Mine, of course.' He and Tumulty look at each other and sort of smile. I got up and I said, 'Gentlemen, I didn't come here to be sniggered at.' And I started to go. Well, Tumulty held me back and said not to take it so big and after all, he was goin' to be up in Frisco all the time and if Johnny and I were both goin' to be in the same city, there was no reason we shouldn't be friends and all that.

"I stuck around a while, then the boy left. Tumulty and I sat there talkin' and drinkin'. Tell you the complete truth, we got stiffer'n a board, and as they say, *in vino veritas*—by God, we had one hell of a lot of *veritas*. He says, 'Y'know, there was one night there I decided the best thing would be to kill you.' 'Is that so?' I said. 'Yes,' he says. And then we had another drink. After a while he says, 'Clay, you and I are enemies, and the hell of it is we're too old and tired, maybe too civilized, to fight it out. I'm sorry for Johnny because our battle has to be fought out inside him. A lot of you is in him and a lot of me and that's where we do our battle.' 'Well,' I said, 'the nice thing about that is nobody gets hurt.' 'Don't be so sure,' he says. 'Don't be so God-damned sure.'

"I didn't know what he was talkin' about much, but hell, I didn't know what *I* was talkin' about either, by that time. It was a damned peculiar night. He went on and on and he was in one of those Irish moods, talkin' like a poet, almost. And he was gettin' off stuff about how we all struggle with what we are and what we want to be and have to take what's in us, what we've inherited, whether we like it or not or believe it or not. I went to sleep, finally, while he was still talkin'. When I woke up, he was gone. I mean, checked out. For a minute there, I worried he might have left me the bill. But he didn't. He paid."

Four: "The last time I saw him was up in San Francisco, not long before he died. I don't know that I ought to tell you about it. It's personal. Well, maybe not personal, *confiden-*

tial. Oh, what the hell, it's all over now.

"BD sent for me, said he had somethin' he wanted me to do for him. I said sure. By then he was slipping, though he didn't seem to know it. He told me he wanted me to go up to see Tumulty. They were more or less on the outs by now, I don't know why. He said to me he'd had a batch of letters from the old boy, still askin' for money. This time the reason was he was sick. Johnny said to go on up there and see if he really *was* sick and if he was, let him know. But if he wasn't, give Tumulty a message that he was in no position to help him out any more, because things weren't goin' too well. BD said he didn't want to write this, for reasons of his own, so that was why he wanted *me* to do the job.

"Tumulty was livin' with some Swedes up there and when I turned up, he was pretty surprised. The first thing was, he was no more sick than I was. He just looked at me, and he says, 'I don't like the message and I don't like the messenger.' Oh, he was a salty old pisser, right up to the end. I said to him, 'The boy says he's done all he can for you right across the years. He claims he's taken care of you to the full.' 'That's right,' says Tumulty, 'I have no complaints.' 'But he can't do it any more,' I said. And he says, 'Well, if he can't, he can't.' Then I said, 'Well, that's the end of the message, John, but I want to put in something of my own. I think the boy's through down there. I don't know if he knows it or believes it, but he's had his day. It's the talkies or squawkies or whatever the hell they call 'em. His voice doesn't seem to go with the rest of him. Several like that. John Gilbert. They're after a whole new kind now and he's been around too long. So what I mean to say is, I think he's on the level with you. If he was doin' any better than he is, I don't think you'd find him mean.' 'No,' says Tumulty, 'he's never been that. He's

113

been generous. On the other hand, I've got to think of my own problems, too. I looked after him for thirty years and he's only looked after me for ten. So he owes me twenty more years. Of course, there's always a chance he might get lucky and I might suddenly cool. I haven't been well. You tell him I appreciate his difficulties and he doesn't have to do anything on the scale he's been doing, but I expect him to do something.' 'I don't think he can, John,' I says. 'I don't give a good God-damn what *you* think,' he says. 'You tell him what I told you to tell him. I'm broke and he's not. He may have to cut down, but that won't kill him. . . .' Words to that effect. So I said, 'Look, I'll tell him anything you want me to tell him. I'm only a measly carrier pigeon, but I've got my opinions. He said if you were really sick, the way you said you were, that was one thing, but if not, he wanted to know. Now, I'm not going to lie to him any more than I'm lyin' to you.' And the old boy looked at me and he says, 'All right, if the only way he'll come through is if I'm sick, then, by Jesus, I'll *get* sick. And don't think I can't do it.'

"Frankly, I think he was beginnin' to go a little crackers by this time. So I went down and told the whole thing to Johnny. I don't know what happened, but not long after, Tumulty died, so the problem solved itself, the way most problems do, if you just *wait* long enough."

I believe some of this, in spite of the source. I don't know why I should be so irritated by every detail that is uncomplimentary to Tumulty. The essential difference between characters in fiction and those in reality is that the latter are inclined to be composed of many more colors. A real person is a mass of contradictions and inconsistencies and a maddening lack of logic. Only in fiction are they ever of a piece.

6/20/52   B.H., Calif.

TMY. A letter from Hobie.

Dear False Friend,

I see by the papers that you are in our state again. But
naturally, you do not inform pals of this unless you happen to want something. I am tempted to withhold all the
superlative John J. Tumulty work I have done, but on the
other hand, it was through this that I met my present
fascinator, Miss Dolores Varro, for which undying thanks.
Will you be best man? May we name first-born for you?
You can see this has gone beyond the jesting stage.

As to JJT, there is a lot of info up here. Or have you lost
interest? The old guitar man is still on tap, and I am trying
to keep him oiled up for you.

Meanwhile, here are a few random scraps I have been
collecting.

TUMULTY, JOHN J. Born: (in a trunk, no doubt) Oakland, California, October 3, 1849. Father: Arthur Lennox
Tumulty of Cork; popular banjoist, minstrel and ballad
singer. Also composer of well-known songs, among them:
WRONG WAY WAGON, HOLE IN THE MOUNTAIN,
LASSIE LASS; ran popular melodeon, San Francisco,
1854–1878; died in great San Francisco fire of 1906.
Mother: Anne (Casey) Tumulty of New York. Singer and
dancer. Partner of husband in variety entertainments,
various parts of America, then with him to California in
1848. JJT educated parochial schools; Oakland, San Francisco, Santa Barbara. No college. Began stage career age

115

of 17 in father's music hall. Played piano and cornet. Later, sketches and imitations. Also protean art—seven Dickens characters. Later joined tour of MAZEPPA with Adah Isaacs Menken. Returned to San Francisco and joined Robinson-Crawley Company which played comprehensive Shakespeare repertory up and down coast. Formed first of his own traveling companies, 1877. A favorite in all parts of California. Among his famous roles: Richard III, Bob Acres in THE RIVALS, RIP VAN WINKLE (own adaptation, many claim he did it before and better than Joseph Jefferson; others say he did Jefferson version. You pays your money etc. This life-and-death point can be checked out), King Lear, Beau Brummel (the Clyde Fitch), George Washington. Also play by Rosamund Manders called THE NEWEST WORLD, and one by Temple Smith: POOR RICHARD in which JJT played Ben Franklin. Never married. Big drinker some years, then teetotaler. Considered great ladies' man but no scandal available. Yet. (Professor at Columbia School of Journalism once said the first things to look for in the subject of an interview are the vices. Whether you used them or not, it would give you an understanding of your pigeon. Pass this on to you, gratis.)

Come on up here. I mean it.

Utmost,
Hobie

I've heard that before. Look for the vices. Not only the vices, but the weaknesses and the errors. This hooks in with the classic advice to actors: When you play a good man, show his bad side, too. And vice versa. There should be a little villain in every hero and hero in every villain. As to T, what have we got? The worst thing is that he was a merciless sponge. Also, there is evidence that he did, now and then, dissemble. But BD owed T his life. No amount of money

116

could have made up for what T did.

As with most characters, there is more than one story here. The trick is to find the right one. A lot more happened to Hamlet than what we see in *Hamlet.* And to Hedda Gabler. Blanche DuBois. Henry Higgins.

There is in T the story of a man's devotion to a boy who might have been his son. Big star brings up the boy, trains him. Bad days come, the boy is now a man, something something, the boy comes through for him. There is also the story of father and son after the same girl. But better if it is his *real* son. On the *third* hand (as HB actually said in a conference the other day!) it might be best to confine the whole story to the early part, ending with T adopting the kid. There is enough to work with there, and might be better than stretching the thing out, which always has the danger of distending the story.

7/2/52   San Francisco.

TMY. I have been here almost a week, but have made no Tumulty notes, because the whole proposition has become discouraging. The things I have dug up on this trip make me wonder what the hell I saw in Tumulty in the first place. To use him as a character, it is necessary to stick to the surface. His façade is attractive, even glamorous, but beyond it is less so; like a circus side show where far more is promised on the outside than you get on the inside.

This was made clear to me on the first day here. Hobie had found three articles about T. They seemed useful. The same night, I went to the Spanish place to talk to the guitar guy.

117

The articles were the appearance. The memories of the guitar guy, the reality. The juxtaposition was not a happy experience.

The first clipping is from the San Francisco *Herald,* September 4, 1895. (T was 46)

JOHN J. TUMULTY TO BEGIN NEW SEASON

Company of 20 Is Assembled

Old Favorites and New
Divertissements Planned

The writer was yesterday accorded the honor of attending the Rehearsal of John J. Tumulty's forthcoming season. Without breaching confidence, for a Rehearsal is, needless to say, a private matter, it may be said that Good Tidings may be brought back.

The first offering, on Saturday Evening, September 14th, is to be *The Merry Wives of Windsor* by Wm. Shakespeare, for the first time in the company's repertoire. There appears to be no record of any recent performance of the play in this city.

A new production is to be *Poor Richard,* a work by Mr. Temple Smith, in which Mr. Tumulty will assay the role of the revered Benj. Franklin. It was a portion of this representation which was on the boards yesterday afternoon. The writer, familiar with Mr. Tumulty's various roles, was nevertheless startled by the complete likeness to

Franklin which has been achieved. For some time, he was indeed unaware of the identity of the player.

There will also be played, in the course of the New Season, Oliver Goldsmith's farce, *She Stoops to Conquer*. In addition, there will be offered the American premiere of *The Newest World* by the British authoress Miss Rosamund Manders, which play has been recently performed in London, England by Johnston Forbes-Robertson with great success.

The good fortune of our City in having this outstanding Company has long been acknowledged. The painstaking care with which the performances are given is apparent, and yet, only by such a visit as the writer yesterday paid, can the efforts be fully appreciated. Mr. Tumulty produces his works with a firm hand.

It was most interesting to observe him darting about the stage, demonstrating to each of the players various details of attitude, speech, and gesture. Although he himself was in the costume and wig of Franklin, he became, at moments, others of the personages involved, men and women alike. This in itself was a rare performance.

Beginning then, on Saturday evening, September 14th, The State Street Theatre will again be one of our City's most rewarding institutions, all thanks to John J. Tumulty, fine actor and good citizen.

The second is from the San Francisco *Ledger,* August 10, 1919:

TUMULTY, JUNIOR
TO PLAY HAMLET

New Season at Tumulty's
Grand To Include Classic

John J. Tumulty was in fine fettle yesterday afternoon, as he discussed his forthcoming season during the course of luncheon at The Fairmont. Bronzed and refreshed by a month in the Arizona desert, he laughed as he said, "Well, now that the labor of holidaying is over, I am looking forward to the restfulness of work!" Asked to comment upon his son's imminent appearance as the Prince of Denmark, he replied, "Suppose we let the performance speak for itself? I will say this, though: one of the principal difficulties in our profession is that by the time the technique and experience required for the performance of the great roles is acquired, one is usually too old to play them. Johnny has the advantage of being a thoroughly seasoned and highly skilled actor at an early age. He began acting at birth!" Tumulty, Jr., is, of course, known to all theatre-minded residents. Those with long memories may well remember his first appearance on October 16, 1896, as one of the child princes in *Richard III.* Later, he was seen in such diverse parts and plays as: Laertes in *Hamlet;* Tom in *Tons of*

Money; Rob Dow in *The Little Minister;* Topsy (sic) in *Uncle Tom's Cabin;* Baker in *The Smiling Lieutenant;* Mosca in *Volpone;* Subtle in *The Alchemist;* Stockmann in *An Enemy of the People* and many others.

Service in the U. S. Navy (1917–1919) interrupted his career and a cordial welcome awaits his return in this acme of parts.

Among the other members of the large company this season are: Sol B. Anders, Daphne Scales, Rose Adriance, Peter Jeffers, Donald Alan Macrae, Amy Gieves, Thurston Gammage, J. Nicholas Findlay, Roger Belmont, Mary Lee James, Maude Adriance, and Patrick Quinn.

The third (October 4, 1924) is a birthday feature with a two-column photograph of JJT.

JOHN J. TUMULTY AT SEVENTY-FIVE

Local Actor-Manager Celebrates Birthday at Work.

The seventy-fifth milestone in the life of John J. Tumulty was passed yesterday in characteristic fashion at Tumulty's Grand. The performance was given as usual, with Mr. Tumulty in the title role of *John Brown.* Following the performance, cast and audience joined in a rollicking tribute, singing "Happy Birthday To You." Mr. Tumulty was then presented with a leather trunk by the members of his company. He responded from the stage as follows: "Ladies and gentlemen before me and behind me, I thank you for remembering this day which I had hoped to overlook. (Laughter)

"It has been said that each of us has what might be called 'an ideal age.' Youth becomes some, age becomes others. I confess that I, for one, feel best suited to the part of a man of seventy-five. (Applause) I should like very much to remain at this age—moving neither forward nor back—and perhaps, with luck, I shall. (Laughter) As to this gift—this resplendent piece of luggage, I am duly grateful—and may I take the liberty of assuming that there is no hidden hint implied? (Laughter) If there is, I must decline to accept, for too many of my years bind me to this place. Here, I have had the blessing of attentive eyes, open ears, patience and understanding —all of which has *almost* made up for the coughing. (Laughter) Dear friends all, this poor player is in your debt." (Prolonged applause) A large reception followed at the Taylor Rooms, attended by His Honor The Mayor of San Francisco, James Ralph, Jr., and Mrs. Ralph; Judge Henry Shannon and Mrs. Shannon; Commissioner Abel Martin and others.

Many messages were read from the platform, including those from Mr. Hartley Manners and Miss Laurette Taylor; Mr. Augustus Thomas; Mr. David Warfield; Mr. David Belasco; Mr. Daniel Frohman; Mr. Lionel Barrymore; Miss Maude Adams; and from Mr. Tumulty's son, the well-known photoplay favorite —— —— [BD].

8/26/54   Edinburgh.

TMY. Here with Ruth, who has opened in *The Matchmaker*. Last night, something extraordinary happened. After watching nine consecutive performances I decided to go to something else. The regular Festival attractions were sold out, so I looked over the list of "fringe attractions" and chose a performance of Marlowe's *Edward II* being given in a hall by The Oxford University Players. I was able to get a single seat. *Edward II* is a play unknown to me, and I was surprised to find how easily it could be followed. I became absorbed in the play and the production scheme— then it happened.

A character entered, spoke his first speech, and I felt a charge of that electricity generated by exceptional theatre talent. The production being one of those thrust-stage

122

affairs, I could not, at first, see the actor's face. Nonetheless, he was thrilling—acting with his whole body, moving in an undirected way, possessed of absolute poise and presence. I searched the program, trying to identify him, but it was hopeless. The cast was huge, and I could not be sure which part he was playing. I gave up and looked back to the stage. He had turned and moved close to where I was sitting. His face loomed before me, suddenly. John J. Tumulty's face!

I have studied photographs of JJT long enough to have his features clearly in mind, and did not think I could have been mistaken. During the first intermission, I doped out his name. Harry Cropper. He continued to live up to his promise through to the end of the piece.

I went back and sent word into the library, which was being used as a sort of dormitory–dressing room. A few minutes later, he came out, wearing a short dressing smock, wiping the melted greasepaint out of his ears. When I saw him without makeup and still closer, my hunch was reinforced.

"Good evening," I said. "Hell of a good show."

As we shook hands, he said, "I'm Harry Cropper."

His words wafted over on fresh fumes of alcohol.

"Yes, I know."

"You quite sure I'm the bloke you want?"

"Oh, yes."

I introduced myself. My name seemed to strike a bell, but a faint one. I numbered a few credits, always an embarrassment.

"Of course," he said. "I've heard of you."

But he still seemed less than friendly.

"What're you doing in Edinburgh?" he asked.

I told him. All at once, he was impressed, because he did know who Ruth is, had seen the invitational preview on

Sunday, and was mad about her performance. I went on to say how much I'd admired *Edward II,* and especially his work in it. He took the praise as though it were no less than his due.

"Can I buy you a beer?" I asked.

He frowned, looked away, then looked back at me with near hostility.

"Sorry. I've got a date with a friend. A *girl* friend."

Jesus Christ, I hadn't blushed in years—but suddenly my face became a hot, uncomfortable mask. I got the idea. Festivals, I gather, bring out the peculiars. I tried to laugh as I replied, "Well, bring her along. I'd like to talk to you. It may be important."

He hesitated before he asked, "Do you know The Albion Rooms?"

"Yes. King Street?"

"Right. In half an hour?"

"Fine."

We shook hands again and I went off to the Lyceum. The show was still on, so I left a message for Ruth with the doorman, saying I would be at The Albion Rooms if she felt up to coming over. Then I walked there, slowly, wondering what kind of a wild-goose chase I was on. How *could* there be a Tumulty here? Was it all a crazy coincidence? How much was my imagination adding to the meager facts?

At The Albion Rooms, I got a table, ordered a drink, and waited. Well over half an hour passed before he turned up. With him, a not-so-pretty girl and another fellow I recognized as having been in the play. Introductions. Drinks ordered.

"Something to eat?" I asked. "You guys must be hungry after all that slaughter."

Cropper grinned at me. "Can you afford it?"

124

"If you don't make pigs of yourselves."

Food ordered. The drinks arrived.

"Cheers."

"Cheers."

We talked about the play, but my mind was not on the subject. Too soon, I heard myself asking, "Is that your whole name? Harry Cropper?"

"No, there's a middle Thomas I lost in the war. Why?"

"I was just wondering. Are you by any chance related to John J. Tumulty?"

"Who?"

"John J. Tumulty."

"And just who might *that* be?"

"An American actor. Long since dead."

"No. What makes you ask?"

"You look like him. Like he looked, that is."

"Oh."

"And there's something about your acting that—"

The waitress turned up and by the time the plates had been wrongly distributed, redistributed, and more drinks ordered—we were nowhere. General conversation. After a while, the friend (Peter) and the girl (Esmé) got up to dance. I gathered *they* were the team, that Cropper had lied about a date with his girl friend—but by this time, I had had three large whiskies and was uninsultable. (In Edinburgh, a large whisky is large!)

"It's uncanny," I began again.

"What is?"

"Your resemblance to Tumulty."

"I probably look like a lot of people."

"No, I don't think so."

Peter and Esmé returned. More drinks. I tried another opening.

"Is your family in the theatre?"

This got a big laugh from all three.

"Not exactly," Cropper replied.

"His father sells carpeting," said Peter.

"And his mother's never *been* to the theatre," said Esmé. "She dreads it."

"Stow it, Esmé. My mother goes to the theatre all the time. At least once a year. Boxing Day. The panto."

Now all three talked and laughed at the same time. I had stumbled onto a private joke of some kind. I relaxed, and tried some arithmetic. Say he is twenty, born in 1934. Say his mother was twenty-five when she had him. So she was born in 1909. The question is: where? Or could it be his father? Cropper—but in this caper, names apparently mean nothing. If it *was* his father, make it born in 1905. When JJT was 56.

My guests were nicely oiled by midnight and we seemed to have been joined by four more. Noisy, dancy. All in pairs, so now and then he and I were left sitting. In one of these intervals I returned to the subject.

"Your parents—"

"Yuh?"

"Were they both born here? I mean, in England?"

"Yes, sir. My father in Roedean. My mother in Stratford. Call me Will. Yes, Roedean, Stratford—don't ask me how they met. I wasn't there, swear it."

"What about your grandparents? Are they English, too?"

He didn't reply. He looked out at the dance floor. I took it that he had not heard the question, and was about to repeat it when he turned back and said, "What *is* this, mate? I only met you a few minutes ago."

"I'm interested."

"In what?"

"In you, as an actor. You've got a large future."

"You don't know what the bloody hell you're talking about. I'm no actor. This is just a piss-up. I'm for the law."

"Maybe you'll change your mind. Listen, I'm no discoverer. *Anybody* who sees you act—anybody who knows, that is—will tell you."

"Tell me what?"

"That you've got it. So why not use it?"

The dancing ended, the group swarmed again. The talk went on in a confusing variety of British regional accents, and I caught only a phrase here and there. The musicians left, the bar closed, our bottle was empty, and I found myself standing out on the sidewalk with Cropper and the original pair. He was the drunkest—the other two had danced some of theirs off, and I had been purposely prudent.

"I know a place," said Cropper.

"Pretty late," I said.

"How do you expect to write the story of my biography if you don't stay with us?"

"Some other time." I knew I'd get nothing more this night, but he was insistent.

"Now, look, cockie, we know you're big Yankee big-stuff —throwing it around—but it's *my* turn to buy—so *don't* walk *out!*"

With this, he grasped the lapel of my jacket and gave it a downward wrench.

"O.K.," I said. "We're off."

Ten minutes later we entered a dark-fronted, law-breaking pub. I recognized its name. It was the place Thornton went the other night in response to an invitation from a group of advanced Scottish poets. "All wearing," TW had reported, "the Marx tartan!" It was comparatively quiet. We ordered lager.

After a while, Cropper said, "I feel rotten."

"Maybe you've had your fill."

"It's not that. I wasn't honest with you, that's why. I lied. I don't like to lie. It makes me ill."

I said nothing.

"I *would* like to act." He looked into his glass and swirled the suds. "But I never admit it, even to myself. I know I'm jolly good at it. *Blast!*"

Peter and Esmé were absorbed in each other. Cropper went on.

"My mother and father—they don't give a damn one way or other, but the old girl—she's got her foot down. *Both* feet."

"Who's 'the old girl'?"

"My grandmother. My mother's mum. She runs the show. Don't ask me why." He looked at his chums and pointed to a table across the room. "Go on over there, you two. I won't be but a few minutes."

They did so, sheepishly.

"Shouldn't we send them some beer?" I asked.

"No more money."

"I think *I* can manage."

"Suit yourself."

I sent over two beers, ordered two more for Cropper and myself, and went to the can. When I returned to the table, he was puffing a pipe.

"I've been thinking," he said. "I believe you. No reason for you to say—come backstage—all that—otherwise."

"Of course."

"My mother's coming up this weekend. Will you still be here?"

"Yes."

"I'd like you to meet her. Appreciate it. Tea or something? And *you* tell *her.* Will you?"

"Gladly."

"Probably won't mean a bloody thing—she won't know who you are—but I'll build you up first. I mean, at least she'll know you're a professional. And married to a famous actress —playing here, in a leading part. That may impress her. See?"

"Sure."

"Where you staying?"

"The Cally."

"Right. Call you."

"Good."

He shouted across the room. "All right, now."

The other two returned. I rose as Esmé was seated, and took advantage of the moment to beat it. I shook hands all around and got, from Cropper, the first friendly look of the evening.

Near the door, I asked the barmaid if it would be possible to call a taxi. She looked at me, coldly.

"We're *closed,* dear," she said.

I walked back to the hotel breathing the Edinburgh smoke, and sorting out the newest pieces of my old puzzle.

His mother, born in Stratford.

His grandmother opposed to the stage for him. Why? Could *she* had been an actress? That would explain Cropper's mother being born in Stratford.

Here are some things I ought to try to find out:

The grandmother's name.

Was she ever in America? Ever in San Francisco?

Was she an actress?

It is too early to tell, but suppose this is *not* all a pipe dream? It might be the best source yet. Home, bed. Late. Sleep fitful.

8/31/54   Edinburgh.

TMY. Ruth has just left for the theatre and this is my first opportunity to set down the details of tea with Cropper and his mother yesterday. It went on until so late that I had to go to the Rubinstein concert directly from there. Afterward supper, and today was full of phonings and doings, so this is the first chance.

Cropper phoned on Sunday. Extremely polite, said he realized we were "in wine" when I agreed to have tea with him and his mum. I assured him I was anxious to do so. We made a date for yesterday at 4:30—downstairs here.

She is basically attractive but lacking in know-how, so gives the impression of dowdiness. She is gentle, even meek, scared of something (probably life), but pleasant. Her negativeness is accentuated as she sits beside her vital, dazzling son.

I searched her face for a touch of Tumulty, but no matter how I squinted, there was not the faintest suggestion.

She had not seen Harry's performance, but was going on Monday. I went on about it.

Finally, I said, "I can't imagine where he gets all that talent. Can you?"

"No," she whispered.

Cropper was loading in the pastry, but seemed to hate the tea.

"A drink instead?" I asked.

"No, thanks," he said, gracefully. "I don't drink."

For a split second, I believed it. This guy is *some* actor! We all settled down to the tea.

"Harry tells me there's some family resistance to his going into the theatre. Professionally."

"Not from me," said his mother.

"I told you," said Cropper impatiently. "It's the old girl. My grandmother."

I wished this young hothead would let me handle it my own way.

"What does she have against it?" I asked. "No one thinks of the stage as disreputable any more. Not these days."

"No, not disreputable," said Mrs. Cropper. "But she does seem to think it frivolous."

"A fat lot *she* knows," said Cropper.

"Has she ever seen him act?"

"No," said Mrs. C. "She simply won't. The last time we discussed it, she said she did not doubt he had the talent for it, but that she wanted him to have a more stable occupation, was the way she put it."

"Stable," said Cropper. "Maybe she'd like me to be a groom!"

(Wit is not his strong point.)

There was a clue in here somewhere—"she did not doubt he had the talent for it."

"She's done everything for Harry," explained Mrs. Cropper. "Putting him through school and college and all."

"I could have put *myself* through," said Harry, morosely.

"I doubt that," I said to him. (Once in a while, it feels good to tell the plain truth.)

"And, of course, if he did want to—" Mrs. Cropper was worried now. "Wouldn't it take time and training and—doesn't one need backing of some sort?"

"It doesn't hurt."

"But don't put your daughter on the stage, Mrs. Worthington," said Harry, absently.

"You see," said his mother, "our own means are quite limited and—"

I interrupted. "But she's rich?"

Harry and his mother looked at each other and exchanged a smile.

"No one knows," he said. "We play guessing games. If you want *my* opinion, she's sitting on plenty."

(Holy Hell! It didn't occur to me yesterday but just now, this minute—is this the answer to the JJT money mystery? Is *this* where it went? Wait. Suppose Mrs. Cropper is JJT's daughter. Her mother one of T's ladies—somewhere, somehow. Slowly, now. Take it easy. Her mother leaves wherever and goes to Stratford. JJT continues to supply her with dough, and, obviously, can say nothing to BD about his needs. This would be a perfect fit—except, God damn it, for the *amount* involved. If it were a third or a quarter—it might make sense. On the other hand, JJT might have wished to provide for her and her daughter over the years and for the time when he might not be around. But—now here comes another damned dip—suppose all this supposition is fact—what good is it in the Tumulty story? That he rears a son who is not actually his son, while his real daughter grows up a stranger to him?)

There was talk of money and its relationship to career. Banal. But then:

"Mrs. Cropper, does the name John J. Tumulty mean anything to you?"

"No. Harry told me you'd ask that. No, I've never heard the name."

I left the subject and fumbled on about acting and actors, dully. When I had gotten far enough away from the idea of

132

JJT, I asked her: "Is your father alive?"

"No." Long pause. "He died when I was very young."

"How young?"

"Oh, *very!*"

I was still in the game! Slowly, I veered around to the subject of travel; Edinburgh, how interesting. France. After a while:

"Have you ever been to the States, Mrs. Cropper?"

"Oh, heavens, no. I should love to one day. Mother adored it."

Those three words absolutely stopped my clock. I heard myself shout, *"What?"*

Poor Mrs. Cropper and Harry were startled.

"Yes," she said, looking at me oddly. "Mother's been out to America several times."

"When?" I asked, trying not to shout again. It came out so softly that I had to repeat it. "When?"

"Oh, not for years, of course. But my father was a mining engineer and his work took him to odd places—and Mother insisted on traipsing along—no matter where. It's a wonder to me I was born in England. It might have been anywhere —Africa, South America—"

"San Francisco?" I asked.

"No, I don't think so."

"California?" I pressed.

"Oh, yes. They went there several times."

"But not San Francisco?"

"No, never."

"Mother," said Harry. "San Francisco is *in* California. It's a city."

"Oh, dear," said Mrs. Cropper, and put her nose into her palm. "My geography."

I was in control now, and spoke carefully.

"If she's been to San Francisco, she hasn't forgotten it. Some people think it's the most interesting city in America. I'm pretty fond of it myself."

"I'll look through the postcards."

"The postcards?"

"Yes, Mother has this postcard collection. At least one from every place she's ever been. There must be thousands. People don't seem to collect postcards these days. It used to be quite the thing."

"I'm sorry your mother didn't come up with you. I'd love to meet her. Maybe I could make some headway with her for Harry."

Mrs. Cropper looked at me curiously, and asked, "Why would you?"

"Because theatre people are interested in theatre."

"Oh. Well, she so seldom leaves Manchester. She *is* quite old, you see."

Manchester! Now and then something happens that makes me believe—against my will—in a design of circumstance. Because from here, we go to Liverpool and then—Manchester. For a week. I took a sip of tea and said, "Well, I'll be darned!"

"Why?" asked Harry.

"I'm going to *be* in Manchester in two weeks."

"Are you really?" asked Mrs. Cropper.

"Yes. Could you all come to see my wife's play there? I think you'd enjoy it. I'd be glad to arrange about tickets and so on."

"That's awfully good of you."

"Not at all. Pleasure. Suppose I call you when we get there." I got out my date book and looked it up. "We get there on Sunday—that's September twelfth. I'll call you on Monday."

"Lovely. I'll ask Mother, but in any case, I'm sure my husband and I would be delighted."

More talk, but nothing. So now it looks as though, before long, I am going to meet a lady who might possibly have known my friend Tumulty.

9/19/54   Manchester.

TMY. We leave here tomorrow morning. If I fail again tonight to set down what happened here, I shall never do so. Every afternoon for the past five, I have resolved to come to grips with the report; every night, I have evaded it. Why? Because it was a disturbing experience and I am not anxious to relive it. Why disturbing? Because my own behavior has been less than admirable. I have become—without meaning to—a meddler and a pry and a disturber of the peace of others. My motive? Lord knows. I am propelled by an obsession, by the need to solve a puzzle on the grand scale. All thought of this as material has long since been obliterated by its complexity and contradiction. What remains is a compulsive drive toward unearthing facts and solving a mystery. There would be nothing wrong in this, except that living people are involved and so are their memories and feelings and sensibilities.

I feel this pen slowing down. In a moment I shall stop.

Later. I remind myself that these notes are private, and, as such, can be freely made. On.

We arrived here on Sunday afternoon. The train trip had

135

been airless and noisy. At the hotel—enormous and impersonal—there is a mix-up about our reservation, so it is almost 6:00 before we can go out and walk. The city seems tired and lifeless and not of its time. We return to the hotel, change, and go down to the dining room. Here, all is different. Manchester becomes the world. The room is filled with a representative assortment of businessmen from everywhere and their parties. There are buyers and sellers and go-betweens. There are turbans and saris, all shades of skin, snatches of many languages and—hold it. Stop stalling. Tell it.

On Tuesday, Harry Cropper comes to the performance with his mother and father. I have dinner with them beforehand at Driver's, a fine oyster house they recommend. They come backstage afterward and say all the right things to Ruth. Especially Harry, who is astonishingly perceptive about the details of her performance, which he has seen twice.

At dinner, they explain that the old lady could not come.

"She hardly goes out at all any more," says Mr. Cropper. "I'd call her infirm."

"It's her leg," says Mrs. Cropper.

"If she ate properly," says Mr. Cropper. "Calciums and so on."

"Let's stow it, shall we?" says Harry to his parents. Then, turning to me, "When do you open in London?"

"You understand," I explain, "I have no official connection with this production."

"I know."

"It opens in London in early November."

"At The Haymarket, isn't it?" he asks—or rather, says. "Yes."

His father regards him. "Now how in hell would you know a thing like that?"

136

Harry shrugs.

"I'm sorry she couldn't come tonight—your grand-mother," I say. "Maybe some other night? Or the matinee on Saturday?"

"No," says her daughter. "I shouldn't think so."

"She's eighty-three, you know," says Mr. Cropper.

My fork hits the plate, as I echo, "Yes, I know."

The following day, Wednesday, I am taken by Harry to call on her. I am given a choice of lunch or tea. I choose lunch, since I hope for an extended session and Wednesday is a matinee day. He picks me up at the hotel and we take a taxi to a large house on the outskirts of the city, where she lives alone. The lower floor has been converted into an apartment so that she does not need to deal with the stairs.

Her name is Mrs. Fielding. (Later, I learn the rest of it: Rosamund Manders Fielding.) She is a bulging old lady who resembles an elderly kewpie doll. Somewhere, in that mass of soft and useless flesh, a long-ago beauty can be discerned by an eye willing to try.

"So you are the American!" she says, offering her hand.

"Yes, Mrs. Fielding."

"Sit there in the light where I can see you. Harry, come and kiss me. There. And you sit here."

Sherry is served.

She put her eyes on me, cocked her head charmingly to one side, and inquired, "And what part of the States are you from?"

"San Francisco," I said, and swallowed my sherry in a gulp.

Her head was erect again when I looked back at her.

"San Francisco," she whispered, and glanced at Harry.

There was a silence during which Harry sipped his sherry, she ignored hers, and I decided that Mrs. Fielding had

137

known Tumulty, that her daughter was *his* daughter, and that Harry Cropper was JJT's grandson. I think so still, although I grant I cannot prove it. Who cares? Some things are known without proof.

Lunch was excellent. A spinach soufflé; a fish I could not identify; and something called a gooseberry fool. A deceptively potent cider was served with this last—two glasses of it loosened me up, and I try to sell Mrs. Fielding on the idea of acting as a career for Harry. She nods politely and smiles from time to time, but I have no idea as to how I am doing.

The postcards come out. There are many American ones, some from California, but not a single one of San Francisco. This, in itself, strikes me as telling.

Later, the stereopticon slides. San Francisco is still missing. Then as we are going through a stack of old Yosemite views—I come upon a shot of Tumulty's Grand! It has been misplaced.

When Harry leaves the room a while later to call for a taxi, I look at Mrs. Fielding and ask, "Did you ever, in your travels, encounter a great American actor named John J. Tumulty?"

She looks at me and smiles, but does not reply immediately.

Then she says, "I have encountered so many persons, in so many places. It has all been so—interesting. Yes. America."

Harry comes back. I see that his grandmother is tiring, and suggest that we leave. Harry kisses her, this time without being asked. He goes.

She gives me her hand. I thank her for lunch and for allowing me to come. As I look at her, tears well up in her eyes.

Her hand clings to mine, and she says, "Yes!"

Harry comes back to the hotel with me, and we sit in the lobby for a while. I tell him to get in touch with me in London. I promise to do what I can for him. He gives me his college address, as well as his home address and phone number. Also the address and phone number of a London chum with whom he stays when there.

Because of Ruth's two-performance day, I did not discuss any of this with her until the following morning. I then related the events and gave her my conclusions. She thinks I am reading more into it than is there.

I brood about it, all the same. For one thing, the inherited talent interests me. For another, if JJT did father a child in circumstances such as these (assuming he knew about it) did he or did he not feel responsible? If he did, what did he do about it? Remember there remains the matter of unaccounted-for money. But what about *Mr.* Fielding? A mining engineer; successful, prosperous. What would have been the need? I would like to know more about Mr. Fielding.

I wish I could get off this kick. It is time-consuming and seems to lead from one dead end to another.

9/22/54/   Leeds.

TMY. The tour continues. I have been working daily and long hours and, it seems to me, well. Although what I am working on is an original screenplay, I am constructing it in a three-act form. Yesterday, I came to the curtain of Act I. Instead of plunging ahead, I decided to take a day or two off and let the whole thing marinate.

Matinee day. I take off early, hire a car—what is the steering wheel doing over *there?!*—and hit the wrong side of the road. I move over and put my mind on the lovely countryside. After a time, I look about to get my bearings and find I am three miles from Manchester. How did that happen? What propelled the car in this direction? I swear I had not been thinking at all about Tumulty. However, since I am so close, I proceed into the city and go to the hall of records. Two clerks help me look up the date of Fielding's death. March 11, 1909. Then to the offices of *The Manchester Guardian.* The requested bound volume is brought to me and on the obituary page I find a continuation. The obit itself begins on page one. I turn to it and go lightheaded as I read:

ANGUS FIELDING DEAD
BY HIS OWN HAND

Body of Engineer Discovered by Shocked Wife

Angus Frederick Fielding, 44, of The Copse, 177 Barnard's Lane, Manchester, died yesterday in the carriage house of his home, apparently a suicide by hanging.

Mr. Fielding, a native of this city, had achieved world-wide recognition in the field of mining engineering. A graduate of local schools and of the University of Manchester, he received his postgraduate training at the College of Palaeontology of The University of Johannesburg in South Africa.

Returning to Manchester in 1894, he founded, in partnership with O. P. Krebs, the firm of Fielding and Krebs, Ltd., which company remains active to the present day.

In 1897, Mr. Fielding married Miss Rosamund Manders, who had appeared briefly on the London stage, but is best known as an authoress of poetry and two works for the theatre: *The Newest World,* a play produced by Johnston Forbes-Robertson; and *The Virgin Queen,* in which Miss Janet Achurch appeared for a short run in 1895.

Their only child, a daughter (Winifred), was born on February 7, 1909.

Mr. Fielding had travelled extensively, often accompanied by his wife. He had supervised projects in

Brazil (S.A.), Ecuador (S.A.), Vancouver (Canada), Arizona (U.S.A.), and most recently had spent a year in northern California (U.S.A.). While there, he acquired extensive holdings for Fielding and Krebs, Ltd. in excavations and mines in the field of aluminium and tungsten. Mr. and Mrs. Fielding returned to Manchester on December 10, 1908, to await the birth of their child.

No cause of the tragedy has been suggested. Mrs. Fielding arose early this morning and was informed by her maid that Mr. Fielding had not slept in his rooms. She immediately ordered a search, in which she took part. In company with Joseph Parran, gardener, she came upon the body of her husband suspended from the central beam of the carriage house. The police were summoned at once.

The mystery is compounded by the facts that Mr. Fielding was and has been in excellent health; that his business affairs (according to O. P. Krebs, his partner) are in perfect order; that, in fact, the acquisition of the California properties has placed the company in the most affluent position in its history.

A memorial service will be held at St. Andrews Cathedral on Wednesday morning at 11:00 A.M. Burial will be private.

Note: "Miss Rosamund Manders, who had appeared briefly on the London stage."

Note: Only daughter is born 12 repeat 12 years after their marriage.

Note: A *year* in "northern California (U.S.A.)"—this must mean San Francisco.

Note: Daughter born Feb. 7, 1909; he is suspended from the central beam on March 11, 1909.

Note: Authoress of *The Newest World,* played in London by Forbes-Robertson—but we know who played it in S.F., don't we?

Note: My theory of T's money to her is demolished. She would have had no need for it.

(Pop always wanted me to be a criminal lawyer; Clarence Darrow was a hero. If Pop were alive, he would approve of my work on this. He'd say, "See?")

I assume the family doesn't know about grandmother's brief appearance on the London stage. If Harry knew, he

141

certainly would have mentioned it by now. How has she been able to keep it dark all this time? Should I try to see her again? No.

I drive back to Leeds and work is out the window as I continue to play with Tumulty clues, using new pieces of the puzzle.

5–2–54   Paris (en route back to London)   Hôtel Raphaël.

TMY. I am here again for a few days after a week in Amsterdam. I went there to meet with the Hacketts, and together we did the necessary research for the production of *The Diary of Anne Frank.*

Since I must spend at least a week here, I mean to pursue a missing link in the Tumulty chain.

I have long resolved that when I got to Paris again I would make an effort to locate Rose Adriance. A number of sources have told me that she lives here; that she is married to a doctor; and that, like many others, she and her husband simply disappeared for the duration of the occupation.

The trouble is that I am neither a born nor a trained detective and, looking back on some of my methods in all this, I am appalled at my clumsiness. I must not make a mistake in the case of Rose Adriance—I must not seek her out. If she has anything to contribute to my investigation, this would be a sure way to blow it. No. What I must do is locate her as soon as possible and then in some way—I don't know how yet—get to meet her. Should she prove congenial, the next step will be to open the subject easily and

142

casually through the fact that I know and have recently worked with BD. And see what that leads to.

How to begin? Possibilities:

1. Bob Blake at The Morgan Guaranty Trust Company, who is acquainted with just about every American permanent resident. He is, or has been, President of The American Club of Paris, and would help, I know. Could I say I am thinking of writing something about American expatriates in France? (He and I have talked a good deal about Gertrude Stein and Alice B. Toklas.) Could I ask him about those he knows who have been here for twenty years or more? Not bad.

2. Irwin Shaw and Marian. Better because they might easily know *about* her, but would be less likely to be close friends.

3. Janet Flanner. She would know if anyone does. Step carefully here. Perhaps talk about silent pictures, mention the name a few times, see if it gets picked up.

4. Ginette and Paul-Emile Seidmann. An excellent possibility. They are dear friends and can be trusted implicitly. I would tell them the whole story. Paul-Emile, who has practiced medicine in Paris for years, would doubtless know many doctors. A French doctor married to an American lady is a combination unique enough to assist his memory, and help to narrow the field.

5. Andrée Valentin. A nurse who is a great friend of Ruth's, and whom I have met. She has spent a lifetime at The American Hospital in Neuilly. Is she still there? If so, I could ask her a simple question: "Do you know a French physician in his late years who is married to an American lady?"

There are the only ones I can think of at the moment, and I had better get going on them at once.

5–5–54   Paris.

TMY. Nothing but strikeouts.

Lunch with Bob Blake. He characteristically offers any help he can give and provides a long list of names, but no one resembling Rose Adriance is included.

Irwin and Marian. Nothing. Irwin says he will nose around. "What's this for?" he asks. "A movie? A play?"

I go over to the Hotel Continental bar, and meet Janet. She vaguely remembers such a couple from before the war, but since she spent most of the war years in New York, she has lost track of them and has not heard of them since her return. Journalist that she is, she suggests that I go to the Sûreté, and offers to introduce me to the right people there. She explains that this is equivalent to our Bureau of Missing Persons, that it has a subsection established to reunite persons separated in wartime. I consider this, but realize I would have to give a good deal of information to the police: why I'm trying to locate them and so on, which would lead to a few lies, and I am not prepared to tangle with the law. When I explain to Janet, she suggests something that had not occurred to me: engage a private investigator.

We talk some more. She begins to remember. She cannot dredge up the doctor's name but recalls that he and his wife lived on the Ile St. Louis. She is sure it was high up, with an extraordinary view. All to the good. Provided, of course, that these are the people I am seeking.

She begins to mention people she used to see there on the afternoons they held regularly and I am making a list of names when, to my dismay, the customary stream of her late-afternoon drop-ins commences. Soon there are seven people at the table. Janet is beginning to collect and collate all sorts of information in that brilliant way of hers and soon has lost interest in me and my problems.

Dinner and the evening with my beloved Seidmanns. Still *another* newly discovered bistro! This one in the Place des Vosges. We talk on my subject. Paul-Emile instantly whips out his Hermès note pad and gold pencil, and makes notes.

"I know *three* French doctors who are married to American girls."

I look up and say, "Hot dog."

"What was that?" asks Paul-Emile.

It is necessary to explain the American argot. Paul-Emile is delighted with it, says it several times, and writes it down.

"What about these three doctors?" I prompt.

"Yes. All married to lovely American wives, but, alas, they are all younger than you say your man must be."

"*How* young?"

He thinks. "Oh, one perhaps twenty-seven or twenty-eight, another perhaps forty, and the third a bit younger, but perhaps also forty. The second one forty-six or -seven."

"They won't do. See if you can find an old doctor."

"I shall try," says Paul-Emile, "and if I find him—hot *dog!*"

This morning, I phoned The American Hospital. Andrée Valentin is on holiday. Hell.

145

5/11/54   London.

TMY. A letter from Janet Flanner today in which she says she thinks she has located the people I am looking for, and that she is sorry to tell me that only the husband, Dr. Albert Duchene, has survived. His American wife died seven or eight years ago.

I am depressed.

6/11/54   London.

TMY. Paul-Emile's telephone call from Paris changes the color of a bleak day.

"Is it a re-*wahrd?*" he begins.

"A what?"

"*Re*-wahrd," he says, shifting the emphasis.

I still do not understand.

"Money!" he shouts. "Money for the finding. Is that not the word? *Re-wahrd.* Not so? *Une récompense?*"

"Reward?"

"I have found your person," he says. "The American lady, the doctor's wife. No. The doctor's widow. *Hélas!* He is dead since a long time. I knew him. A great man. The Doctor Joseph Saint-Blaise. He was a professor to me long ago. The world is small, *hein?* The lady's name—the widow—is Rose, as you said."

146

(I damn near fainted. Could I believe it? Was Rose Adriance alive, actually sitting there across the Channel, reachable in an hour's time?)

"Go on," I say. "What else?"

"She lives still in the Ile St. Louis. As you said, she is old, but a colleague has told me she has still her 'Tuesdays.' "

"Good."

"The people who go to her are a strange mixture—so it is amusing. They are: *or* Christian Scientists *or* cinéastes. These are her two worlds. She has become Christian Scientist since the Doctor Saint-Blaise has died. She is active in the Church and in the Cinématèque Française."

Movies, I think. There's an entrée. And suddenly, luckily, I remember Neil Martin, who acted with Ruth in *Seventeen* and now lives here with his French wife, Hélène, and is high up—very high up, I believe—in the Christian Science movement.

So. Luck on two counts. In through Neil and stay through films.

"Paul-Emile," I say, "you are a wonder. I'll be over in a day or two—and I'll bring your *re*-wahrd."

"Your English," he says, "is becoming poorer. Re*ward*. Say after me."

12/11/56   New York.

TMY. A letter arrives today after what a journey. On the envelope, my name is typed; then follows, in an ornate hand: "Care of: The Society of Playwrites, The City of New York, State of New York, United States of

147

America." And the damned thing arrived.

Pinned to the sealed enclosed letter is a card which I gather has been sent inadvertently. It reads:

Harry, Send this, if you please, to the funny-looking American you brought to lunch. I cannot recall his name, but I should think the address I have provided would be sufficient. Thank you, dear.

(Is she dead, I wonder?)
This is the letter:

Dear American,

I cannot recall your name. Forgive me. I remembered it for some time after we met, but now, when I need it, my memory fails me. I do not wish to consult Harry. It would open other matters.

I am told that I am ending, and I believe it to be so. Would it interest you to know about the sensation? It is simply a fading away. Periods of lucidity become shorter each day—this is being written during one of them (I trust!). For the rest, the condition is one of pleasant fatigue—the sort one experiences after lovemaking.

It is, in point of fact, a near-perfect time marred only by loose ends, unanswered questions, and one or two regrets. I do not regret anything I have ever done, only those things I *failed* to do—out of modesty, timidity, or lassitude.

You came, a stranger, into my quiet retire, and asked disturbing questions out of the long past—of a time before your birth. Why? Did you know the answers? I expect you did. How? Who are you? What do you want? How do you know what you already know? Why do you want to know the rest?

148

In my long life, I married one husband, and took one lover. This, as I write it, seems frugal enough, even circumspect. Unfortunately, the arrangement of time was not fortuitous. Had the lover preceded or succeeded the husband, all would have been well. Had the husband been more of a husband, or the lover less of a lover—. But I am running on.

You know his name. I loved him and, in his way, he loved me. His way was fraught with impermanence, since he believed, foolishly, that he had lost the single love of his life. It was a subject he discussed with candour—with me and, doubtless, others. I would have left my husband and stayed with him. Is it not rather comic that my husband would have approved? It was my San Francisco gentleman who would not consent.

In the City of New York, en route home, my husband and I tarried for a week before we achieved passage. During that time, Angus and I lived through our crisis. He asked for his freedom and suggested that I remain in New York. To both these conditions I agreed, but on the day prior to sailing, he had a reversal of feeling and insisted I accompany him. Again, I acquiesced. The journey was long and pleasant and we spent the time making our peace with ourselves and one another, as well as making plans for the future.

The birth of Winifred ended our dream. Three days following this event, Angus left and did not return for twenty-three days. From the time he returned until his death six days later, I did not hear the sound of his voice. He came in to see me each morning and kissed my hand. He then looked at the child, often for five or ten minutes.

His agony conveyed to me something I had suspected but had not known for certain: the fact that it was not possible for him to have fathered a child.

(Two days have passed since I wrote the above.)

149

Winifred is the daughter of John J. Tumulty, although the fact is known neither to her nor was it, ever, to him. I thought it best.

Harry resembles him, not only physically, but in spirit. I have many photographs of John, and it has interested me, as the years have passed, to observe the growing resemblance. It has been, at times, terrifying. Harry came in one afternoon and woke me from a nap. As I opened my eyes and saw him there in the dim light, looking down at me, the whole of my life with John returned.

Monday week. I pick up my laggard pen once again after an interval of illness, during which I contemplated the destruction of what I have thus far committed to paper.

But my concern for Harry's future impels me to continue. So I address myself to you, a total stranger. My own connections with the world of the theatre have long since been severed.

Harry has talent. He has John's talent. I have seen Harry in all he has done, although he is not aware of it.

My observation of his development has caused me to alter many of my ideas on heredity and environment. I was, long ago, active in the Fabian Society. Beatrice and Sidney Webb were close friends until my marriage. As Fabians, we were rather given to placing the greater emphasis upon the environmental factor. We believed that our sharply defined class system was self-perpetuating in that it prevented men (and women) from changing station.

But consider Harry, as a case in point. Nothing in his life has led him in the direction of the theatre with the exception of the blood in his veins, the instinct in his genes, and the atavistic magic of the ages. It has astounded me. Has he told you of his wife and child? At 18, as an act of revolt, he married Esmé (a chambermaid at

The Mitre in Oxford), who bore him a son a year later. He is, as you see, a thoroughly independent own-man sort.

Once, in another century (literally), I composed a play for the theatre. (All Fabians wrote plays!) It was called "The Newest World" and was concerned with the American revolution. The leading role was that of a young British subaltern sent to put down the rebels. As he lives and works and fights with them, he becomes sympathetic to their cause, renounces his commission and his King, and joins them. The role was taken in London by Johnston Forbes-Robertson; in New York by Maurice Barrymore; and in San Francisco by John J. Tumulty. Although the last was an American, I preferred his performance to the others. But I ramble.

To return to the question of Harry. As I saw him becoming more and more like his grandfather, I made strong efforts to divert him from his course. I hoped that it would be possible to snuff out these tendencies and inclinations and replace them with solid, albeit conventional, aspirations. For I could not persuade myself that he would be fulfilled by becoming another Tumulty. John was an entrancing man, but lacking in moral fibre. He was given to alcoholic excess. His relationships with women were mendacious. He gave the best of himself to nothing, to no one—only to his work. And what, may I ask, was that? A powerful display of self, in many forms and guises.

No, I concluded, this was hardly the life for my only grandson. And thus my plans to abort his aims proceeded.

I see that I erred. There is no holding back nature or talent. Harry must go on to do what he must.

At the appropriate time, you may apprize him of the facts. Perhaps they will assist in bolstering his confidence. You may, if you choose, show him this missive.

I am not, as you may have gathered, a formally religious

151

creature, nor have I ever been. Perhaps if I had accepted with literalness the teachings and precepts and warnings and admonitions of my elders, this matter which now involves us would not exist. Nor would Harry exist. Who is to say if that would be a good thing or not? However, since one cannot live a long life without the sort of pattern which organized religion provides, I was led to Humanism; to a study of Buddhism (that delightful godless tapestry of wit and wisdom and eternal common sense); briefly to Christian Science (until your Mark Twain's treatise on the subject laughed me out of it); to Art (in all its wondrous forms and passionate implications); eventually and finally to The Fabian Society. This, too, had its pitfalls and disappointments; but, by and large, I am convinced that some good was done, some small progress effected, and, above all, what congenial company it provided. I can well remember a *red*-bearded Shaw: talking, talking, talking. Wells, the Webbs, Granville-Barker—oh, dear. Names escape me, although so many living faces are here before me.

I apologize if I give the impression of maundering. But it is all to a point. It is this. My religion (if it can so be called) in this waning season of my life is simply a prayer for order and form; a belief in man's capacity to achieve it; a sense that nature assists him in doing so in many mysterious and magical ways.

Our immortality lies, not in ourselves, our souls, ghosts, spirits—but in our progeny, in our works, and in the memory of those whom we have encountered. It is enough.

Harry is—shall be—my future. And John's.

Is it not meaningful that you and I should have encountered one another?; that you should have been not only in Scotland, but in Edinburgh, at the Masonic Hall at the moment when Harry was acting there? You recognized him. Who else could have done so? You do see, do you not, why I am obsessed with the idea of form and design? Is there not something in the fatalistic view which holds that there is only one possible course of events? Do you know that splendid exposition of this postulation by Mark Twain: "The Mysterious Stranger"?

Perhaps we shall meet again and this hurried (I hear you laughing) message will prove to be an anachronism. If not, I give you Harry—perhaps, after all, the best of me.

I greatly appreciate your indulgence, your many favours, and your great courtesy. I shall dream for Harry a tomorrow in which his bloodline may take pride.

I hope not goodbye.

Faithfully yours,
Rosamund Manders Fielding

It goes without saying that this letter has had a profound effect on me. Never have I felt so in touch with the past. Never has the idea of design in events seemed so arresting.

>>> <<<

Inventory. In 1909 JJT fathers an illegitimate daughter. She, in turn, produces a son who, not unusually, possesses attributes of his grandfather. Now what?

Are there other illegitimate offspring of JJT? Most probably. Where? Who? Never mind all this idle speculation. Deal with what you have, know.

What is Harry to BD? Actually, nothing. Technically? I am easily confused in trying to dope out complex relationships. It is one of the many dead keys on my piano. I can remember taking twenty minutes to figure out the answer to the puzzle of the man pointing to a portrait and saying:

Brothers and sisters
Have I none
But that man's father
Is my father's son!

—and even now I get mixed up thinking it through.

Harry Cropper's mother is BD's half-sister by adoption. So Harry is his—what?—half-nephew? Is he Harry's half-uncle? Look it up.

I wonder if the findings would interest BD enough to give Harry a leg up. Think about it.

5/7/57   Paris.

TMY. I have just returned from Mme. Saint-Blaise's Tuesday and have much to set down. I find it hard to believe that three years have passed since Paul-Emile located her. Where have they gone? I had fully intended to go to Paris at once—on the day he told me he had found her—then all sorts of things happened. Ruth fell ill, but insisted on continuing to play. Next, complications about the *Diary* starting date. Tumulty and his story receded from the scene (as has happened so frequently).

We did go to Paris on our way back to the States, but the lady had gone off to Abano to take a cure and would not be back for some time. I looked up Neil Martin and asked him about her. His report was glowing, mainly based on her devotion to the Church. He knew something of her American background, but not as much as I know. I did not press very hard, as I knew I would be returning before too long

154

and would deal with it then. All at once—three years. (I am reminded of Charlie Butterworth's remark about Hollywood: "You make your first hit on Broadway, sign up, come out here, take a nap by the pool, and when you wake up— you're forty-seven years old!") But today, I met her.

Many interesting things happened this afternoon in that astonishing apartment atop the Lambert on the Ile St. Louis. The most interesting, to me at any rate, is that I fell in love. I did not expect, after 15 years of near-perfect marriage, ever to experience again the unsettling phenomenon of infatuation. Rose Adriance Saint-Blaise is, according to my best calculations, in her late sixties. She radiates beauty of body, mind, and spirit in the most encompassing way. Like all great works of art, she has a unity of tone, a unity of intention. Everything she has is hers alone and fits perfectly with everything else. Her voice and the shape of her head; the trim, lithe, sensuous figure; the acquired French gestures; the eager, hungry-for-life, humorous expression on her meltingly beautiful face—are all part of a single design. How to describe that listening look on her face and in her eyes? She appears to be ever intent, even when she herself is talking. Why not? Are those eyes lavender? Blue-violet? Above all, her overpowering femininity! In her seventh decade, she disturbs my spine. She is a vivifying woman, a stimulating female, a libidinous lady, an irresistible she. (And, I perceive, a dangerous influence on writing style.)

When, seven weeks ago, it became clear that we were going to get to Paris, I wrote to Paul-Emile and asked him to assist me in arranging a meeting with the lady. He wrote to her, identifying himself as a former student of her husband's, and asking if he might phone her. (French *politesse*.)

She sent a *petit bleu* to say yes. He phoned and said that a friend of his had expressed an interest in Christian Science, and could she recommend a course of reading? She did so and invited him to her Tuesday. He went and went again. By the time we arrived in Paris, he was able to take me along.

Wonder of wonders, she has heard of me. Vaguely. I watched, from a corner of the room, a vermouth cassis in hand, as P-E quietly recited my history, my credits, my relationships. His face near her ear, her eyes on me, my awareness of all this as I pretended to study the collection of *presse-papiers* in a cabinet on the wall.

Later, she said to me, "I am so glad you could come. I see fewer and fewer Americans. I miss them. In so many ways, they are the best of people."

"Now, now," I said. "None of that Yankee Doodle chauvinism."

She laughed—what a laugh!—a sort of musical ripple with a built-in echo—and went on.

"No, no. I'm quite serious. Americans are much maligned but oh how I admire their vitality and generosity and, above all, their humor."

"Well," I said. "We're all inclined to get patriotic when we're away from home."

"But *I'm* not American."

"You're not?"

"I'm English."

"I always thought—"

Her bright eyes were upon me. "Always?"

"You're not exactly a stranger to me," I said carefully.

"How so?"

"Well, let's say that Madame Saint-Blaise *is*—but that Rose Adriance is not."

She was gone. Had I seen her get up and walk away? No, but there she was, across the room, in spirited conversation with a small, semicircular group.

About twenty minutes later, she came up to me and with no little apprehension asked, "Who are you?"

"An old admirer," I replied. "Among other things. I'm a silent movie buff and I know all your films. Some of them I've seen many times."

"What a curious day," she mused. "I thought that world to be as dead as mutton, and here you are—dear me, *dear me!*"

"I don't mean to trouble you."

"No. Not that, but—that particular past is so distant. Another world, other people. They seem like characters in fiction for the most part, including myself."

"Fascinating characters, though, don't you think?"

"Some of them. My mother, and—" She stopped. Tears in her eyes. "Forgive me," she said, got up, and left the room.

I talked to Juliette and Marcel Achard for a while. Other than Paul-Emile, they were the only ones there I knew, and he had left half an hour earlier. By the time the hostess returned, her party was thinning out.

I was reluctant to leave, and hung about trying to think of an excuse to remain, when she appeared before me and said softly, "Stay and talk to me. Is it possible?"

"Yes."

I stepped aside as the last of the guests took their leave. Now that I was more relaxed, I began to register impressions more clearly. I became aware that her English had taken on an ever-so-slight French accent.

When we were alone, she led me into a small room, completely windowed, overlooking the Seine. It was filled with flowers and potted plants; a miniature winter garden. It was clear that this was where she lived, for the most part. Books and magazines and records, baskets of letters, a desk, a file, address books, Kleenex, Contour chair, a record player, a tape recorder, reading lamp, two telephones.

She settled into the Contour chair, pressed a signal button, and motioned me to a facing armchair. Why was it, I wondered, that she looked even more beautiful in this room?

"Are you comfortable there?" she asked.

"Oh, yes."

"Good, because that is where I want you. Where the light flatters me."

There was the answer.

Her butler appeared. *"Un Jack Daniel's pour m'sieu,"* she said. *"Avec de l'eau. Et moi, je prends un scotch."*

"Entendu, madame."

He went off. I smiled at her and asked, "How do you know I drink Jack Daniel's?"

She put her head back and replied, "We seem to know a good deal about each other, don't we?"

I was still mystified, but dropped it.

"I was born in Rottingdean," she said. "My mother and father were both in the theatre. But Rottingdean because my father believed in the sea—in sea air, sea water, sea food. I don't suppose I had a bath in fresh water until after he died. So there we were—on the sea—although his work, and my mother's, was largely in London."

The drinks arrived and were served as she continued.

"And then in the summer of 1896, came a splendid offer. Henry Irving and Ellen Terry were off on an American tour. Their business manager was Bram Stoker, a friend of my father's."

"Bram Stoker?" The name was familiar.

"Yes. Later on he became quite famous as the author of *Dracula.*"

"Oh, yes."

"Stoker offered Mum and Dad rather good parts and off we went. I was six and I have vivid memories of the journey. Trains and strange foods and pink scenery. We reached San Francisco in September, my mother used to tell, and they played at The Grand Opera House there for two weeks. A California debut for both Terry and Irving and greatly exciting. When the company left, they left without Maude and Colin Adriance. My father had fallen in love with San Francisco—probably because it was a city on a sea—and decided to settle there. Odd, isn't it? The place he so loved killed him in the end. Swallowed him up ten years later, during the disaster."

We were silent for a time. The light was beginning to fade in the streaked sky over Paris.

She went on. "We're so often swallowed up, sometimes killed by what we love, isn't it so?"

"I don't know."

"My mother and I thought of going home, but our roots had grown deep and there was something infinitely thrilling about being part of the determined spirit of rebuilding the great city. It took years—was rather like being involved in the creation. I was sixteen, and I'd become an actress, too. And, oh—all sorts of things. Does any of this interest you?"

"Immensely."

"Why?"

"It just does."

"Have you known Paul-Emile a long time?"

"Not long enough. I wish I'd known him and Ginette all my life. I have a feeling it would've been a better life."

"Come and see me again. Not on a Tuesday. I only go on with the Tuesdays because I don't know how to stop."

"Whenever you say."

"Tomorrow."

"What time?"

"Four."

She offered her hand. I took it, held it long enough to convey that I did not consider our meeting casual, and left.

I walked back to the Raphaël, slowly.

5/8/57   Paris.

TMY. A report on my second meeting with Rose Adriance.

I arrived at four and was ushered into that same small room. There was a tray of liquor, a bucket of ice, and glasses. Also an elaborate tea tray: Limoges service, scones, sandwiches, tarts. Fresh flowers. Everything conveyed sumptuous, civilized hospitality until I became aware of the chill emanating from the lady.

"Well," I boomed, far too heartily. "This is all very festive!"

"Yes," she said coolly.

"Is something wrong?"

"Just what is it you want?"

"Want?"

"What are you after?"

"Nothing."

"Are you sure?"

"Friendship," I said, bumbling badly. "Conversation.

160

You're someone I—I've known about and—. As a matter of fact, BD and I have worked together. I did a film with him back in—"

"I know," she interrupted, naming it and the date and the cast. "I looked it up this morning. Looked *you* up. I find it strange and suspicious that you should not have mentioned your relationship to him yesterday."

"It didn't occur to me."

"That's untrue!" she said sharply. "Perhaps you'd better go."

"But why?"

"You make me *most* uneasy. You seem detectivy, in a nasty way."

"I apologize."

"What are you up to?"

"Nothing, I promise you. I don't want anything of you and I'm terribly sorry to have troubled you." I got up. "Goodbye."

"Sit down."

I did so.

"What is he like these days?"

I thought for a while and replied, "I'd rather not say."

"Oh? Why not?"

"Well, I don't want to dissemble, since I'm already suspect around here; and I'm worried about telling the truth."

"Try it."

"The fact is, I don't like him much. We did make a successful movie together, yes—and our dealings are perfectly cordial, but I don't admire him as a man. As a talent, yes."

"Are you writing something or planning to—about him or me—or John J. Tumulty?"

I have no idea as to how long it was before I replied. That name, falling from her lips, gave the man a life and a reality

161

and an overwhelming immediacy.

Finally, I said, "Yes. Not about him or any of you really, but a fiction based on the Tumulty story."

"And what *is* the Tumulty story?"

"I don't know. I know parts of it, pieces, but not all of it."

"Why didn't you say so at once? Why this game?"

"I've no idea. It was stupid of me. I'm sorry."

"Will you have some tea?"

"No, thank you."

"A drink?"

"No, thank you."

"No?"

"Yes."

She laughed her laugh and said, "Help yourself."

As I fixed myself a drink—strong—she said, "All that about your animosity toward BD. Did you say that to endear yourself to me? Or is it the truth?"

"It's the truth."

"Very well. I choose to believe you. It's not difficult. He is one of the least likable creatures I have ever known."

"But you married him."

"Only to please his father, whom I loved."

My reaction to this must have been strange indeed, because it made her laugh.

"No, no," she said. "Not loved, simply *loved*. He was not my lover. He was my mother's lover. Do you follow?"

"Yes."

"He became my father, so to speak, the day after my father died. What a superlative man! He was a father and beyond—to me and to BD—partly, I suppose, because he never had children of his own. He worried about us constantly; about our health and futures and education. He said to me once, 'Help BD. You're the strong one. And one of the

162

things the strong are meant to do is help the weak. Just as the rich should help the poor; and the fortunate, the unfortunate. He's going to need your help and mine as long as he lives, because he's weak. He can't resist temptation, he won't learn the lesson of work, and yet he's worth helping because he's talented and unlucky.' Years later, he somehow engineered our marriage, I don't know how."

(*I* know, I thought, and considered telling her. I will, someday.)

"*Now* will you tell me?" she asked. "How he is? Or rather, how was he when you last saw him?"

"That would have been about six or seven months ago. He's holding on pretty well. He keeps up with things. Works some, as much as he wants to, I gather." I paused before adding, "His marriage is dead, in my opinion."

"It would have to be. The poor man has no idea, never *has* had, of what women are for." She looked at me. "Do you?"

"I hope so."

"So few do. We are—can be—so useful, and valuable. We've so much to give, and our men—they turn us into domestics or tarts and let it go at that. Or playthings or pets. Pity. BD was one of the worst offenders."

"But he didn't turn *you* into any of those things."

"You're bloody well right he didn't! Even so, I didn't leave him until I had Tumulty's permission to do so. Think of it! The power of that man."

"He was somebody," I said.

"The war was my great good fortune. The *Old* War—or as some of us call it, the *Real* War. I was fired by patriotism, so I volunteered my services to one of those great pageants that were being staged everywhere in the country. I played the part of a Red Cross nurse and by the time the tour ended, I had become so involved with her that I insisted upon becoming a Red Cross nurse in fact. And I did. Mr. Tumulty used to tease me and call me the female St. Genesius—he was the actor, you know, who became a Christian by acting one in an anti-Christian play. A fascinating character. They used to perform a classic piece about him here—by Rotrou, I believe. So I trained for a year, then was sent overseas. And it was here, at The American Hospital, that I met Doctor Saint-Blaise."

She took a deep breath. When she spoke again, it was in a new voice. "He was rare. He had a reverence for the human spirit that equaled his awe of the human body. To see him perform surgery was watching a great artist at work. He looked upon it as creative, and in his hands, it was. The human body was his religion." She smiled distantly as she looked out the window. "I recall a time in Germany at a medical convention. There was an impressive display of new equipment. One machine in particular was near to miraculous and I chided my husband, saying, 'Now even *you* must admit that's better than a human body.' 'Really?' he snapped. 'And if it's damaged, can it repair itself?' He was divine. I met him during my first morning in France, worked with him that afternoon, and went to bed with him that night."

I must have reacted oddly, because she smiled and added, "It was *most* unlike me. But we were all war-weary in those days and behaved strangely and, in any case, I thought: 'Ah, well! France. Why not make the most of it?' In a week's time, I was his mistress. Frenchmen, by tradition, know how to arrange such matters and so, without delay, there we were in our little flat in Neuilly—our *'cinq à sept'* as they're called —except that our hours were rather different. Often bizarre. What with the hospital on the one hand and his wife and children on the other—our life had to shift for itself. It was exciting—and enjoyable. What went wrong was that we hadn't augured *love*. For me, it was an adventure; for him, routine. We didn't fall in love, we grew in love. It took time and trouble. By the time the war ended, we were hopelessly intertwined.

"We went away together for a week; to England, to Clovelly in Devon—where we thought and walked and talked and helped each other. We considered every avenue and decided on a simple one. We would separate, and resume our lives as before—richer always for having had what we'd had. So it was. We corresponded regularly and shared a part of each other's life. Then, after about nine years, in 1929, his wife died. A year later, he sent for me, and we were married. We had twenty-three heavenly years together. I've had *such* a lovely life."

"Yes, you have."

She laughed again. "Do you remember that line in old plays—'I don't know why I'm telling you all this!'?"

"*I* know. Because the playwright has to tell the audience, that's why."

"Yes," she said, "but in this case it's something else again. My friends are nearly all gone, or gaga. It's becoming lonely. Old people like to talk—have you noticed? It helps them to feel still alive. And they love to linger on memories, and reveal secrets. It gives life a meaning, in a manner of speaking. And then, too, we don't want the secrets and memories to die with us. So we talk. Foolishly sometimes, I expect."

"Not at all. You can't imagine how all this interests me."

"Ah, yes. But then you're something of a special case, aren't you? A professional Nosy Parker."

"Call it that."

"I've hurt your feelings. Forgive me. It was only badinage. Have a drink."

"Tell me about Tumulty as a businessman," I said, pressing on.

She bit her lip and smiled. "It was not his strong suit. Money was unreal to him. The things one bought with it or did with it represented the only reality. A prop or a light, a play or a costume, a meal. But money itself, even the *idea* of money, bored him, irritated him. He seldom carried it. It used to be said that he never carried *anything* in his pockets because he was vain and peacocky and wouldn't allow *anything* to spoil the line of his clothes."

"Yes, I'd heard that somewhere."

"Not a word of truth in it. Oh, he *was* rather a beau and dressed smartly, but his having no money in his pockets can be explained far more easily."

"How?"

"For one thing, it was never much on his mind; and for another, he seldom had any."

"But surely he earned a great deal?"

"Yes, and spent it."

"On what?"

"On productions and commissioning plays; on theatres; equipment and repairs; advertising; rights and translations. He fed his theatre whims endlessly."

"When you were married to BD—"

"Yes?"

"Did BD give him money?"

"I've no idea. Why?"

"Well, there's a huge discrepancy. Two versions—actually more like *twenty* versions—but they fall into two categories. BD, for instance, claims he constantly gave Tumulty money

—for years and in vast sums and—"

"*Most* unlikely."

"Why?"

"Because BD was *never* generous."

"He claims Tumulty was forever at him for loans to pay judgments and liens—"

"Nonsense!" Her face was flushed with anger. "That *couldn't* be true."

"Why not?"

"Because nothing could be less like Mr. Tumulty than what you describe—*he* describes. What a cad!"

"But if—"

"John Tumulty was a proud man. The idea of his asking BD for help for *any* reason is beyond my *imagination*. BD is lying."

"Still, he has records—showed them to me, for what they're worth—"

"Worth nothing."

"—according to which he turned over to Tumulty something like six hundred and forty-seven thousand dollars. Now, that's quite a—"

I stopped talking because Mme. Saint-Blaise, who had been sitting stiffly, was now on her feet. Her eyes had become glazed and her face had gone white. The change was startling, and brought me to my feet as well. She swayed slightly and held on to the back of her chair for support. I moved to her and asked, "Are you all right?"

"No," she said. "Not. Please—call—and—"

I looked around for a bell or a signal, found nothing. She was pointing about, vaguely and ineffectively. I ran out into the hall shouting (in pretty good French, to my surprise), "*Vite! Vite! Quelqu'un! Madame est malade! Vite!*"

167

The butler and a small, lumpy, thick-bespectacled woman (the cook?) appeared. I motioned them to follow me.

We found Mme. Saint-Blaise sitting exactly as she had been an hour earlier, sipping tea.

The servants looked at me and at each other.

"I'm quite all right," said my hostess. "Now." She turned to the servants. *"C'est rien,"* she said. They went off, whispering. About *me*, I had no doubt.

"You went pale," I explained.

"Yes," she said. "I'm apt to do that from time to time." She smiled again. "I'm an old lady, remember. Strange things happen to old ladies." A sip.

"All the same," I said, "I think I'd better go."

"Must you?"

"I should. You must be tired."

"It's curious," she said. "Talking does tire me as a rule, but talking to you has been relaxing."

Did that "has been" mean this was our last meeting? I wondered, but decided not to ask.

2/15/60   Beverly Hills

TMY. We arrived here a week ago and have rented Frank Orsatti's house on Roxbury Drive for six months. The house is comfortable, but I am not. The reason: a bad joke that has gone too far.

A little pink envelope in the mailbox this morning. Nothing else. No stamp on it. It has been privately delivered.

I dread opening it, but do so without delay and read—typewritten:

SO YOU ARE BACK AGAIN. WHAT
FOR? IF IT IS FOR MINDING
BUSINESS NOT YOUR OWN YOU ARE
HEADING FOR TROUBLE. MME.
SAINT-BLAISE IS A LYING BITCH.

For a minute there, I couldn't remember who the hell Mme. Saint-Blaise was. I haven't so much as thought of her for some time, or of Tumulty.

I am sure now that my tormentor is BD.

What does it matter? I have no further interest in the subject.

But I wonder how he knew about my meeting with Mme. S-B? And if he knows that, why doesn't he know that I have not made so much as a one-line note on Tumulty for—how long is it?—good God, nearly three years. I have been otherwise involved and have plenty on my plate now. Too much.

Three years. Where does time go? Never mind that. Where does *my* time go?

4–18–60   Beverly Hills. Roxbury Drive.

TMY. BD is ill. He has been in the hospital—The Good Samaritan—for five weeks. At the moment, there is apparently no telling when he will be getting out. His wife phoned me yesterday.

"I saw it in the trades this morning that you are here. How are you?"

"Fine. You still read the trades?"

"Oh, yes. We are all creatures of habit, isn't it so? And

169

often I find it valuable—as today. How else would I have known you are here? You never would have called me, surely?"

"Of course I would."

"Ah, but you didn't. BD is sick, you know."

"No, I didn't. What is it?"

"I'm not sure. They tell us so little. It is to do with his bones. For a time there was talk of inflammation, but it has gone beyond that. They have been making tests for weeks."

"I'm very sorry."

"Could you find time to go down and see him? I know how it would give him such pleasure."

I'd rather see you, I think, but I say, "Of course. When's a good time?"

"In the afternoon. Between two and four. That is best for the friends. Ena and I spend evenings there."

"Every evening?"

"Certainly."

"How *is* Ena?"

"The same."

"I'll go tomorrow."

He is not in his room when I get there. A male orderly, making the bed and readjusting the complicated rigging around it, tells me BD has gone down to therapy.

"How long will he be?"

"Search me."

"O.K. if I wait?"

"Ask the desk."

I go out to the desk, where no one pays any attention to me. Looking down the hallway, I see a nurse enter BD's room. I go back to talk to her. At last, a pleasant note. She is Irish and pert and charming. A chubby girl who likes her work.

"I'm afraid he'll be down all the afternoon," she says in a soothing brogue. "Would you like to see him there?"

"Is that all right?"

"Oh, I think so. If you'll wait a wee moment, I'll take you along."

She makes a few notes on his chart. Presently we are on our way.

"How is he?" I ask.

"Oh, you know. We have good days and bad. He's a smashing, lovely man. He makes me laugh."

"Is he going to get out of this all right?"

A pause. Too long. "You'd be better off to ask his doctors about that."

"Sure."

We reach the therapy section in a sub-basement. I hope I never see it again. I can think only of Rowlandson prints, or the Gustave Doré illustrations for Dante's *Inferno*. It is, in a word, Hell. Moans and groans; the sound of running water, of electrical devices; the sight of crippled, misshapen, suffering fellow men.

I am so upset that I have no idea as to when the nurse left me. I find myself standing alone near a sheeted-off section. As I peer in, I recognize BD lying on his back. A physiotherapist is carefully manipulating his leg.

I step into the area. BD studies me for a long spell. It is difficult to begin, but finally I manage to get out a false and hearty "Well, how are *you*, young man?"

He does not reply, but continues to look at me. Tears fill his eyes. He blinks them out and continues to stare. I have always had the uneasy feeling that he dislikes me, but now, after all these years, it changes. Time has erased all memory

171

of friction, of our abrasive contact, of the battle of egos. In a place like this, at a time like this, what matters? Nothing. We are reminded that we are all in the same boat, and for a damned quick cruise at that.

I am overwhelmed with pity for this talented man; by commiseration for what lies beneath his pain-racked face; by shock at the portrait of the vulnerable human condition. Without forethought, I lean down and kiss his forehead. It is cold and damp and clammy.

"Bullshit," he says.

"O.K. if I sit down?"

"Help yourself," he says, hoarsely. I wonder if his voice is gone for good.

He asks me what I am doing in California. I tell him, in some detail, about my United Artists picture.

"Well, *that'll* be lousy," he says.

I shrug to cover my embarrassment and say, "Who knows?"

"*I* know!" he says, and emits a cry of pain so piercing that I jump up. At the same moment, I see him kick out violently, catching the physiotherapist just below the stomach. The poor man falls back against a cabinet, and holds on to his middle as he looks at BD and says, "*Jesus*, fella!" He moves out of the area.

"Can I do anything?" I ask.

"No, no. Sit down."

I do so. BD moves slightly, and grunts with pain.

"Drink of water?" I ask.

"He does that on purpose, that bastard. Hurts me."

"Come on, now. You don't really believe that, do you?"

"Certainly I do. That bastard. Dirty Jew bastard."

"Well, if he is, he's the first one I ever ran into named MacNamara."

"What?"

"That's the name on his badge. MacNamara. Probably an Irish Catholic, like you."

BD explodes a laugh, sounding as he did in the old days. The laugh increases in volume and intensity. I know he is laughing at something other than what I have said, and ask, "What?"

"Remember what Bill Fields said that time about Irish Catholics? 'They're the worst *kind* of Jews!' "

The therapist returns, accompanied by a large, over-weight, gray-haired man. I squint and read his badge, "L. H. Beddington, M.D."

"Hiya, doc, m'boy?" says BD, all charm.

The doctor, unsmiling, asks, "What's the trouble?"

"Your physical torturist threw me a fifteen-hundred-watt jolt, that's all."

"Let's have a look," says the doctor, and takes his place beside the table.

BD looks at the therapist and says, "Had to blow the whistle on me, huh?"

The doctor raises his hands, but before he touches BD's leg, he looks at him. "I want to say one thing to you, mister. We're doing our best for you. In the course of it, we may hurt you. If you kick *me*, I'll bash your teeth in."

There is a long moment of almost unbearable tension.

BD reaches into his mouth, and brings forth a full set of dentures. The lower half of his face collapses. He looks a hundred years old as he smiles up at the doctor, sticks out his chin defiantly, and says, "Try it!"

The doctor shakes his head and laughs. Even the therapist laughs. The doctor proceeds with a careful, tender examination. BD winces from time to time, but that is all.

"Apparently some sick nerve ends in there," the doctor

173

says, "but look here, you've got to go on with your course. I'll give you something. A deadener."

"Watch your language."

The doctor said, "Demerol. All right?"

"How about one of those delicious little suppositories?" suggests BD. He turns to me. "This guy's a real pusher, y'know. Well, come to think of it, I'm quite a pusher myself —when I *get* one, I mean."

General laughter.

"No," says the doctor. "We'd better save those for sleep. I'll give you a pain killer."

"A brain killer?" asks BD, and howls.

Pressing, I think.

He looks at me and says, "Pressing, huh?"

An eerie moment. The doctor and the therapist leave.

We talk about Frank Capra for a time, and about John Ford and George Stevens and Willie Wyler and others of his colleagues. A nurse comes in, gives BD an injection in his right buttock, and goes out. Within five minutes, BD is phenomenally changed.

His voice is no longer hoarse, but has returned to full vigor. His articulation, which has been thick, becomes clear.

He peers at me and says, "I'm going to beat this, y'know."

"I know. You're going to make it fine."

"You don't think I *am*. You think I'm going to go from this slab to another slab till the last slab, but you're *wrong*. You've been wrong before, buddy-boy. You were wrong about the goddamn finish the first time we ever did anything together, weren't you?"

"I guess I was."

"Bet your ass. And you're wrong again."

"I said I thought you were going to make it fine. Didn't you hear me?"

"Sure I did. Not only what you said, but what you thought. What makes me a genius. I can always tell what they *think*. What do I care what they *say*? I'm going to walk out of here on my own sweet power and back to work. What do you know about *that*? I've got my picture all finished—in my head. Every goddamn scene, every fucking shot. They think I've been sacked out here on my butt, jerkin' off and feeling sorry for myself. A lot *they* know, those assholes. I've *got* my *picture*, buddy-boy! Every goddamn line. Every goddamn trick. I'll show 'em a few tricks. All those new punks—they think they invented celluloid. Why, for Christ's sake, they haven't done a goddamn thing in the last five years we didn't do thirty years ago, *forty*. If I wanted to, you know what I could do? I could start and say: 'Fade in. Close Shot: A male hand holding a female hand. The other male hand comes in and places a wedding ring on the third finger of the female hand. The camera pulls back to reveal—' You want to hear the rest of it?"

"Sure."

"You do, huh? Well, up yours, Maybelle. This is *my* picture. I wrote it and I directed it—in my head. It runs an hour and forty-eight minutes. Exactly right. All I have to do now is photograph the goddamn thing. A cinch, a piece of cake. No stars. *I'm* the star. I'll make 'em *all* look sick. I'll tell you one more thing about it, and that will be all—where it's laid. It's laid in San Francisco. Have *you* ever been laid in San Francisco? Goddamn, what a city. That is, without a doubt, no contest, the single best city in the world—not only because of buildings and hills and geographical location, but it's got the best people, descended from the best goddamn stock this country ever produced. People with imagination and courage and a sense of what the hell it's all about. Civilized. I never should've left it. Never. So let's go up there."

"All right."

"I mean just the two of us. Let's go on up there. I've got to scout a few locations anyway, but no wives. Not yours, not mine. I want to show you that city and I'll show you what I'm going to do with it. There it is, the best goddamn movie set that ever was and it's never been shot, not a bit of it." He pointed a powerful, threatening finger in my face. "And if you start telling me about that crock they called *San Francisco* at Metro, I'll bash your teeth in."

"I wish I could pull my dentures out the way you did," I said. "I bet it would get one hell of a laugh."

He ignored my attempt at the kiss-ass joke, which was all right with me because I regretted it the moment I said it.

"*San Francisco,*" he went on in the most scornful possible tone. "They offered it to me before they offered it to anyone. In fact, Hoppy—you ever know him? Hoppy? Robert Hopkins?"

"Just met him."

"Best goddamn idea man they ever had out there. Well, he had this idea—brought it to me first, in fact. I said, 'Hell, no! I couldn't do anything that's got the San Francisco fire in it. Too goddamn painful. I wouldn't want to live through *that* again.' But when they finished the script, they sent it to me. Naturally, they would. I was hotter than a firecracker in those days. I *still* am, but in a different way. Well, I read it—tried to read it—some of it. It was God-awful. I said to L.B., 'This isn't a script. It's a one-way ticket to disaster.' In those days they thought if you put Gable, Tracy, and Jeanette MacDonald into one, you couldn't miss because you were giving people so much for their money. They found out later it's possible to give them *too* much for their money."

"It was a big hit, though, wasn't it?" I asked.

176

"A hit?" he echoed. "No, you're one letter short. Put an 's' in front of that and you'll have it."

"I thought it was a—"

"Don't *think* so much!" he shouted. "I've told you before, but you never listen to a goddamn thing. In your business, you're not *supposed* to think. You're supposed to feel and describe, and write and care and worry and question. Don't *think* so much. That's for philosophers and economists and sociologists and the men in white and all those cockeyed wonders in their shirt-sleeves trying to figure out how to blow up the world before someone else blows it up. They want to be the first, see? That's their kick."

The shot had taken complete effect. He was euphoric. He looked younger, perhaps because the drug had brought about a relaxation of his recently tense face and body.

The therapist returned and resumed his routine. BD was not aware of his presence; or of mine, after a while. Still, he rambled on. He did not seem to mind whenever I attempted to get him back onto the track. He took the prodding and prompting easily. Did he assume my voice to be part of his own thought process? Had he known I was steering him, he most assuredly would have resented it. He went on talking and I was even able to make fat notes.

"Christ," he said, "they didn't even *go* to San Francisco, those stupid bastards. They were all so tied to their back lots back then. You know why, don't you? Because they wanted to keep an eye on everybody, every minute. Everybody was an employee. It didn't matter if you were Wally Beery or the guard at the gate. You were working for the front office at so much an hour or a day or a week, to do such and such a job, and you were supposed to be on time, and do what you were told, and shut up.

"And L.B., *that* old buzzard, he couldn't *believe* it when

177

I told him to shove it. He looked at me through those milk-bottle-bottom glasses, with those big popeyes, and he kept saying 'Gable, Tracy, MacDonald' over and over again as though it were a Hindu mantra of some kind. You know, one of those magic incantations: 'Mene, mene, tekel. Gable, Tracy, MacDonald. Hocus-pocus, alakazam. Gable, Tracy, MacDonald.' And when I still said, 'No,' he started to press me for a why not, and I said to him, 'Because it's a phony baloney, L.B., that's why not.' That made him sore as hell, and he started to get purple in the face, that way he used to, and yelling, 'Damn it, don't you use the word "phony" around me! I'm no phony!'

" 'I didn't say you were.'

" 'What the hell do *you* know about phony? We've spent two hundred thousand dollars on the research.'

"And I said to him, 'Sure, so you've got the facts, but what you haven't got is the truth.'

"He screamed some more. 'Do you know what you're talking about? What the hell're you talking about? Hanging around with those stupid intellectuals all the time. You're losing your touch, that's *your* trouble.'

"And I said to him, 'Never mind *my* touch. And my trouble is *nothing* next to *your* trouble. You're going to lose your balls on this thing. All three of them. I was *there,* you stubborn Hebe hothead. I was *part* of it. *In* it. I was goddamn blown up. You want to hear about it? Sit down and I'll tell you about it.' And what do you think he said to that? He said, 'Get out. You're barred from this lot as of today. You and your agent both. Whoever he is. Even Myron Selznick.' And I said, 'What do I care? I hate your shitty chicken soup anyway.' But imagine him not even wanting to *listen!* I could've told him. I could've told them *all.*

"I told my wife about it once—one of my wives, I forget

which one. We were on a cruise. A beautiful yacht I'd chartered. The Greek islands. I got to telling her about that fearful *Walpurgisnacht* in San Francisco, and it took all night. We drank some and ate a little and the sea was calm and the stars were near, and I told her about that night, and I didn't finish until the sun was right over our heads. I remember she looked at me and she moved her head from side to side. God, what a beauty she was—and she said, 'How can you remember it so?' And I said to her, 'How can I *forget* it?'

"You know, a thing like that happens to you maybe once in a lifetime. Changes you. It teaches you things. You find out about people and you begin to believe in them more than in God, because a thing like an earthquake, you have to figure that's the kind of thing God is responsible for, and you wonder why when you see the misery and the agony and the pain and the waste it causes. And then you see how people behave, some of them, and it puts you on a path of thinking. Yes, yes—I know I told you no thinking, but I meant about your work, not about your *life,* you dumdum. Mostly, people *help* each other in a crisis. There turns out to be more unselfish ones than selfish ones and more brave than not. Mind you, it's no great feat for me to remember all that. I was no babe in arms. I was seventeen. And not a Booth Tarkington seventeen, either. I was whatever they used to call a swinger in those days. A sheik? No, that was later. A dandy? Buck? Dude? Rake? I don't know. What's the difference? Hell, I'd been working in the company for ten years or more. I was a well-known little actor around town. I'd been screwing for three years, so what the hell? I was no thumbsucker. And I'd had my share of booze by then. In fact, I was a little boozed up that night and in the kip with this ugly Japanese piece—I like 'em ugly once in a while, don't you? They're almost always better. Stands to reason. A dame's got looks, that's all she needs. Without, she needs talent, or at least skill. And they're so *grateful!*

"Anyway. She made up for her ugly with her action, this Asiatic wiggler. There we were, in the middle of the night, in the middle of a whale of a ride, and *wham!* Five in the morning, it was—something like that. I tell you, for the first couple of minutes of it, I thought: 'My God, this may be the greatest fucking that ever *was!*' I mean with the whole room going and the walls trembling, but when the ceiling came down, I knew something was wrong, because I knew even *I* couldn't be *that* good!

"I'd been out that night. Not with the Japanese number, it wasn't considered the thing around San Francisco in those days. We all fraternized a mile a minute, but in private. No, I'd been out to see a show; a good show, too, *Babes in Toyland* by Victor Herbert. It was at the Columbia. What a city! There was something at the Alcazar and something at the Tivoli. Then there was a wow of a burlesque, The Cherry Burlesquers. They were at the California. And, naturally, a lot of crap too, there always is, like *Dangers of the Working Girl* at the Central, I think; and something called *Queen of the Highbinders* at the Alhambra. But The Metropolitan Opera Company was at the Opera House, doing *Carmen* with Caruso. I tried to get in, but they were sold out. So I went to *Babes in Toyland.* And I went back after to see some of my cronies and that's where I met the Japanese bimbo. She was in it. She looked fine when she was on but when she got the makeup off she was a one hundred percent Olympic champion Oriental dog. So we knocked around in the dark, and around one A.M., I was ready to get to it. Now I couldn't very well take her back to my place because all of us in the Tumulty company lived at the same boardinghouse; and she was somewhere in Jap town, which didn't thrill me; so we

180

checked into one of my little hides on the Barbary Coast—
it was right across the street from The Midway Plaisance
that featured the best hootchy-kootchy dancers in town—
and there we were, having at it, when it happened. Five-
thirteen A.M. April eighteenth. Nineteen-oh-six.

"When we caught on that some kind of ungodly cataclysm
was in the works, we grabbed some clothes and tore out, and
when we got to the street, I was convinced that either I was
asleep and having a nightmare, or else that I'd died and gone
to Gehenna. Dust and smoke and screaming and rubble and
hysteria. I lost the Japanese broad right away, never saw her
again. I tried to find my way home to Powell Street but on
the way, these two big grimy cops grabbed me and said they
were organizing rescue squads and ordered me to stick with
them. So I did, and we pulled people—living and dead and
in-between—out of the fallen-down houses and tried to help
the firemen; but I still wanted to get back and see about
Tumulty, so I kept switching from squad to squad, working
my way back to the center of town. I was with one squad—
listen to this, you'll love it; weren't you once some kind of
a mediocre musician?—when we saw a man sitting on a
trunk. A dark little fat man, shiny face; and he was dressed
in a long nightgown and holding on to a big alarm clock and
a gold watch and chain in one hand and in the other hand
a pitch pipe and what do you think he was doing? He was
vocalizing! I don't mean singing. I mean vocalizing, scales
and exercises and so on. Well, nobody paid much attention
because all kinds of people were doing all kinds of crazy
things, but a fireman and I walked over and I saw right away
that it was Caruso. That's right, Enrico Caruso. The most
famous tenor in the world. And it turned out that not only
was he scared shitless, but that the main thing that worried
him was the shock. He thought maybe the earthquake might

181

have ruined his voice, so he was sitting there trying it out. "Well, it *hadn't* ruined his voice. If anything, it probably made it better. I'll bet he found high notes in it that night that hadn't ever been there *before!* I took him by the arm, started leading him away. He kept worrying about his trunk, and jabbering away in Italian. How the hell he ever got his trunk down there, or found it down there, I'll never know, but I managed to get him away. I kept yelling for somebody who spoke Italian, eventually located somebody—a Salvation Army girl—and we took Signor Caruso along until we found a police captain. I told the captain who this was. I had to pick a captain who'd never *heard* of Caruso. He'd heard of *me,* though. So he took my word for it that this roly-poly man in his nightgown, crying like a baby, was one of the most important people in the world, and had better be looked after. I heard later that he'd had to keep identifying himself all day—till he got out on the Oakland ferry—by singing a few bars every time. What a scene, huh? And did you see it in the M-G-M turkey? Of course not. And not in the Caruso thing they did, either. Those airheads.

"I ran into him, Caruso, a couple of times after that. One night in New York I went backstage and introduced myself, and talked about that night. He didn't remember me at all. I don't think he remembered much about the night, either. He went on for years and years after that—he didn't die till 1921—but he never set foot in San Francisco again. *Never.* Whenever the Met came, they came without him.

"Later on that night—well, morning actually—I found Tumulty. He was hurt, but not badly. In some ways I wish he *had* been hurt, because then his attention would've gone to that. Instead, he stood some distance from what was left of his theatre, and I don't think he could've felt more bereft if he'd lost *me.* But hell, *every* theatre was leveled that night.

182

Every single goddamn theatre in San Francisco. There was only one—The Chutes—that was on the outskirts on Haight Street between Clayton and Cole, part of an amusement park. After a while they reopened it, and called it the Orpheum. But—you won't believe this, I'm not sure I believe it myself—within four or five months there were theatres all over the place. Some of them in tents, some in shacks. And in a couple of years, there were more new theatres put up than there'd been before. That was the beginning, the real beginning, of Tumulty's Grand. We lost four people out of our company that night—Colin Adriance, Rose's father, he was one of them—but I'm damned if I don't think Tumulty cared more about his theatre than them. So listen, will you call over to the main house and ask Greta to come over here?"

"Who?" I asked, startled.

"Greta, you nitwit!" he shouted. "And then, when she gets here, blow, will you? I'm going to give her a bounce and she doesn't like people watching. She's a Lutheran."

"All right."

"And don't worry too much about the preview. I've seen previews go great, and then the picture lays an ostrich egg —and the other way around. The main thing is voice lessons! There's nothing wrong with it for the stage, you understand. But when they record it for these asinine talkies, it doesn't sound right. It's too high. Tumulty, *that* stupid son-of-a-bitch, was always trying to get it higher for me. He said voices penetrate better from the upper register. But now, with this goddamn talkie craze going on, it's no good. I know there's a teacher somewhere could help me. It's simply a case of exercises—voice exercises, I mean—to get it down. Everybody around here is panicking. All they're interested in is stage people. They forget *I'm* from the stage. And Jesus

183

Christ! That hungry Equity mob is on its way like it was the gold rush all over again. Hell, maybe it is. So don't tell *me* about San Francisco. Let's have a drink."

He turned and looked at me. "Hiya," he said, and winked. "Glad to see you. Come in. Sit down. What's new?"

"Thanks a lot," I said. We shook hands. "I'll be in again." I left.

I mean to go back and see him, but never down in that therapy place if I can help it. I do not ever want to see that place again, in the same way that Caruso never wanted to see San Francisco again.

I shall have to trust to luck, and hope that in this new state of his, he will continue to talk as he did today.

2/6/61   Beverly Hills.

BD is not going to recover. Rosella told me this today. She has it as a consensus from the team of doctors that has been caring for him. It is not one thing, she explains, but many, and they complicate one another.

"Will he be able to come home?" I ask.

"I have wished to know the same thing, but they tell me they cannot say as yet. And when they do, they tell the house will have to be made into a hospital. He needs much care, much equipments, machinery, nurses. Many hands. Ena will be my great help, but he has never liked things done for him, always preferred to do for himself. It may be one of the reasons our marriage was not a success." She smiled a Gioconda smile and added, "Of all his productions, the least successful."

"It didn't seem so from the outside."

"Ah, yes. But marriages are lived *inside.* Isn't it so? Italian women love to serve. It is so that we are trained. My husband, he did not like that idea, ever. When we were working together, in the cinema, and were partners, it was well, always well. But when the time came that I thought it wise to step aside and let the others, the younger, take part—the public was telling me this in any case; politely, but telling me —I was happy. I wanted much now to be a wife, perhaps even a mother. It was not his way. We lived together, quite pleasantly. We traveled, sometimes together, sometimes separately. It has been, as they say, all right. But we missed, both of us, a great deal. Above all, family. Mine is far away and after so much of separation—strange to me; and he has no one, has had no one for such a long time. He has been very much alone."

"Did he ever talk to you about John J. Tumulty?"

She laughed. "I can remember long ago when he warned me you would ask me that question, and I was to say nothing. Ah well, after so long a time, you have asked it, and it seems not to matter so greatly, does it?"

"No."

"Yes, he talked to me of John J. Tumulty. So much and so many times and it was never quite the same. I could not tell which was the truth. Perhaps *he* could not tell, either. Once, long ago, he spoke of Tumulty, his father; showed me the photographs, and the scrapbooks filled with praise. Another time, he told me Tumulty was *not* his father, that he had been adopted. He told me he did not know who his real father was, had never known. Then one day, while we were making a picture together, there was a man; not a nice man, rather drunk and disagreeable, in a small part, and he made things most difficult. We had to stop for a time and BD came

185

into my dressing room. I was in a temper and said, 'Why do you support such behavior?' And he said, 'Because the bum happens to be my father.'"

"Clay Bannister," I say.

"Yes. Remember my husband made a life of stories and fantasies and dreams. Those were his life more than his real life, even about such things as his past and childhood. As to happenings, he would elaborate and change and invent. Not lying because poets do not lie. They tell something how they feel it, and it is possible to feel it in different ways at different times. He is a good man. Sad but good. I have made him happy, I hope, sometime, for an hour or a day or longer, but still, he is a sad man and now he is to have a sad ending."

1/6/65   Holmby Hills.   Delfern Drive.

I have had Frank Chapman, who has been working with me on the Nez Percé film research, write one of those letters to *The Saturday Review*. It was published in the issue that arrived today and reads:

> For a biographical work on the subject of JOHN J. TUMULTY, American actor (1849–1930), the undersigned would be grateful for clippings, programs, documents or letters. Photographs would also be welcome, as would the opportunity to interview persons ac-

quainted with the subject. All
expenses with regard to copy-
ing, Xeroxing, or photostating
will be reimbursed. Frank
Chapman, Box 903, Beverly
Hills, Calif. 90210.

A shot in the distant dark.

1/16/65   Holmby Hills.   TMY.

Frank's letter to *The Saturday Review* has opened up
a new channel.

It begins with a postcard, and, of all things, a *penny* postcard. I have not seen one in years. A five-cent stamp is
pasted next to the imprinted one-cent stamp and both the
address and the message appear to have been typewritten
on an antique machine. The type is unfamiliar, the spacing
wayward. The message reads:

Sir: In re your letter on page 32 Saturday Review of Literature, issue of 6 January 1965, please be advised that the
undersigned, who had the inestimable pleasure of much
converse with John J. Tumulty, Esq., will be pleased to
receive you for the purpose of mutual exchange. For appointment please telephone Mrs. Gino Brosio, 629–9401.
Respectfully yrs:

Walton M. de Young, M.D.

It is one of those cards that bears study; full of tantalizing
mystery. Walton M. de Young, M.D. Mrs. Gino Brosio. How

187

do these two fit together? A housekeeper, a nurse, a companion? How about a daughter who married an Italian? Frank guesses nurse. I choose daughter.

And the word "converse" sends me to the big dictionary. I was sure he was not using it in the sense of conversation, and so I am glad to find that in addition to conversation it also means:

> . . . . 2. *Obs.* a. to maintain a familiar association (usually fol. by *with*). b. to have sexual intercourse (usually fol. by *with*). c. to commune spiritually (usually fol. by *with*).

We had better stick to a. Lord, how the language changes! We no longer commonly use that Esquire thing of his; or "converse" in that sense; "Respectfully yours" has gone.

The card troubles me in other ways because it is a hint that should this work ever be undertaken in any form it will be necessary to move with the greatest caution in the matter of period language.

Later, gooseflesh. I called the number, spoke to Mrs. Brosio, identified myself, explained that I was the one doing the project and that Frank Chapman was working with me. She could not have been more cordial and identified herself immediately as Dr. de Young's daughter. That was the gooseflesh.

She suggests early morning for the meeting, but when I explain that I am not available mornings, she seems troubled and explains that his best hours are in the morning. I am about to break a rule, damn it—(William James: "In the formation or breaking of a habit, beware of the single excep-

188

tion.")—when Mrs. Brosio, sensing that I am discomfited, suggests tea tomorrow and adds, "Why not try it and if it doesn't work out then perhaps you can find a morning? Sunday?"

"Thank you. What time tomorrow?"

"Four. Let me give you the address. Do you have a pencil?"

January 17, 1965   H.H.   Delfern.

I returned, half an hour ago, from tea with Dr. de Young. He may be a better character than Tumulty! He is 91 and if, as his daughter insists, he is better in the morning, he certainly must be *something* in the morning.

He is a native San Franciscan, and did not retire from his practice there until the age of 85.

He says: "One day, I was looking into this overly wealthy woman's throat: slightly infected, partially removed tonsils. I was trying to get a proper look, she was gagging away, I was ducking spittle, and I thought to myself, 'Good Lord, I've seen this hellish throat thousands of times over.' And all at once, I was sick of it. I told her to close her mouth and I sent her home and I sent *myself* home and I said, right out loud, 'That's *it.*'

"I called up Prudence here, her husband had died about ten months before, and I said, 'Pru, put a mess of house plants into the guest room. I'm moving in on you. For good.' She nearly fell out, didn't you?"

"No nearly about it. I *did* fall out," said Mrs. Brosio. She turned to me, "You won't change your mind and have a

189

madeleine? I baked them this morning."

"I *will* change my mind. Thank you."

She left us.

"Good man," said the doctor. "I'm ninety-one and hale, eat her baking every day. People ask me constantly for my secret. There's no *one* secret, there are hundreds. And they're not secrets, they're simply applied common sense. I'll tell you one of them: By and large, the people who live longest are the ones who—barring accident—*want* to."

I pull out a pad and make a note. One, I want to get the words exactly right. Two, I am anxious to see if he has any objection. None. He takes it as a matter of course, as though he were being interviewed. So I hang on to the pad and scribble away for the rest of the visit.

"There's no *one* thing," he repeats. "Don't you see? It's an *attitude* that eventually involves many things. Nutrition, exercise, rest. Sexual activity, mental activity, spiritual posture. Discipline and habits of life. Good habits make for a good life and the other way about . . . I believe in moderation in all things, including *moderation*. . . . Are you in the movie business?"

"In a way, yes."

His daughter served tea.

"We go to all the pictures—don't we?—now that there are so few plays. We take what we can get. I miss the theatre, though—the excitement of it. It was always a great part of my life and meant much to me. It was in theatres that I learned to laugh and feel and see that I was so much like others and that they were so much like me. It was to my love of theatre that I owe my friendship with John Tumulty. My father before me had been his physician; in fact, he was my father's very first patient. I was twenty-four years his junior, yet we were fast friends, and after my father's death in 1919

190

—good Lord, almost fifty years ago!—I became John's doctor."

At last. I was hoping he would introduce the subject. But he leaves it at once.

"We're all lazy, aren't we?" he says. "And everything in modern science appears to be aimed toward cosseting that laziness. Automobiles to keep us from walking. Prepared dinners to keep us from cooking. Ready-made dreams on the television box to keep us from exercising our imaginations. But let me ask you—do you know any greater joy than those of walking or cooking or using the imagination? And what about the thing they've put into our hands so that we can press a button to change channels? Now they don't even want us to *move,* by God. We'll atrophy. First our brains, next our bodies."

"Excuse me," says his daughter and carries the Jersey jug into the kitchen to get, I suppose, more hot water.

"Speed Reading," said the doctor. He makes a scoffing sound. "Next thing you know, they'll be giving courses in Speed Fucking!"

I nearly dropped my cup. I saw him scrutinizing me in the manner of an expert diagnostician.

He asked, "How'd you happen to hit on Tumulty?"

"I heard about him from several sources, and he began to interest me more and more. I love actors. And then, some years ago, I had occasion to work with his son."

"With whose son?"

"Tumulty's."

"He had no son."

"Well, adopted son."

"Adopted *bastard*—in both the literal and the opprobrious senses of the word."

Two splotches of red appeared on his cheeks. His daugh-

191

ter returned, glanced at him and said, "*Now* what?"

"Nothing," he said loudly.

"We're talking about someone Dr. de Young dislikes."

"Dislikes, hell!" he said. "Despises."

"All right, Pa, settle down."

"*You* settle down. I'm talking."

She laughed and poured tea.

"That wretched lousebub," said the doctor, "broke Tumulty's heart. He used him as a father when it suited him, and denied him in times of crisis."

"Please, Dad," said Mrs. Brosio, watching me writing away as fast as I could. "Do be careful. This is all for publication." And to me, "Isn't it?"

"I don't know. It may be. But you can trust my discretion."

"I don't give a damn," said the doctor, and went on. "I looked after John for years. Not that he took much looking after. He was a well-made, vigorous man. The great life force was in him and he used it not only to benefit himself but to benefit a good many others. Me, for example."

"What sort of actor was he?" I asked.

"Glorious! Large. He never let us down. Played trash from time to time; I expect he had to compromise at times for business reasons. But I saw him be old when he was young and young when he was old. He made me laugh and cry—and—best of all, sometimes both at the same time."

"Was he a generous man?" I asked.

"With himself, yes."

"With his money?"

"He never *had* any money. He was always stone-broke. Way early on we worked out an arrangement. I provided him with medical attention, he provided me with theatre tickets. As many as I ever wanted or needed, whenever. I believe he had the same sort of barter understanding with

192

a good many others. Restaurants, tailors, bootmakers, and a few hookers."

"Dad!"

"If you don't care for the conversation," he said, "if you find it too strong—you may be excused. Give me some more tea. This is cold. It's *worse* than cold, it's *tepid.* A fresh cup, please."

"Was he a gambler?" I asked, digging harder.

"I've no idea. We most of us have a secret vice or two, isn't that so? But the idea of gambling doesn't seem to fit Tumulty; at least not the Tumulty *I* knew. We were out together frequently and he never suggested a visit to a gambling house, although I can assure you there was a plethora of them thereabouts at all times. No, I strongly doubt it. Gambling is such an *occupying* activity and Tumulty never had time. Still, as I say, it might have been a private matter. Why do you ask?"

"Well, only because there's a money mystery about him. He seems to have used up a good deal of it which can't be accounted for."

Dr. de Young regarded me with unfriendly eyes.

"And how does that concern *you?*" he asked.

"There're conflicting accounts about him. I'm trying to find out which are true and which are not."

"He was a scrupulously honest man and anyone who says nay to that is a malicious son-of-a-bitch."

"Dad!"

"Oh, are you still here?" he said, glaring at her.

I pressed on. "When was the last time you saw him, Doctor? Do you remember?"

"Of *course* I remember. I'm not *senile,* for Christ's sake! I called on him the day before he died in 1930 and, to put it plainly, I was astonished to find him alive. He'd been

193

letting go for some time. That's when most patients go—when they *let* go. We live when there's something to live for. Detective friend of mine up home once told me he'd handled over two hundred suicides. 'And never a one of them,' he told me, 'had a mutuel stub in his pocket—of an unrun race, that is.' That saying, 'Where there's life, there's hope'? Well, it's ass-backward. Should be, 'Where there's hope, there's life.' Tumulty had decided his life was over, that his usefulness on earth was at an end, and that he would be better off dead."

"Did he speak of BD at that time?"

"Not that day, no. But a few days earlier, he'd talked of nothing else. The boy—he still called him 'the boy' even though the prick was over forty."

Mrs. Brosio rose quietly and slipped out of the room.

Dr. de Young went on. "The boy, he told me, was having professional difficulties. John had been trying to reach him, he was sure he could help, but the boy, he told me, was inaccessible. . . . I'm tired now, young man. I have greatly enjoyed our visit. I suppose it's because I love talking about John. Or just talking . . . You must come again."

"I'd like to."

"Meantime, I'm going to lend you a few things that may be of use. Some programs, a number of cuttings, and a few letters. Please handle all carefully. I treasure them. One letter especially, written by John to my father, who was still in the East after completing his service in the Medical Corps of the Union Army. After his discharge, he'd stayed on with the government for the purpose of setting up veterans' hospitals. He'd become an expert amputator and was much needed. He and John corresponded. Many of their letters are lost and some are meaningless, but I think you'll find this one rewarding. And one other, an earlier one, limns John's personality so well that I chose it for you. The letters are Xerox copies I had made—what a useful invention!—so you may keep them. The other items I expect you to guard with your life, and return."

"Of course. Would you let me pay for the Xeroxing?"

"No, thank you. I'm quite well off, really."

We shook hands. I found Mrs. Brosio in the kitchen, thanked her, and said goodbye. (Reminder: Send flowers— or house plants? Yes. Flowers for her, house plant for him.)

Here, then, before me, is the material. Not much, really. The talk was better. The programs are mainly interesting because of the jottings they bear. Dr. de Young's. A phrase, a word—often an undecipherable scrawl, probably made in the darkness of the theatre. Comments, apparently, to help fix details of the performance in his memory. What a methodical man!

A program for the performance of October 30, 1896. (The precise day of Ruth's birth!) The Alcazar. *Camille.* Tumulty as Monsieur Duval. The title role played by Nance O'Neill! A current tingles through my body. I met Nance O'Neill in the late forties when we were casting *The Leading Lady* and she came in to see about a part. (Ruth told me later that Nance O'Neill had been Lizzie Borden's one great friend throughout the course of her life, even long after the New Bedford slaughter.)

More arithmetic. JJT was then 47. The program includes photographs of him in the part. He played it straight. At that time, 47 was considered old.

I once found, on the back of a research clipping, this item:

195

> OAKLAND, CALIF. August 14, 1891. J. M. Hudson Murdoch of this city died today at the home of his nephew, Oliver Cram, City clerk. Mr. Cram stated that his uncle had not suffered illness but had met his demise of natural causes due to his advanced age. He was 51.

In the program photograph, JJT looks as Gallic as Guitry. As I browse further through the program, my eye catches a name listed among the "Supernumeraries"—Master J. J. Tumulty, Jr. He would have been seven. The original text of *Camille* includes no children, but I suppose they worked some into the country scene.

There is a letter with a newspaper clipping pinned to it. The clipping is from *The Alta* (S.F. theatrical weekly), September 8, 1856. A series of items in a column of miscellany, separated by tiny trumpet devices. One of them is circled in blue crayon:

> Edwin Booth will leave on the steamer today for the Atlantic States, whither he goes on a professional tour. Mr. Booth has now been in this State nearly four years, during most of which time he has been playing at our theatres. He is a young man of undoubted genius, and, with care, time, and study, bids fair to reach to the very head of his profession. We wish him a pleasant journey, and a speedy return to California. We learn that he will play his first engagement at the Broadway theatre, New York.

The letter is dated March 2, 1864, on the ornate stationery of Stockwell's Theatre, Mason and Eddy Streets, San Francisco, California:

My dear Wally,

You are much missed, the more so since I, for one, do <u>not</u> approve of your present action. <u>Nothing</u> will be gained by the Carnage you are now witnessing. The land will be ever divided North and South. The elements of climate, agricultural practice, accessibility by sea, and the originating stock of each population cannot be changed by defeat or victory or treaty. Still, I respect the dictum that a man must follow his Conscience if he possesses such a Rare Jewel. I pray you be prudent in all actions and soon make a safe return.

The enclosed cutting from *The Alta* is sent along to amuse you.

Note: September 7, 1856. I made my theatrical debut at The Union Theatre, San Francisco, playing (?) one of the murdered little Princes in "Richard III" with Junius Brutus Booth, Jr. in the title role. He was called "Mr. June" and was an exceedingly amiable man. As an actor, however, he left a great deal to be desired. His performance was poor and the press, next day, said as much. What I liked best was staying up until after <u>Midnight</u> with my parents and eating the Welsh Rarebit made with beer; as well as being allowed to sleep until noon of the following day.

Note: September 8, 1856. San Francisco. Edwin Booth leaves the city for a voyage to the Atlantic States.

If you ponder the proximity of these two events, perhaps you will conclude, as have some others, that they are not <u>entirely</u> unrelated, nor necessarily co-incidental.

Dear friend, once again my hand in yours. May God be with you.

Faithfully yours,
John

P.S. The great Edwin Forrest is to play a Season here beginning in mid-May. I am hoping that kind Providence will allow me to take part in it. <u>Pray for me</u>.

A second letter. The paper on which it is written is edged in black.

April 16, 1865

Dear friend Walton,

I need not tell you of the state of <u>shock</u> in which this City finds itself as a result of the Foul News by wireless from Washington. All theatres were closed last night. (Junius Brutus Booth, Jr., playing at Pike's Opera House, does not plan to resume.)

Groups of incensed men and women went about last night stoning the offices of anti-Republican newspapers, some of which were <u>demolished.</u> They further vented their wrath upon each and every house which failed to display some sign of mourning.

What is far worse is the <u>disgrace</u> which has been brought upon my profession.

The attitude toward all players is hostile. My Father has <u>forbade</u> my Mother to leave the house unaccompanied. Actors and actresses have been openly insulted, turned away from hotels and restaurants, and <u>spat</u> upon in the streets.

The City is dressed in <u>mourning</u>; virtually every building is draped in purple and black. Flags are at half-staff. People speak softly or in whispers. Rumors abound. One has it that the City Council will <u>not permit</u> theatres to re-open.

Another maintains that Edwin Booth will retire <u>forever,</u> never to face the public again.

If the theatres here are to close, I shall have no option but to leave the City and travel Eastward, in which unhappy event, I shall have no joy other than the anticipation of seeing you once again.

Yours truly,
and in sorrow,
John

July 4, 1866

Dear friend Wally,

Independence Day. Not alone my Country's, but <u>mine</u>! I am free at last of my damnable association with the benighted Edwin Forrest and his <u>doomed</u> season.

You will recall with what anticipatory <u>joy</u> I wrote to you in March of my hopes of achieving a position with Mr. Forrest's company. At the eleventh hour, due to a change in the repertory plan, I was engaged. (2nd Juvenile and 3rd Business).

At the first reading rehearsal, I was <u>dismayed</u> by the appearance and the comportment of my Employer. His famous power and soaring spirit have been greatly diminished by the effects of the scandalous divorce action in which he has been so long involved. The fact that he has been roundly <u>trounced</u> in that sordid affair by his trollop-wife Catherine Sinclair adds to his chagrin.

The Irishman McCullough appeared to be "running the show" and Miss Lillie (Mr. Forrest's paramour) was <u>greatly</u> in the forefront.

Mr. Forrest was <u>old</u> beyond his years; his frame <u>ravaged</u>;

his once-powerful voice but a puny echo and his manner, of another era.

He complained constantly of the weather and of the climate. He coughed and spat so constantly, that the stage director was obliged to place brass spittoons at various points on the stage.

Maguire, ever the optimist, had caused 400 additional chairs to be built into the Opera House. As it eventuated, he failed to attract the 400 arses to fill them!

The hapless Mr. Forrest opened with "Richelieu" in which he disappointed, and began to change the bill so frequently that we scarcely left the confines of the theatre and often slept (or collapsed) in our dressing rooms. "Virginius" was no better. He moved on to "Lear," "Othello," "Damon and Pythias," "Macbeth," "The Broker of Bogota," "The Fall of Tarquin"—but press and public alike were not content.

After six weeks of this nightmare (with the curtain up!) Mr. Forrest declared himself in need of a holiday and went off to the Northern desert with Miss Lillie. He has announced he will return to fulfill his engagement at a later date, but McCullough, who has secretly joined forces with Maguire, whispered to me that this is a gross canard.

Thus I have wasted time and effort, and learned little. I err. Observing the decline of this once-great player, the lesson of the dangers of excessive womanizing is clear. The Female has a place in the scheme of an Artist's life, but when that place is put first, the sickness unto death has begun.

I hope now to return to the Company of that roaring creature who has been called "The Dramatic Cocktail"— I refer, of course, to the estimable Miss Lotta.

(in a whisper) If only she would not insist upon playing, ad infinitum, "Little Nell and the Marchioness"!

She is <u>far</u> more effective in "The-Ticket-of-Leave-Man," "Captain Charlotte," "The Pet of the Petticoats," "Nan-the-Good-for-Nothing" and "The Female Detective." In short, any piece which affords her the opportunity to sing, dance, or play her plunkety banjo.

Did I write you about the storm she raised when recently she tied a hat to her hips and actually <u>"wiggled"</u> it across the stage? She is a <u>caution.</u> I admire her and learn <u>much</u> from her.

I trust that my next to you may contain more affirmative news.

With all profound good wishes, I beg to remain,

Yours,

ever truly and devotedly,

John

The last letter is dated May 9, 1869. The stationery is that of the Orpheum.

My dear old Wally,

You grow more <u>foolish</u> with each passing year. Who would have imagined that well over three years following Appomattox you would still <u>insist</u> upon absenting yourself from family and friends, pursuing the dubious career of Medical Carpetbagger Extraordinary? Does it not give you pause when you consider the burgeoning events in your native City which are occurring <u>unobserved</u> and <u>unenjoyed</u> by you? Or are there compensatory events at your latitude-longitude? We often speculate as to whether you are in the thrall of <u>A Siren Song</u>.

You missed, five nights ago, the opening of the new and resplendent California Theatre (thus named, I gather, because the required lucre for its construction came from none other than Ralston of The Bank of California. If the theatre's appellation does not sit well with you, take comfort in the thought that it <u>might</u> have been dubbed The Bank Theatre or even—God save us!—The Ralston).

It was a <u>rousing</u> occasion. I attended in company with my new friend Dave Belasco. (I await <u>impatiently</u> the opportunity to share him with you!) He is some four years younger than I, but <u>forty</u> years more brilliant. He is a Jew who was, somehow, educated in a Canadian monastery, giving him a curious <u>double</u> advantage: Jew blood and Catholic discipline. We sat up among the Gallery Gods and were thus afforded an <u>excellent</u> bird's-eye view of the proceedings both on and off the stage. Dave said that the auditorium performance was <u>infinitely</u> superior to that which was offered on the enormous stage. The piece was "Money" by Bulwer-Lytton. I thought it was <u>creaky</u>, as did Dave. Marie Gordon, of the Haymarket, London, was attractive enough, and, I thought, well-spoken; although many in the entr'-acte complained that they found her unintelligible. The so-called British accent, I suppose. John McCullough provir'ed his usual <u>bombastic</u> rant. I am bound to say that Dave disagreed and found him Vital. "Nothing," he said, "matters more in the theatre than true Vitality. It reminds the spectator that he, too, <u>may</u> be alive."

We saw Leland Stanford, James G. Fair, James Flood, John Mackay, and even the poor <u>demented</u> Emperor Norton. The latter was accoutremented in the manner of a Napoleonic Marshal, yet was one of the <u>least</u> spectacularly dressed! The aforementioned gents bid fair to outdo him, attired as they were in full dress, Diamonds, Pearls, Emeralds and Rubies.

One of them, I cannot remember which, wore in his lapel a boutonniere made of actual, genuine <u>Diamonds</u>! The ladies were pulchritudinous in the extreme—showing more bosom than I have seen outside of The Pacific Museum of Anatomy on the Barbary Coast (do you re-

member?) and, needless to say, ¾ of the powdered poi-
trine of a San Francisco swell is more stirring to the male
member than the full business being <u>flaunted</u> in one's
face by a harlot. Silk and marble blended elegantly, and
fully three of every four ladies wore their headdress in
the new so-called "follow-me-lad" style. Have you seen it
in the East? Long, sensuous curls dropping over one bare
shoulder. <u>Hurrah for fashion!</u>

The carriages and clarences and barouches clogged all
of Bush Street and the performance began <u>considerably</u>
late.

The structure itself is <u>mighty</u>. The depth of the stage
some 77 feet; sidewall to sidewall, 80 feet. A <u>fine</u> theatre
—if only Dave and I had it and not these two ancients!
Perhaps one day we shall. We have been discussing a
possible partnership, with only Dave's feeling that he
may have a future with McCullough (and my fear of
Dave's endless relatives) standing in the way. <u>Beware</u> of
<u>relatives</u>, say I.

This may be an historic epistle, for if all goes as planned,
I shall post it in the <u>new way</u> and it may thus become one
of the <u>first</u> in the sacks of mail to travel from California
to the Eastern Seaboard entirely by <u>Rail</u>. <u>Think of it!</u>

To be safe, I mean to prepare one fair copy of this and
post it in the <u>ordinary</u> way.

Meanwhile, be of good cheer and return as expediently
as you can.

Believe me,
affectionately,
your friend,
John

Rereading this stuff, I see that it is better than I first
thought. It does, indeed, help to fill in the outlines of his
personality. Also, material from this early part of his life is

valuable, since it is possible to observe him in his professionally formative years. I suppose nothing ever came of the Belasco relationship, although they both worked mainly in San Francisco for the next fifteen years. JJT sounds like another person in these letters; another, that is, from the one I have in my head. Actually, these letters sound more like BD than JJT. Interesting. This was JJT before he was 20. When BD got to be the same age, he had the same slant, the same sauce, the gift for the put-down. A whole set of acquired characteristics.

The trouble is, I am having difficulty making both JJT's into the same man. I think of myself at 20. 1932. Confident and terrified by turns. Opinionated. Scornful not only of the Establishment, but of the established. Quick to criticize. Intolerant. Impractical. Impatient. Careless of time and health and emotion. Rebellious and independent. Foolish in too many ways. In sum, a mess. I look back upon another being. I am told that even physically, not a cell is the same. Can it be? And what if it were possible for the 20-me to look forward and know the present-me? Would he not be as contemptuous of me as I am of him? Probably.

March 21, '65   Holmby Hills.

A second visit to Dr. de Young.

I thank him for the material, return the programs and the photographs.

"Was BD ever a patient of yours?"

"Yes," he replies, "but I will discuss no aspect of that. I abominate him. Nevertheless, I cannot violate that confidence. He is alive, don't you see?"

"What did your father think of him?"

"My father brought the son of a bitch into the world and told me afterward how much he regretted it. He was close enough to John to sense every nuance of their drama. He turned on BD at the moment BD turned on his father. My father, remember, was a man of a different time. He lived when there was a considerable reverence for age. One respected the wisdom and the experience of one's elders and, at the same time, felt a sympathy and compassion for their failing powers and their inexorable approach toward the end.

"This has faded through the years. Older persons—and the irony is that there are more and more of them—are objects of neglect. I have felt it daily for a long time. You and your interest in the past are unusual. Why, for instance, are you pursuing this Tumulty history so avidly?"

"I honestly don't know," I reply. "It began as an idea for a movie—still is—but it's gone beyond that. I got caught up in it and I'm afraid I'm permanently enmeshed. But it has its rewards. Meeting you has been one of them, Dr. de Young."

He nods and says, "Thank you, my boy."

June 10, 1967   Delfern Drive, H.H.

A shattering day. The shape of life has changed, and its size has been diminished. Spence is gone. Lloyd Lewis once said you can always tell the quality of an actor by the size of the hole that remains when he leaves the stage. The void caused by Spence's sudden departure is simply immeasurable.

Carl arrived early this morning to help us get ready to move. When he came upstairs I saw a curious expression on his face. I made a joke about it. Since he did not laugh at it, I did.

He looked up and said quietly, "I take it you haven't heard about Mr. Tracy."

"Oh, hell!" I said, and thought at once that Spence had been taken ill again. "Hospital?" I asked.

Carl shook his head, and I knew.

I went into the bedroom and said to Ruth, "Spencer is dead."

A cruel way to convey the dreadful news, but it was she who taught me never to build up to shocking announcements with "I have something terrible to tell you" or "Please don't get too upset but—"

She sat down heavily and burst into tears. I got her some water and did what little I could to comfort her. Ten minutes later we were on the phone to Kate and five minutes after that, on our way to St. Ives Drive.

It was only six days ago that he phoned me at ten minutes to six. I remember it indelibly because our routine for the past year has been for *me* to call *him* every evening at six. He had never called me before.

When I answered the phone, he began to shout, "I did it, Jasper! I'm *finished.* I'm sitting here with a beer. What do you know about *that?*"

"Where's Kate?"

"One of those parties on the set, but I can't handle it. I said goodbye and left." He began to laugh. "What a day! Stanley cried. I cried. But I've finished it. You never thought I would, did you?"

"I thought nothing else."

"Bull. I tell you who must be giving the biggest party of all: the front office. Those poor suckers had no insurance on me."

"Yes, you told me."

"You know what I'm going to do when I finish this beer? I'm going to have *another* beer."

"Are we going to see you later?"

"Sure, and every night now. I'm finished and that's it. Never again. That was my—thank God—last picture."

"Bull."

His voice changed suddenly and he spoke in an unaccustomedly serious way. "It's the truth, ol' pal. I wouldn't put people through that strain again. I'm used to it, but to see everybody around all day worrying about the next five minutes is too much."

"You've got one more coming up," I reminded him. "For me. Tumulty."

There was a long pause before he said, "It's a deal."

"Deal."

"Something tells me you're never going to finish the goddamn thing, anyway, so it's a safe shot."

"I'll finish it," I said, and felt instantly irritated.

"I don't think so."

"Why not?"

"You've been farting around with it too long."

"I'll finish it. Just you drink your milk and keep in shape."

"Speaking of milk," he said, "excuse me. This bottle's empty. I've been sucking on an empty, for the love o' God."

"See you later."

"Did I tell you I finished the picture? I didn't? Well, listen. I finished the picture."

When we saw him a few hours later, he kept giggling and grabbing everyone in sight. There had been bleak times in the past few years, but that night he was the happiest of men.

We all talked about that night today, and about other nights—in Paris and London and New York. I recalled our long walks in Paris, and nights in St. Jean–Cap Ferrat when we would stay up until sunrise discussing religion, sex, or George M. Cohan. Spence was one of the few original thinkers I have ever known. His ideas and his opinions were formed within himself, out of the crucible of his own experiences and agonies. He was not one to paraphrase what he had read in the latest issue of *Time* magazine or to report what someone had told him. His way led him to a deep and personal belief, which was why it was usually so unshakable.

It has been a too-long day and perhaps I should not be doing this now but there is nothing else I want to do.

Several times in the course of the day I have considered the weight of my loss. Selfish? Yes, I suppose so, but I could not help thinking that to me it is a double death.

I see now how much Spence was tied into the Tumulty story. Whenever I thought of Tumulty, I pictured Spence. I have never heard Tumulty's voice, but the sound of him in my ears was the sound of Spence.

My own desire to see this figure theatrically reincarnated by Spence was doubtless the driving force toward solution and completion. All that is hopeless now.

June 12, 1967   244 Ladera, Beverly Hills.

Spencer's funeral. For some reason, it is held early in the morning; for another, in an obscure out-of-the-way church. I have not been able to learn the answer to the first question, but the second is because this is the church of Monsignor John O'Donnell, who was Spencer's steadfast friend throughout the roller-coaster ups and downs of his life. Thus Louise—most appropriately and touchingly—has arranged for the services to be held there.

We pick up George and drive down together. He looks at me strangely as he gets into the car. Is it because there is some giveaway of the fact that I have had a couple of drinks?

I realize what an idiotic thing it was to do, particularly since I have not had a drink in the morning since buzz-bomb time in London. However, I had to do *something* this morning and that seemed the simplest, even though the stupidest. I began to shake shortly after I awoke and had trouble shaving and trouble tying my shoelaces, so I went down to the bar and carefully poured a bourbon and plain water. Within ten minutes the improvement was so marked that I went down and had another. A welcome numbness set in.

George and Ruth and I stopped for a cup of tea on the way to the church. I tried to pretend that mine was another bourbon.

We arrive. George and I are among the pallbearers and

are directed to our positions. Many familiar faces. Some look as though they have been skillfully aged by Perc Westmore in the makeup department. Many strange faces. I wonder who these people are. I wonder even more about certain parties who should be there and are not. I note, too, the absence of Hollywood funeral nonsense. Very few fans, cameras, gawkers. Can this be the reason Louise chose this hour? If so, bravo.

At best, there is little dignity in death. Turning funerals into opening nights manqué, as is so often the case with theatre and film folk, is unforgivable.

All at once a voice behind me.

"Where's your yarmulke?"

I turn and am astonished to see BD standing there with Rosella and Ena. He smiles his oppressive smile, winks, and lights a cigarette. He *is* wearing a full makeup. It is artful and discreet, but a makeup nonetheless. He is wearing the large white carnation denoting that he is also a pallbearer.

We shake hands. His is ice-cold and clammy.

"You're looking well," I say.

"It cost me a fortune."

"Terrible day, isn't it?"

"Yeah," he replies cheerfully. "I'm next, so I thought I'd come down and give it a little dry run."

I am in no mood for gallows humor and am about to step away when I realize that everyone else has moved away from him for one reason or another and it seems rude to abandon him, so I stand there.

What with the emotional strain, the two drinks in me, the unexpected BD, and the unsettling ecclesiastical atmosphere, I am beginning to feel lightheaded. The strangely intertwined drama of BD and Tumulty and Spencer begins to take on disturbing proportions.

210

I catch George's eye and convey to him, I expect, some sense of desperation because he comes over and joins us. He greets BD, who shakes hands with him and says, "Where's your yarmulke?"

Once this son-of-a-bitch gets hold of what he thinks is a joke, he doesn't let go. It gets no recognition at all from George, who seems to be framing a crack of his own. BD, enormously sensitive, feels it coming, turns abruptly and walks away.

"Isn't he a disgrace?" mumbles George. I shrug. "Coming to a funeral drunk."

"He is?" I ask.

"Couldn't you smell it?" asks George. "I can *still* smell it."

For a moment I consider confession, but decide against it.

The service is extended and tedious and, to me, meaningless. I have time to think of many things. This is more than the death of a man. It is the death of a talent. (I recall another funeral. Lubitsch's. Billy Wilder and Willie Wyler out on the sidewalk afterward. What is there to say? Finally, Billy: [a sigh] "Well, no more Lubitsch." Willie: "*Worse* than that. No more Lubitsch *pictures!*") What is important about talent is that it nourishes the rest of humanity.

Later. The pallbearers in this case actually do carry the heavy coffin for some distance and considering the line-up, it is a wonder to me that we make it. Some are pretty old; others have bad backs and say so; still others are known cardiac cases. At one moment, I have the distinct impression that Chester Erskine and I are carrying it between us. Finally, mercifully, the hearse is loaded.

I have some difficulty locating Ruth in the crowd at the exit. BD has no difficulty in locating *me*. He lights a cigarette with a trembling match and says, "I swear I thought this guy

211

would bury us all. He was a selfish bastard, and they're the kind last the longest. Like our mutual friend Tumulty."

"Oh, you think so?"

"No, I don't *think* so. I *know* so. First picture Tracy and I ever made together was a Donnybrook. You couldn't tell him a goddamn thing. He knew everything. He wouldn't let you show him anything, or give him a piece of business or a reading. Nothing."

"It turned out all right, though, didn't it?" I say tightly.

"Oh, I forgot," he said. "*You* know everything, too. Yes, it turned out all right. Sweat and blood and spitting cotton and wearing out four Moviolas. I swore I'd never get on the same set with him again, or even in the same studio, and then, you know how it is, I got hold of a script and as Sam Harris once said, 'Let's never use that son-of-a-bitch again until we *need* him.' So before I knew it, there we were in Round Two."

"And what about the third one? How did that happen?"

His expression changed. He threw away his cigarette and said, "I've never understood it. I never got around to asking him, and now it's too late, but the fact is *he* sent for *me*."

"He did?"

"He'd got onto this book, and read it, and wanted to do it. He called me, sent it to me. I read it. He was right. It was a natural. So we met and talked it out and took off. I think it was the best either one of us ever did, but he got pissed off and stayed pissed off because I got an Oscar for it and he didn't."

"I don't think he was like that. He got his share—of Oscars and everything else."

I saw tears in BD's eyes. "I'd like to live a little longer than I'm going to," he said. He began to sway slightly,

212

reached out, and held on to my shoulder for support. "I've found the whole thing—life, I mean—miserable but interesting. Y'know what I mean? And one of the things I'm sorry I didn't get to understand is the difference between like and love. Now, I never liked this guy and he certainly didn't like me, but I can tell you this. I loved him." His voice caught in his throat on the last two words. He paused. I continued to look around for Ruth as he went on, "I don't know why, and I've only got one little clue. There was something about him that always put me in mind of John J. Tumulty." I tremble.

"But the curious thing is, I never loved Tumulty. I couldn't because he was a crook and a sponge and an all-round Olympic pain in the ass, but I *liked* him. So the question is, Why should I have *loved* Tracy for reminding me of him?"

Ruth suddenly stood before us. I introduced her to BD, whom she had never met. He took her hand and bowed in a most courtly way. "I'm honored," he said. "You're a great lady." He glanced at me, and continued to her, "And you certainly deserve a hell of a lot better than what you've got."

He bowed again and disappeared into the crowd.

Tumulty occupied my thoughts all the way to Forest Lawn and during the brief ceremony there.

We spoke to John and Susie, Spencer's children, to his brother Carroll, and to Louise. The rest of the day and the evening with Kate, me drinking too much and dealing with the fading Tumulty in my mind.

12 Jan 68   Beverly Hills

Yesterday, a call from Dr. de Young. He wants to see me. I have abandoned the Tumulty search but—well, what can I do? I go.

He took to rambling and it was difficult to keep him on the subject. Now that he has taken to talking more loosely might he let something go which he might otherwise have guarded? In pursuing this story, attempting to get to the bottom of it, I am like a wino reaching for alcohol even if it happens to be in a can of Sterno, or in his wife's bottle of perfume; like a compulsive gambler in Vegas, or a born thief; like so many (most?) who know what is right, yet do what is wrong. Well, no harm done—yet. It does not matter what I find, only what I eventually use. Further, if I ever do, it will be in fictional form and probably revised out of recognition anyway. I console myself or cop out by reminding myself that I am, in a sense, legitimately practicing my profession; that "the proper study of mankind is man."

He gives me *his* version of the earthquake (referring to it, of course, as "the fire"). It is all fairly standard stuff that I have heard before, except for one small nugget.

"Charlie Field wrote a little poem soon after; well, doggerel, really. I think it shows how we preserved a sense of humor even in the face of catastrophe. There is nothing in life—I repeat, *nothing*—more important than a sense of humor. The best people have it, the worst people lack it. Charlie wrote—and recited at the drop of a hat:

214

If, as they say, God spanked the town
For being over-frisky,
Why did He burn the churches down
And spare Hotaling's Whiskey?"

I am planning a suitable exit line when he gets onto the subject of adoption. I can see possibilities of getting from that to Tumulty's, so I stay.

"In some ways," he says, "I consider the act of adoption one of the most noble in all human expression. Adoptive parents are saintly; and, in the main, adoptive children are loving and grateful."

I seize the opening.

"You'd call BD an exception, wouldn't you?"

"*I'd* call him more than *that*," said Dr. de Young. "An ingrate, a megalomaniac, mean and selfish and petty."

"He claims—and has a hell of a lot of evidence to support it—that he took care of Tumulty right through the years."

"Took care of? What does *that* mean?"

"Provided for him. Financially. Gave him money, a great deal of it."

"I don't believe a word of it. Tumulty lived like a damned pauper throughout most of his days. He was extravagant—yes—but it was always with his work. He'd spend more than he had to get the right setting or effect; bring players all the way from New York, sometimes London; he was constantly commissioning authors to prepare plays—but he owned two suits of clothing. His collars were generally frayed and he ate in cheap restaurants unless he was someone's guest. Even when his son—yes, I say his son because I recognize no distinction between adopted children and natural offspring —I say even when that son of his became a movie star and lived in the lap of luxury—a millionaire many times over, some said—his father lived in one rented room and often found it necessary to ask friends for small loans to tide him over. Yes, from *me* sometimes, if you want to know how I know. That friend of yours—a complete rogue, he was—hell, he *is*—but it doesn't shake my faith in the process of adoption."

4 April 68   The St. Francis Hotel   San Francisco

Every time I come to San Francisco, the Tumulty juices begin to flow. I should have thought by now my spirit would be tired of the subject. But no. Tumulty and the characters surrounding him have become old and captivating friends.

Moreover, it has turned into a long, lifetime game; a 75-volume whodunit; a three-and-a-half-acre jigsaw puzzle. It holds, for me, a never-ending fascination.

Last night, for instance.

We came up here two days ago on a sort of last-minute let-go, along with Nela and Arthur Rubinstein and their friend, Bronnie Kaper. We wanted to hear Arthur play again. Whitney Warren had invited us all to a postconcert supper at his house, one of the most charming in all San Francisco.

(At the airport, an exchange with the porter: "Are you free?" I asked. "No," he replied, "but I'm reasonable." It has all the earmarks of an old joke, but I have never heard it before.)

A light dinner at Trader Vic's. The concert is surpassing.

Afterward, we wind our way up Telegraph Hill to Whitney's. A small party. Whitney and a Mrs. Folger. Our bunch. And a most amiable couple, Mr. and Mrs. Freer. (Her name is Janice.) He is a stockbroker, but he and his wife are involved in the arts. Mrs. Freer serves with Whitney on the board of directors of the opera company. Both Freers are active in the lively regional-theatre movement, and spend endless time raising money for the museums, for the symphony, and so on. Mr. Freer has a new enthusiasm: The San Francisco Film Festival. He talks about it at length.

After supper, the Rubinsteins are being shown about the house and I find myself standing out on the closed terrace overlooking the romantic view. Mr. and Mrs. Freer are with me. The city is spread out before us and I begin to inquire as to the whereabouts of certain places and buildings, especially theatres. Mr. Freer asks how I know so much about old San Francisco theatre. I tell him about my interest in Tumulty.

"Of course," he says. "Tumulty's Grand."

"You knew it?" I ask.

"I was no more than a little kid when it flourished, but I remember being taken there quite often. It was considered one of our most distinguished companies. At the time, we were surrounded by theatrical trash. Melodeons and music halls and third-rate road companies, but Tumulty's Grand was our own and much respected."

The rate of my heartbeat increased and it was not only the brandy.

"Tell me more," I urged.

"Well, to tell you the truth, I don't recall Tumulty himself on the stage. I'd be fancifying if I said I did. There might have been *Peter Pan* with him as Captain Hook. I'm not

217

certain. But I do have definite recollections of him at our home."

"At your home," I echo stupidly.

"Why, yes," he says, pointing down and to the right. "We all lived down there on Powell, in what was called a four-family. My father and his family, his two brothers and a sister. Each family in one-half of one of the two enormous, adjoining houses. We all shared the yard in back and the kitchen garden and the garage. Also the attic and the basement, which was mainly coal and laundry." He chuckles, and goes on, "I suppose I must have been ten or eleven before I comprehended that we were all different families. I'd thought of it until that time as one complicated unit. I seemed to have four fathers, four mothers, and a continuing supply of brothers and sisters. We were all in and out of one another's rooms at all times. It was a dandy way to live. My Uncle Fred was a stockbroker. That's how *I* got into the business. I had no aptitude, apparently, for architecture, which was my father's field, and Tumulty, you see, was a client of my Uncle Fred's."

My hearing apparatus goes dead. Mr. Freer keeps talking but my thoughts are racing. This bolt from the blue, named Freer, whose path has accidentally crossed mine, has given me the solution to a twenty-five-year-old mystery.

Crystal clear. Tumulty was a speculator and played the market. Like most amateurs, he was probably in constant difficulty. I don't know much about the workings of the stock market in those days—but I believe it was possible to buy stocks on low margins, which increased the gamble. I must double-check the last year or so of Tumulty's life. The stock market crash in October, 1929. Was there a call to BD around that time? And didn't Tumulty die shortly afterward? Is there a possibility he knocked himself off? Could he

218

have been one of the many who were wiped out by the crash? He would have been eighty or eighty-one at the time and the strain of it could easily have killed him.

"I'm sorry," I say to Mr. Freer, "I didn't hear that last."

He smiles. "I *thought* you were wool-gathering."

"Would you know anything more about Tumulty as a speculator?"

"Did I say he was a speculator?"

"Didn't you?"

"Certainly not. In any case, I couldn't discuss a client's affairs, now could I?"

"No. It's only that I'd often heard from his son—*adopted* son—what a financial genius he was and how brilliantly he played the market."

Mr. Freer takes his time lighting a cigar.

"John J. Tumulty," he says, "was a great actor. He was *not* a financial genius. Nor did he play the market brilliantly. And now suppose we say no more about it."

◆

I awoke this morning still considering the talk with Freer, wondering if I could learn anything more from him. Probably not. He is a stolid, conservative broker. I begin to see that I owe BD an apology on this score. He was telling the truth about the money he advanced. Playing the market in the way Tumulty did was akin to gambling. And that was his vice—well hidden. The solution is reinforced by the way his death related to the '29 crash and the look in Freer's eye when he said Tumulty did not play the market brilliantly. That means Tumulty went broke.

The hell of it is, he becomes less attractive when you consider that all the time he was carrying on these financial manipulations with Freer and Company, he was borrowing money from the people around him, his friends and co-workers, sometimes even his employees. This is his dark side and I wish it weren't so bound up with money, an unattractive theatrical subject, unless it can be made comic.

15.X.69   Goldwyn Studios.

It is the morning after and I am still thrown. Last night, the season at The Ahmanson Theatre opened. Hume Cronyn in *Hadrian VII.* This is the touring company, which opened in Montreal. (Hume, being Canadian, wanted it so. The troupe is largely Canadian.)

During the intermission, I glanced through the program. All at once a name came up from the page and struck me between the eyes: John J. Tumulty!

I heard Ruth ask, "What's the matter?" and myself reply, "Nothing."

I spent the whole of the second act attempting to pick out Tumulty. When I succeeded, I longed for a pair of opera glasses to bring his face closer.

Later, at the reception in The Founders' Room, I could hardly wait for Hume to turn up so I could ask him about the guy.

Hume was besieged by congratulators. It was difficult to get his ear and, when I did, his attention. I decided to find Tumulty myself, but the room became too crowded. I returned to Hume and asked him to help me. He sent someone off, and a few minutes later, the someone returned with young Tumulty. Could it be my imagination or does he indeed resemble the red-haired, square-jawed, blue-eyed Tumulty I have seen in portraits?

He has never heard of me, but Hume gives me a considerable build-up, and we move off into a comparatively quiet corner.

He is remarkably youthful; hair, long; eyes, suspicious; manner, nervous.

"Are you Canadian?" I ask.

"English," he replies.

"What happened to your British accent?"

"Scuttled it. I cahn't bear the sound. Any rate, I'm going to make my way here in the States, so I may as well get to sound like one of the natives, what?"

"I'll bet you can get to sound like anything you like."

"What makes you think that?"

"I get the feeling you're an exceptionally good actor."

"You're bloody well right I am," he said.

I proceeded carefully. "How does it happen?" I asked. "Are your people in the theatre? Any of them?"

"My father, but he only *thinks* he is."

"How do you mean?"

"Because, mate, he hasn't got it. He's a loser. He ought to give it up and try something else, but he won't. Stubborn bugger."

I swallowed before I asked. "What's his name?"

"You've never heard of him."

"What's his name, anyway?"

"Cropper," he said. "Harry Cropper."

I had to lean against the wall. Finally I asked, "How old are you?"

He dripped charm as he smiled and countered, "How old do you *want* me to be?"

"The truth."

"Seventeen," he said. "Soon to be eighteen."

"You look older."

"Well, I *am* older, you see; or younger, or taller or shorter. Just give me your order."

"Come in and see me, John." I wrote my name and telephone number on a card.

"Jack," he said.

"What?"

"Call me Jack."

"All right. Give me a ring. I'm going to be doing a production here in the spring and there might be something in it for you."

"Good."

"But you'll need a British accent for what I have in mind. Can you learn one, do you think?"

He laughed a personality laugh and went off. Suddenly, there was too much to deal with. How long ago was it that I met Cropper? Contradictions. Didn't I think him talented? Could the boy be right? Could it be that we are both right? Isn't it true that talent is not enough? Haven't I known many outstanding actors and actresses who have never made it? Why? The luck of the game? No. You make your luck, and if you're not lucky one day, there's a chance you may be lucky the next. The failure of the talent to connect is usually due to a single inherent weakness or fault or lack.

. . . I have just returned from a long walk, trying to slow down my thoughts. This John J. Tumulty. His name is Cropper, surely; grandson of Mrs. Cropper, who is the daughter of John J. Tumulty. This kid is his great-grandson. The continuing line, the seed of talent. This lad has Tumulty's blood in his veins. BD has none. Is he lying about his age? He is probably no more than fifteen or sixteen at the most. A maverick, probably a runaway. I can understand his going to Canada first and planning his professional assault on the U.S.A. from there. I believe Orson Welles was about fifteen when he left Woodstock, Illinois, and went to Dublin, of all places, to begin his remarkable career.

I wonder if BD would be interested in meeting him?

Later.

This afternoon, I phoned Hume to congratulate him properly. I asked him about young Tumulty.

"He's a genius," said Hume, laughing.

"I don't know what that word means."

"It means that the bloke can act; naturally, instinctively. He hardly needs to rehearse or practice. He understudies several parts, and I've seen him in them. He's terrifyingly good." Hume laughed again. *"My* understudy was out one day and Jack filled in. I happened to be at the theatre doing an interview, and I heard my part out there, so I went and had a look. In a way I'm sorry I did. He was burning up the damned stage. Imagine it, in *my* part. I think he's all of seventeen. Are you thinking of him for something?"

"Possibly," I said. "Hume, you were superlative last night. I was proud of you. What's more, Alec McCowen thought so, too, and considering he created the part, it's better praise than mine."

"Any praise is welcome," said Hume. "It's a hard job."

17.X.69   Goldwyn.

TMY. My new JJT left here a few minutes ago and I am beset by mixed feelings. He phoned this morning, asked if he could come by. I said 2:30. He said, "Fine," and turned up at 3:45.

Maybe punctuality is not so important. Transportation is difficult out here, especially for strangers. Still, it rankles. I am sure he would not have been late had it been for a performance or a screen test. In any case, I am nettled by the time he arrives and the first fifteen minutes added up to a *mauvais quart d'heure* indeed. It was not until Mrs. Ellis fixed tea at four, and brought out the box of Carr's wheat-meal biscuits, that the atmosphere changed and we were able to make civilized contact.

"Where'd you get the name Tumulty?" I asked.

"Odd about that," he said, stuffing biscuits. "It's actually most of my real name. Damn, these biscuits are good! Remind me of home. May I have another?"

"Have them all."

"My birth certificate read 'John J. T. Cropper.' Rather posh, wouldn't you say? But that's how I was christened. By church law, I believe, they don't accept initials and make you string out the whole bloody things." He became a British provincial clergyman: face, expression, gesture, all, as he intoned, " 'I christen thee John Joseph Tumulty Cropper, and may God have mercy upon your soul.' Of course, I never knew all that till long after. It wasn't till my first year at Eton

224

—there's a hole to skip—I went out for Dram and, of course, landed Rosalind in *As You Like It.* "

"Why 'of course'?"

"Because it's the lead. And because I wanted it. I always get what I want."

"I see."

"And on the night, my father was there. And my mother. Funny it was, too. He with some Eurasian bird, and ol' Esmé with her new Bank of England spouse."

I recalled the young girl I had met in Edinburgh—a few months ago, it seems. Now she is "ol' Esmé" to this young man coming on strong. He went on.

"They took care to sit at opposite sides of the house. My mother came back for a quick peck and a soggy 'Well done, Jackie.' My poor square stepfather could scarcely speak, he was so upset at the sight of me in drag. They cut out pretty fast. Then my dad came in and introduced me to the Queen of Siam or whoever the hell she was and started giving me a lot of God-damned notes. Imagine that! I took it for a minute, then I looked at him and said, 'When's the last time *you* played Rosalind, ol' cock?' And all *he* could think of was 'Mind your manners!'

"Naturally, he was a bit sloshed. He usually is. And invited me out. So we all went round to the Crown and Anchor and started to tank up on shandies. And it was right there at the table I got my first look at the program. And where my name was supposed to be it said, *John J. T. Cropper.* And I said, 'Here, now! What the hell's all this? A typo?' And my father looked at it and said, 'Not in the least. It's your name.' And he said it out and I heard it for the first time. 'John Joseph Tumulty Cropper.' 'Why all that?' I asked him. And he said, 'I'll tell you one day.' And I said, 'When?' And he said, 'When you're a little older.'

225

And I said, 'I'm a little older now.' But he was mulish and wouldn't speak up and it was several weeks before I got to him.

"He took me over to Paris for a bit of a piss-up and one night, walking back from the Comédie-Française where he'd taken me to see *Chapeau de Paille d'Italie*—smashing play, isn't it?—we walked all the way from there across the bridge to the Brasserie Lipp. He Scotched it up nicely and I didn't discourage him and after a while he started to tell me. About my name, that is. God, it was fascinating! He told me that *his* mother, my grandmother—she's dead now—"

"Did you know her?"

"Just. Sort of dumb, she was, but no trouble. Gave me money all the time, rather pleasant. Anyway, it turned out she was a little something her mother picked up in San Francisco. I've never been to San Francisco. We're going there. Is it any good?"

"Yes, it is."

"Any rate, *her* father—real father—was somebody named John J. Tumulty. He was an actor of some sort, they say. I've never been able to find out much about him."

"Are you interested?"

"Yes, I am, funnily enough. I've got his name. He's actually an ancestor and if he was any good, I'd like to know about him."

"He was good, all right."

"How do *you* know?"

"I've heard of him."

"And then my father told me there's a mogul out here; BD or something like that, who's his son. Is *he* still alive?"

"Yes."

"Maybe I ought to look *him* up. We're related, aren't we?

What is he, anyhow? My grand-uncle?"

"I believe he was an adopted son."

"The hell you say! When my dad told me about him, I went and looked him up at the National Film. And there it was: 'John J. Tumulty, Jr.' He changed his name later, when he went into the flicks."

"Yes," I said.

"I wouldn't mind meeting him. Maybe he could give me a leg up. But he must be as old as Noah by now, wouldn't you say?"

"Not quite."

"Know where I can find him?"

"Let me arrange it. He's a friend of mine."

"He is?"

"Yes. He hasn't been very well."

"I should think not, at his age."

"Let me look into it."

"What was this thing you had in mind for me?" he asked.

"I'm doing a production of *Idiot's Delight* here in the spring."

"Where?"

"At the Ahmanson, where you're playing now."

"*Idiot's Delight*, did you say?"

"Yes."

"What's that?"

I contained myself and said, "It's a fine play written by one of our best playwrights, Robert E. Sherwood. Have you heard of *him?*"

"Afraid not."

"You *should* be afraid."

"New play? Old?"

"It was written in nineteen thirty-five."

"Thirty-five!" he repeated incredulously. "And you say it's *good?*"

I took a deep breath. "Yes. There were a number of plays written around that time that were good. Some of them great. And the same goes for nineteen forty and forty-five and fifty-five."

"Yeah, well, I suppose so," he said, unconvinced. "What's the part?"

"There's a young English honeymoon couple, and I think you'd be right for the husband; not the wife, even though your greatest triumph up to now seems to have been Rosalind in *As You Like It.*"

He laughed disarmingly. "Good part?"

"Well, it's a damn sight better than the part you're playing *now,*" I said, unable to conceal my annoyance.

"Take it easy," he said soothingly. "I only *asked.* Anyway, what I'm doing now is nothing. Odds and bods. I only did it to get to the States."

"O.K."

"What about Equity?" he asked. "Can you swing that for me?"

"I think so. Here, read it and we'll talk again."

"And you won't forget about fixing a meet with my Hollywood relative?"

"I'll do what I can."

We shook hands. His grip was firm and confident. I knew he was going to say, *"Ciao."*

"Ciao," he said, and left.

Through the window, I watched him walk toward the main gate. He was leafing through the play; not reading it, but in the way actors have done since Sophocles' time, I suppose—hunting for his part. He bumped into a half-naked showgirl, appeared to mutter something, and moved off without looking up.

18.X.69   Beverly Hills

A sad meeting with BD today. I had phoned yesterday to try and set it up. Within ten minutes, Rosella called back to say he would be glad to see me.

"I should warn you," she said, "you may not be glad to see him."

"Why is that?"

"He is not at his best in these days. His body—it is disintegrating. Decalcification, they call it. He is much aware of what is happening and it makes him angry."

"I should think so."

"And especially, he hates anyone who is healthy."

"Well, he won't hate me. I seem to be falling apart, too."

"Tell him that!" she said eagerly. "He loves so much to hear about others who are ill."

"And who're flopping."

"Yes."

"How are *you?*"

"I am fatigued."

Late this afternoon I went over. Nothing has changed. The collection of Academy Awards and other trophies are, perhaps, less shiny than they were when I first saw them. It is clear that death is living in the house.

I greet Rosella and Ena and start up the stairs. Rosella stops me. "Oh, no. He lives out back, in his cottage."

"All the time?"

"Shall I take you?"

"Don't trouble. I've been there many times."

"I remember."

I kiss her cheek and start out. Memories and impressions come flooding back. The cottage seems smaller as I approach it.

I remember the afternoon when I was sent away abruptly to make room for a quickie with the maid. Or, I wonder now, could that have been a put-on? Men who want to build reputations as cocksmen are given to this kind of playacting. They talk about it, constantly intimating sexual adventures. They derive a vicarious excitement by creating envy in others. BD often did this with me. I could scarcely mention a star or a featured player or a producer's wife that he did not wink or indicate in some way that he had been there. That afternoon with the maid, was it all part of this sick scheme? No.

I knocked. It was opened immediately by an attractive young nurse who wore no makeup, and needed none.

"Do come in," she said.

English.

The place had been enlarged and repartitioned. I was in a small office. The door to the left was open. A bedroom, deserted.

"I'm Mrs. Harcourt," said the nurse. "Would you come with me?"

I followed her through the door on the right into a small gym filled with complicated equipment. Beyond it, a new room, large and unlike any I have ever seen. A glass room: fireplace, pictures, shelves—all part of glass walls. A glass ceiling.

230

BD sat facing the spacious loggia. He was on a large thronelike armchair, his feet spread out on a hassock before him. There was an Exercycle in the room and a walking machine, a trapeze, and three television sets piled one atop the other. They were all on, tuned to different channels. No sound. There was a desk fitted over his chair, three telephones, and a complex control panel from which apparently every appliance in the room was worked.

The visitor's chair was carefully placed. The nurse motioned me to it.

"Will you be all right there?" she asked.

"Thank you."

She looked at BD. "Anything?"

"I'll get rid of this bum as soon as I can, baby. And we'll pick up where we left off."

She shook her head, smiled at me, and pantomimed, "Isn't-he-incorrigible?" before leaving.

"What about that 'Mrs. Harcourt' bit?" he asked, dropping his voice. "Isn't that a kick?"

"How do you mean?"

"She's no Mrs. *Anything*. But when they go out on these jobs they think it's safer if they pretend to be married. She's been here seven months. It took me about seven minutes to figure that one out. I've got her trained like a seal. Aren't you going to ask me how I am? Or don't you give a shit?"

"I do, but I'm not."

"What?"

"I *know* how you are."

"I look *that* bad?"

"You look fine."

"My Merry Widow-to-be's been popping off, eh?"

"Come on."

"How are things with *you?*"

"Bloodcurdling. I've got the beginnings of some kind of arthritis."

"Arthritis?" he said. "For that there's a great man out here. Dr. Sidney Grant."

"I've seen him."

"And what does he say?"

"He says I've got the beginnings of some kind of arthritis."

Rosella was right. He was instantly sympathetic and interested and ready to help in any way possible. He questioned me as to my symptoms. I tripled them in the telling and within fifteen minutes had scored a real success.

I then told him of having talked to Frances Goldwyn earlier in the day and of her concern about Sam's condition. He had been doing extremely well, but recently had had what amounts to a relapse and now again there are nurses around the clock.

BD responds to this account with a mystifying mixture of concern and relief; pleasure and pain. He admires Sam Goldwyn, and respects him, and wants him to be well; yet it pleases him to hear of an illness more serious, perhaps more advanced, than his own.

I pick a propitious moment and say, "Guess who I met the other night."

"Who?"

"John J. Tumulty."

"Who?"

"John J. Tumulty—the third, I guess. Or maybe the fourth."

"Or maybe Henry the Fifth," he says. "What the fuck are you talking about? Do you know?"

"Yes, I do."

And I tell him in detail not only about young Tumulty but about my first meeting with Harry Cropper in Edinburgh in 1954; and subsequently with his grandmother, Mrs. Fielding; about my research in Manchester and about Mrs. Fielding's letter to me, written shortly before her death.

The account takes the better part of an hour. Mrs. Harcourt comes in three or four times to check on things.

The second time, he asks her to bring drinks, which she does.

I come to the end of the story.

He says, "Are you making all this up, you bastard?"

"No."

"Can you prove any of it?"

"To myself, yes."

"Get the fuck out of here!" he yelled. "Out! You hear me?"

I got up and started out.

"Wait a minute!" he roared. "Who do you think you are? What's your God-damned game anyway? You write one bloody word without— Where the hell do you come off, digging into people's lives? Is any of this any of your business? All right, now beat it. Take off. And stay off. And don't call me up. I'll have you waylaid, you God-damned nosy yid! *Out!!!*"

Mrs. Harcourt came in, and I went out.

Rosella, with Ena, was waiting at the main house. She touched me and said, "Yes, I know."

I did not know what she knew or how she knew it and at that moment I could not have cared less. I was eager to get away from the atmosphere of the outburst.

Damn it, setting it down has upset me again. I had better go out and walk.

19 Oct 69   Sunday.   TMY

BD wakes me early this morning.

"Hello," I say sleepily.

"Wake you?"

"Yes."

"Good."

"Who is this?"

"It's me. Bring him over. Bring the pipsqueak over and let me have a look at him."

I am speechless.

"Hello?" he says.

"I'm here."

"What's the matter?"

"I don't know. I thought after yesterday—"

"Oh, me bursting into song?"

"Yes."

"Well, you hit a nerve, doctor. But never mind. I'd like to see this so-called Tumulty clown."

"How's five o'clock? And then let me see if I can get him."

"Don't *see*. Get him. Tell him I want to see him. Tell him who I am."

"He knows who you are."

I cannot locate Jack. He is not in his room at his hotel. No one seems to know where to find him. I leave messages asking him to call me.

2:00 P.M. He does. I invite him. There is a problem about transportation. I arrange to have a car sent for him.

He picks me up and, together, we drive over to BD's place. Jack surprises me. He is neatly dressed and carefully groomed. His shoes are shined; his necktie, carefully knotted; the creases in his slacks, sharp.

The other day when he came over to the studio, he reminded me of another young man, another meeting, but I could not remember who, what, where. Today, the contrast throws it into perspective. The other young man was Marlon Brando when he first came to see us at the instigation of his sister, Jocelyn, whom we had interviewed and who asked us, as a great favor, to see her kid brother, Bud. "He's an awfully good actor," she said. "And he needs a job." He came a few days later, smoldering with talent, and resentment that it was taking so much trouble to get to use it. He was flip and fresh and enormously impressive. Unfortunately we had nothing for him and he had to wait almost a year before he cracked through in Max Anderson's *Truckline Café*. Jack is the first one since Brando who has struck me with the same degree of impressiveness.

I doubt, however, that Brando would at any time have got himself up in this conventional way for the purpose of an interview. He was and is a true independent. Young Tumulty is a practical, practicing opportunist. He senses, correctly, the sort of man BD is, and for the moment at least is going to do nothing to antagonize him.

On the way, I said, "Remember, the man's an invalid. Beyond that, he's important out here. He expects a certain deference."

"He'll get it."

"Another thing. He's dying and knows it and hates the

235

idea and it puts him on edge. He's an exposed nerve. He may lose his temper and throw us out five minutes after we come in. On the other hand, you may find him charm itself."

I was wrong. BD did not blow his cork. Nor did he drip charm. He simply sat there, looking and listening.

Aware of my role as a go-between, I remained on the periphery of the meeting. It was left to Jack to keep the game going—and he did.

"Beautiful place you have here," he said.

"Yes," said BD.

"I understand *your* name is John J. Tumulty, too."

"What do you mean, *too?* It's not *your* name."

"It is *now*," said Jack, and laughed so infectiously that BD and I joined him. "This is good and funny, wouldn't you say? One for the book? Here you are, a guy who *had* the name and dropped it; and here I am somebody who picked it up. I guess that name just wants to be kept alive."

"Yes," said BD, studying him.

"It goes without saying, sir," said Jack, putting it on a bit, I thought, "that I'm interested in finding out all I can about my great-grandfather, not only because I've decided to use his name but because he represents my roots in this country and this is where I'm planning to live and work."

"Are you any good?" asked BD.

"Yes, sir. *Exceptionally* good."

"How do you know? Your girl friend tell you?"

"No, sir. The *audience* tells me. When I speak, they listen. When I want them to laugh, they do. And when I want them to shut up, they do. *That's* how I know I'm good."

"But if you ever get in front of a camera," said BD, leading him on craftily, "how will you know? There'll *be* no audience."

"The director. In a film *he's* the audience."

He had played a trump card brilliantly. The hand was won.

BD gave him two file folders, and said, "These are for you to keep. One of them has a lot of articles, clippings, interviews, stuff like that. The other one is full of stills."

"I'll treasure them, sir."

"I don't know," said BD, "whether you're related to him or not, but it doesn't matter for the moment. If you're interested in him, there's some material to look at. Leave your phone number with Mrs. Harcourt. I may call you. Thanks for coming over."

Jack rose and said, "It was a great honor, sir. I appreciate it."

When he was gone, BD stared at me.

"Jesus Christ," he whispered. "He might just be. He just might be."

"Is that your hunch?"

"No, my eyes. What they see. And what I hear. His voice. It could be a fluke, but, Holy Mother of God, he's the spitting image of Tumulty."

10.XI.69   Beverly Hills.   TMY.

BD and young Tumulty have had a row, the subject of which is so astonishing that I have been unable to deal with it. Each has indicated he would like me to patch it up.

They had been meeting regularly. BD exhibited an overwhelming interest in Jack, his father, his grandmother, and his great-grandmother, Mrs. Fielding.

BD remembers her (as "Rosalind" Manders) quite well. She made a great impression on him when she worked with Tumulty. Jack remembers her only vaguely but has filled in his knowledge of her with considerable invention in order to give BD what he wants.

BD proposes to leave the considerable Tumulty collection to Jack. This includes the portrait that used to hang in his office, letters, programs, scrapbooks, clippings, souvenir props, jewelry, and costumes.

About the row: I was present, about two weeks ago, when BD informed Jack he was setting up a trust fund for him. It had been worked out with care: a regular income (modest but generous) immediately and certain parts of the principal to be paid on his 21st, 26th, and 31st birthdays. Jack looked over the documents, thanked BD politely, and told him he wanted no part of it.

BD was astonished. (So was I.)

"Why not?" he asked.

"Why should I take anything from you?"

"Because you're going to need it."

Jack's anger was soft, taut, passionate, and terrifying. "I don't need money," he was saying. "I need a part, a job; a play, a film. I need a good director who doesn't bug me. I need a chance to grow and develop and learn something. I need some friends and lots of balling (but not the kind you can buy) and some love and a good agent. I don't need money. I certainly don't need yours. I want my own. Then it'll mean something to me. I'm sorry if I sound ungrateful but I have to say to you what I've said to my own people: Shove it!"

And he left. Mrs. Harcourt came in and gave BD some medicine. He asked for a drink but did not offer me one. He was stunned. He had expected, I suppose, a hug and a kiss.

We were silent for a time.

Then he said, "Son-of-a-bitch is off his rocker."

"No. Principled."

"Same thing, isn't it?"

"I don't think so."

"Would you, in your wildest dreams, if you were writing this—do you think you could make this scene believable, acceptable to an audience? That a nobody, a punk just starting out turns down a legacy of six hundred and forty-seven thousand dollars? I mean to say, there's not a person in the world would ever . . ."

647. The exact figure he claims to have turned over to Tumulty.

He stopped talking, and sat morosely drinking.

"Why six forty-seven?" I asked.

"Why not?"

I shrugged. "Such an odd figure."

"What's odd about it?"

He was playing cat and mouse. I was the mouse.

"Why not six fifty, or seven, or eight?"

"Guess."

Two conversations were taking place; one spoken and one unspoken.

Stalling, I asked, "Why don't you offer me a drink?"

"Oh, sorry."

He buzzed a signal. Mrs. Harcourt appeared almost at once with a tray, and put it down.

"Help yourself," he said.

When Mrs. Harcourt had gone and I had swallowed half a strong drink, BD looked at me craftily, and said, "Go ahead. Guess."

I finished my drink and put down my glass. "Well, in for a dime, in for a dollar—or in this case, six hundred and forty-seven thousand dollars. That's the same amount you gave John J. Tumulty, his great-grandfather."

"He was great, all right."

"Am I right?"

"You've got a fine memory. Fine. What you *haven't* got is any kind of a brain. Memory is nothing—a machine. They build machines now with memories ten million times better than *any* man's. And faster. There used to be guys out here made a living—hell!—made *fortunes* with their memories. They used to remember old pictures and turn them into new pictures. A switch on this. A twist on that. A scene from here. A line from there. Memory is nothing—a side-show act. But faith and understanding—above all, imagination. Those are the gems."

What was all this? Was he trying to get me off the track?

I looked at him in the eye and repeated, "Why six hundred and forty-seven thousand dollars?"

"I'll tell you. The thing about you is that you don't know as much as you think you know. That's the trouble with your writing and with your thinking and with your life. It's surfacy and specious and jejune."

"God damn it! You *would* use that word. I never know what it means and I've looked it up I don't know *how* many times."

"Look it up again!" he shouted.

"I will. Right now."

I walked out as fast as I could.

"Wait a second!" he called.

But I didn't.

10.XII.69   San Francisco.   TMY.

I flew up here late yesterday afternoon, remembering just in time that it was the night John J. Tumulty was going to act in San Francisco. Hume told me a few weeks ago that there had been a few shifts and replacements in his company. Some of the Canadian actors have found movie and TV jobs, some have gone home. So Jack has taken over one of the better parts, and I saw him in it last night.

I have never been as sure of anyone's future as I am of his. A young John J. Tumulty playing on a San Francisco stage again—just as a young John J. Tumulty did in 1869—a hundred years ago! The whole thing was a considerable experience, but I am not going to try to put it into words today.

Christmas Day, 1969   Beverly Hills.   TMY.

BD died today, in his sleep. He was 80. Driving home, after visiting Mom, I heard the bulletin on KFWB. I pulled over, stopped, and sat for a few minutes, thinking about him. A dramatic touch, I thought, to die on Christmas Day. W. C. Fields is the only other one I can recall. I turned around and drove over to BD's house.

Rosella was there with Ena, packing. A few others. Dr. Charles Carton, who had been his physician and friend. Dr.

Richard Thomas Barton. Ellie, BD's secretary for as long as I can remember. Also, three businesslike strangers, probably funeral directors. Mrs. Harcourt.

Ena seemed to be in complete charge, ordering everyone about—including me—in a terribly butch way. Hold it. I did not mean to write that word. It just ran down my sleeve. Too easy a description, and yet . . .

In the past year or so I have paid many such visits, but this one was different. It lacked feeling. The only one grieving was Ellie. Strange, because he was always sharp and short-tempered with her. I stayed about fifteen minutes and left.

It occurred to me I ought to cable Mme. Saint-Blaise. If I didn't, who would? When I got home, I did.

BD DIED PEACEFULLY TODAY AFTER LONG ILLNESS.

I added the widow's address and signed it.

I wish BD and I could have become friends, but he was not anyone's friend. He was bitter, unhappy, unable to derive joy out of his work. He takes with him many answers to many questions.

Whatever other problems it solves or creates, his death ends that unnerving game of his little pink notes to me. (Whatever our disclaimers, we are all, in the end, selfish.) I wonder why he didn't come clean on it toward the end. Many times, when we exchanged a look, I knew that he knew I knew. Ah, well.

BD's funeral. A bleak day and a bleak occasion. The church is the one where the mass for Spencer was said. The atmosphere, however, is different; even the building does not seem the same. There are few mourners. Thirty-four, by my count, and that includes people connected with the mortuary and church staff. I see Billy Wilder and Frank Capra. No actors, no actresses. I am not surprised. Correction. Gregory Peck was there, in his capacity as President of the Academy. And Charlton Heston as President of the Screen Actors Guild. So far as I can remember, neither of them ever worked with BD.

The day is damp and a nerve-testing gale has possessed it. At the cemetery the number of mourners has shrunk to fewer than half. Because of the weather, the officials and the priest make the services mercifully short. My attention goes to Rosella and Ena. Rosella is beautiful in black; contained, impassive. Ena is a reflection of her except for the faint, victorious smile on her face. Or am I imagining it? Studying her for the better part of half an hour, I am more convinced than ever that I have met her before. But, if so, why wouldn't she acknowledge it? An actress? Agent? Hooker? And, of course, I may be all wrong. I don't think so.

So ends this complex man, whose life-journey was so long and tortuous, whose relationships were destined to be ambiguous; who was cursed with more than his share of the guilts and fears with which all of us live.

It was not until I was alone and on my way home that I wept for him.

2 January 1970   Beverly Hills

In the mail today, another pink note.
It was nearly lost in the late-arriving Christmas cards
(from abroad, mostly) and New Year's cards and first-of-the-
month bills.
But that color leaped out of the pile.
The message, typed:

```
NOW WILL YOU STOP?  OR WILL YOU
CONTINUE, LIKE A VULTURE, TO FEED
ON THE FLESH OF THE DEAD UNTIL
ONLY BONES AND DUST REMAIN?

"AND YET FOR SOME, THE FIRES OF
HELL COME AS WELCOME RELIEF AFTER
TORTURES OF HELL UPON EARTH -- "

                        DANTE

YOU ARE WARNED.
```

Who would use a Dante quotation? Pretty obscure
writer around here. What's his last credit, after all?
Dante. Italian. Rosella. Rosella? Ridiculous. What would
be her motive? Money. That's generally a good one. Is
she concerned that digging into the Tumulty story might
turn up others who might encroach on her rights to BD's

244

estate? Indeed, it already has. She came within an inch of losing that 647.

Has the time come to try the police? No.

14 Jan 70   BH.   TMY.

I am flabbergasted. I offered the part of Mr. Cherry in *Idiot's Delight* to Jack Tumulty, and he turned it down.

He is not doing anything else and has no prospects, but does not feel the part is good enough!

I invited him to lunch at The Bistro, and explained I would like to understand his reasoning.

"The fact is, ol' boy," he said, "I'm in a position now to hold out for the right thing, something suitable. I don't see how I can make a score in your piece. That's what I need to do—send up a rocket."

"What do you mean, 'now'?"

"I don't need the money. I am actually, as they say, financially independent."

"You are?"

He looked at me incredulously. "Don't you remember? You were there. The settlement."

"The BD money?"

"What's the trouble? You've gone all peculiar like."

"You turned it down, made a big screaming scene."

"So I did. I thought better of it later on, though. I went in to see him several times and he showed me the error of my ways." He called off, snapping his fingers, "Check, please."

"*I'll* take it," I mumbled automatically.

"No, no. Don't be silly."

While we waited for the check, I thought of how sorry I was for so many people in the future; those who were going to have to deal in one way or another with John J. Tumulty the Third. The Fourth? What does it matter?

5.II.70 (A.M.)   B.H.   TMY.

A cable this morning explodes my day. It is from Rose Saint-Blaise and reads: "COME AND SEE ME REGARDS."

What timing. Five days before rehearsals. What if I flew over, using the direct polar route, saw her, and flew back? Jack Lemmon is already rehearsing the numbers with the girls and I am not needed for that. Yes, I am. Further, we have been meeting nightly at Jack's request, going over the text inch by inch. Could I explain the situation to him? An emergency? Is it? The tone of the cable makes me think so. It is a command, not an invitation. There's something there I need—no, *want*—and I suspect she is ready to give it to me.

I could go later, after the opening, but that seems a long way off and in dealing with elderly people there is a certain amount of risk involved. What if Rose Saint-Blaise does not last until late March?

5.II.70 (P.M.)

I tell Ruth about the situation and sketch my plan for a quick dash over and back.

She says not a word, but looks at me as though I have gone bananas.

There is no discussion. It is clear she considers my idea professionally insupportable and, in the cool light of evening, so do I.

I shall cable the lady that I cannot come before March 20 and set up a routine of daily prayer.

19.III.70

The play is on. All is well.

Jack Tumulty was at the opening, dressed in a tartan dinner jacket, and accompanied by two small dazzlers: one blonde, one brunette. He came back afterward and bestowed reserved approval.

Before he left, he said to me, "Do tell me where I might find the chap who played Mr. Cherry. I *must* present my compliments. *What* a performance!"

And there was I, without a weapon.

30.III.70   NYC

Travel plans all day. So much going on here that I begin to wonder what the hell I'm doing. And the expense. Should I try to phone? No. She specifically said, "Come and see me."

I try to phone, anyway. No luck.

The beginning of every trip is plagued with misgivings. Should I? Shouldn't I? What will I miss here? What may lie ahead there? The most comfortable posture generally is to stay where you are.

But no. The trip is on. I cable the lady:

> AT LAST. ARRIVE APRIL TWO. WILL PHONE AT ONCE.
> MEILLEURS SENTIMENTS.

5.IV.70   Paris.   Hôtel Raphaël

I phoned Mme. Saint-Blaise within an hour after our arrival, but she was not available. She called back a while ago and said she hoped to be able to receive me tomorrow.

Later, someone else called. I couldn't tell at first whether it was a man or a woman: one of those odd voices. It turned out to be a woman. She identified herself (in French) as Mme. Saint-Blaise's companion and asked me if I would be

—I think the word she used was *prudent*—when I visited tomorrow. She explained that Mme. Saint-Blaise has been not at all well and that I was to use my discretion if the meeting took place.

It was a difficult conversation because my comprehension of French is at its worst on the telephone. I may have got some of it wrong, but the sense of it was that she was being protective of her friend.

The part I liked least was that *if.*

6 April 70   Raphaël, Paris.   TMY

A bad day.

All my efforts to see the lady are frustrated. There are people around here who are trying to postpone our meeting until it fails to materialize. I have talked to the companion again and to a Christian Science practitioner and to a young man who says he is her nephew. What nephew?

Ruth says that in my place she would go on over there and pretend that the appointment had been made. This strikes me as an absolutely ridiculous idea. I tell her so and it provokes a minor quarrel.

This afternoon I went over to the apartment on the Ile St. Louis. On the way, I stopped and bought some extravagant flowers.

The forbidding lady who opened the door—the companion, I expect—was rocked when I presented myself. I pretended I spoke no French (could she have been pretending she spoke no English?) but made it clear I had an appointment. I kept pointing at my wristwatch, pantomiming telephone, and somehow blustered my way in to the room where Mme. Saint-Blaise sat.

She greeted me with "Oh, I'm *so* glad you're here. They told me you couldn't come this week."

"They were lying. All of them. What is all this? Are you ill?"

"They think I am, so they build this wall. One would have thought they might have learned by now, walls are never impregnable. Do sit down."

I gave her the flowers, sat down, and asked, "How are you?"

"How *could* you have known jonquils are my favorites?"

"I looked it up in the Encyclopaedia Britannica."

"And where on earth did you find such beauties?"

"At La Chaume. My wife is a flower child, told me where to go and what to get. She knows about such things."

"Thank her for me, won't you?"

"Certainly. You realize that I came six thousand, six hundred miles, because your cable said, 'Come and see me'?"

"Yes," she said. "I do. There are some things I want to tell you and some things I want to give you. One doesn't like to die and leave loose ends hanging about."

"You're not dying."

She gave me her gentlest look and said, "We're *all* dying."

Her companion brought a vase, and left. During the next quarter-hour, Mme. Saint-Blaise arranged the flowers as we continued to talk. I have never seen anyone do it so beautifully. It troubled me that she seemed to be more interested in the flowers than in me, but I got used to it.

"I was so saddened to hear of BD's death," she said. "And thank you much for sending the address. That was most thoughtful. I wrote to his widow, though there was little I could say. We have never met." She looked from the flowers to me. "Perhaps now we shall. Would that be a good idea or a poor one?"

"She's a fine lady. I think you ought to meet her. And simple to arrange before long, I should think. She's going back to Italy to live. To Florence."

"Yes," she said absently. "What I have to tell you I could have told you long ago, when we first met. But at that time it was not seemly."

"I see."

"The fact that BD was alive made it an embarrassment. For reasons of his own he might not have wanted it known."

"What known?"

"Why, what I'm going to tell you."

"When?"

"Now. Do you know much about pride? Are you a proud person? It's a difficult word in our language. It can be complimentary or uncomplimentary. Tumulty was *not* a proud man. He took pride in his work and in his accomplishments and in the achievements of his friends."

"Yes."

"BD, on the other hand, is a—I should say *was* a—*desperately* proud man; easily offended, easily bruised. What is most regrettable, it damaged his work. I've often thought—and I've had *such* a long time to think—it might have been better for all concerned if Tumulty had not insisted upon revealing to BD the circumstances of his birth. But that was not possible because of *Tumulty's* brand of pride. He lived by a certain code—outmoded now—which had to do with honor, probity, a man's word as his bond, and the truth. I never knew him to tell an untruth."

"*I* did," I blurted out.

"But you never knew him!"

"I'm sorry," I said. "I mean I know of an important matter in which he certainly *didn't* tell the truth."

"Will you tell me what it was?"

"Of course."

She leaned back in her chair, finished with the flowers. I got up and moved about the room as I told her the long, complicated story of Tumulty's sponging and cadging; about Whitman and The Old Actor; about BD's explanation. Finally, about meeting Freer in San Francisco, hearing about the stock market speculation, and solving the puzzle.

"What bothers me," I said, "is that I never got a chance to apologize to BD or explain it to Frank Whitman."

I stood looking out over the most entrancing city in the world. I turned back into the room, took a step toward her, and saw that she was in tears.

"What is it?" I asked.

She shook her head. The companion came in, accompanied by a short, thin young man whom I disliked on sight. He was one of those who attempts to disguise his baldness by a careful forward combing. His clothes, although elegant, were of another time. He wore a diamond ring and a gold bracelet. He and Mme. Saint-Blaise exchanged a few lines in rat-a-tat French of which I could catch not even my customary quota of one word out of five. The young man came over to me, bowed stiffly, and said, in infuriatingly good English, "I am Pierre Saint-Blaise, Madame's nephew. I must ask you to leave. She is not well."

"But I *would* like to explain that—"

"You have upset her," said the little mint. "As you see."

He pointed to her as though acting in a French courtroom drama.

The companion was forcing her to drink some water in an effort to stop her crying.

I saw there was nothing for me to do but go, although it damn near killed me to leave the rest of what she had to tell me. I took a couple of steps toward her to make my farewell, but her nephew intercepted me. I tried to move around him. He put his tiny white hands on my chest and gave me a rather ineffectual shove.

I moved closer to him and said, "How would you like me to knock you on your faggoty ass, buster?"

I heard a spluttering sound behind me, turned, and saw that Mme. Saint-Blaise was laughing. She was still crying, but laughing, too; had apparently splattered the companion with some of the contents of the glass, which made her laugh even more.

She looked up at me as I said, "That's what used to be called a water-doh in the silent days. Remember?"

She nodded vigorously as she continued to laugh and cry.

I went to her, kissed her cheek, said, "Call me tomorrow," and left.

There were plenty of taxis in the street, but I walked all the way back to the Raphaël, sorting it out. It is going to be more difficult to see her now, although I have changed my mind about there being anything sinister in any of this. The people who surround her are fond of her and are trying to protect her. They have no idea as to who I am or what I want. The fact that my visit today upset her will reinforce their determination to keep me out.

11.IV.70   Raphaël.   Paris.   TMY

Still here. I have added nothing because there has been nothing to add. I did not want this notebook to begin to resemble a diary I kept when I was ten and which Mom found and sent me a few years ago. It is filled with page after page upon which has been carefully written the word "Nothing."

The time here adds up to nothing because I have not been able to reach Mme. Saint-Blaise. The telephone is hopeless. I have sent wires, *petits bleus,* flowers. No reply.

13.iv.70   Paris.   TMY

At precisely 9:15 this morning, as I was going out the door, the phone rang and the concierge said, "M'sieu Kah-nan?"

"Yes."

"Is a young lady to see you."

"Where?"

"Downstairs here."

"Well, send her up."

"Un moment." A pause. He returns. "No. She wish you to come down."

"What's her name?"

"Un moment." Another pause. "She don't give it. She ask you please to come down."

There was no one in the lobby as I approached the front desk. The concierge pointed out the front door and said, "She goes to her car."

I went out. Directly in front of the hotel, a small Bentley was parked. I approached it and saw, sitting at the wheel, a young woman in widow's weeds, complete with veil. It occurred to me that this was a dangerous way to drive. The window of the door on my side was open. I leaned in and said, "Yes?"

A familiar voice said, "Get in."

It was only then that I recognized Mme. Saint-Blaise.

No wonder that both the concierge and I had mistaken her for a young woman. Her face, seen through the opaque veil, was indeed a young face, and everything else about her: her figure, her verve, her voice, was young.

"Please come with me," she said. "It has all been such a strain to arrange and I don't know that I can do it again."

In two speedy, reckless left turns we were on the Avenue Foch, heading toward the Bois de Boulogne. I was relieved when she threw back her veil and put on her glasses.

"I know you've been trying to reach me," she said. "Please don't resent my friends and my family. They mean well."

"How did you manage this today?"

"I'd been planning it. This is the anniversary of my husband's death. I told them I wanted to go to his grave alone."

"Thank you."

255

As we entered the Bois de Boulogne, I asked, "Where are we going?"

"Why, to my husband's grave."

The park rustled by on both sides. Suddenly, a pond. Ducks. Birds in flight. Ancient little structures. All these began to give the day a sense of unreality. Yet I felt I was approaching the answers I had so long been seeking.

"Since you cabled me," she said, "I've lived with strange emotions. And only recently have I been able to sort them out. As you know, I had no contact whatever with BD for many years. Yet the fact of his death leaves me bereft. I suppose we're all joined in life, to the earth, by the persons and places and things we know. Then we begin to lose them, one by one. The people first, then the places change or disappear or become unreachable, so we cling to our *things* for a time. Then *they* wear out, or we lose them or tire of them. Do you follow? Each day there are fewer ties that bind me to the earth, to life. BD, or perhaps the memory of my life with him, was one of those. Have you had breakfast?"

"Yes, of course."

"So have I, but let's have another, shall we? I know just the place."

She turned onto a side road and within a few minutes pulled up in front of a tiny *auberge*. We entered and sat down. She was greeted by the personnel in a way that made it clear she was a regular.

We began a second breakfast—a basket of toast and croissants and brioches, gobs of fresh butter, an assortment of jams and jellies, huge pots of coffee and hot milk.

Suddenly she said, "On April third, 1931, I had an extraordinary phone call." (Where was *I* in 1931, April? What doing? I wanted to orient myself, somehow. I remembered: working as a comic with Maxie Furman and Joey Faye at the

Eltinge burlesque theatre on 42nd Street.) She continued. "It was from BD. He was here in Paris at the Crillon and said it was imperative that he see me at once. I didn't think the request unusual, since there were a good many matters of business between us which remained unsettled. I told him I would try to arrange it. I talked it over with my husband, who took a dim view of the matter and was, in fact, nettled. He flatly forbade me to go through with such a meeting. Finally, he relented and made a joke of it. You look surprised."

"Do I?"

"Remember I was much younger, and we were, in a sense, newlyweds. The next question was where and when. I thought the proper thing would be to invite him to our house for tea or a drink. My husband vetoed this and suggested I lunch with BD at a public restaurant. Later he phoned me to say he had decided on Maxim's and had made a reservation. The next day BD and I met there.

"I was shocked by his appearance. In the year since I'd seen him he had aged ten. He had, to put it bluntly, lost his looks. He was not much over forty. I wasn't prepared for it at all, because men as a rule grow more attractive in middle age, and I should have thought this to be the case with BD especially, because he certainly was one of the handsomest men ever. But it was more than his body that had deteriorated. It was his spirit. It was as though all his vital organs had been cut out of him. There was an aura of panic about him.

"I had kept up with the doings in the film world. I always have. One needs an interest in life. And although I gathered he was suffering—along with so many other film actors and actresses of the time—from the difficult transition into talking pictures, I had assumed he would be able to make it.

257

After all, his basic experience and training had been in the legitimate theatre. Unfortunately, his first talking picture was a failure. The technicians had not yet mastered the methods of recording. The sound was frequently out of sync. Do you remember? And almost every comedy for a time had people crunching on celery to get laughs. The film he made was a drama—a stark father-son story—and the fact that the sound went funny and sometimes dead caused laughter in the wrong places and the picture failed badly. There always has to be someone to blame for failure and in this case they blamed him. It shattered his confidence and I'm afraid it shattered our marriage as well.

"He'd always been a difficult man to live with. Now he became impossible. He was bitter, jealous, vindictive, horrid. He moved out of our house and into a great suite in The Ambassador Hotel and gave a party that lasted for about ten months. I lived in hope, as do all cast-off wives, that the trouble would run its course and that we'd somehow patch it up and go on making the best of it, in the way most married couples do. But all that changed when Doctor Saint-Blaise sent for me. His wife had died. I had to believe then that some Providence was at work.

"I remember going up to see BD, to discuss it with him. His place was filled with raffish characters. Whores and starlets, and creatures who were *hoping* to become whores and starlets. Awful sycophants and professional laughers. It didn't seem very merry to me. I wasn't able to achieve privacy with him. They all came floating in and out. And that's how our marriage ended. With a handshake. And as I turned to go, he gave me a ringing slap on my bottom, which made everyone laugh.

"From that day until the day at Maxim's I had seen him only once, in San Francisco, at Tumulty's funeral. He took the occasion to change completely and had never been more sensitive or kind. He arranged everything in grand style, sent his Rolls-Royce and chauffeur to meet me and put them at my disposal, had reserved an enormous suite at the Fairmont, sent flowers, gave a small dinner in his suite, which was far more grand than mine, for a few of Tumulty's closest friends, and saw me off on the train." She finished her coffee and said, "Shall we go?"

As we approached the car I offered to drive, and she accepted. We drove in silence for several miles. I glanced at her from time to time. She seemed to be deep in thought and I considered it best not to interrupt. Now and then she would direct me to turn left or right, but that was all.

Then she said, "Our luncheon at Maxim's was rather soggy, as you can imagine. He drank rather more than he should have but, knowing him as I did, I understood that it was because he had something vital to say and was having a hard time getting it out. And then, too, we were sitting on a banquette in the little gallery and a party of American tourists was having a jolly time beside us. Their presence seemed to intimidate him. The moment they left he turned to me and blurted out, 'Look here. I'm in trouble.'

" 'I'm sorry,' I said. 'What sort of trouble?'

" 'I'm broke.'

"I couldn't help smiling. You'll see why in a moment. And it infuriated him.

" 'I'm glad you think it's funny,' he said.

" 'I don't. Not at all.'

" 'Can you help me?'

"And I said, 'Yes. I think I can.'

"At this he took heart and said, 'I need twenty-five thousand dollars. Can you lend it to me? *Will* you?'

"And I had to smile again."

I interrupted to ask, "Why?"

She went on. "I said to BD, 'Meet me tomorrow afternoon at The Morgan Guaranty Trust Company.'

" 'Where's that?' he asked.

"And I said, 'Right around the corner from here.'

" 'I'll be there,' he said.

"And then, although the bill was a long time in coming and I had to wait endlessly for a taxi—he had a car and chauffeur, of course—we could not find a single thing to say to each other until 'Goodbye.' Here we are. Slow down, please."

We drove through the old stone gates of the cemetery. Following her directions, I parked the car. We walked a short distance up a hill, and came upon the Saint-Blaise family plot. She got out a key and opened the gate in the fence that surrounded it. A wide tombstone bore the legend: "JOSEPH ALEXANDRE SAINT-BLAISE 1884–1953" and under it: "ROSE ADRIANCE SAINT-BLAISE 1890–   ." With her standing there beside me it was an unsettling sight.

She put the fresh flowers she had brought into metal vases, and tended to a few weeds. As she did so, I looked again at the tombstone and wondered why anyone would want to follow such a macabre custom.

We sat on a comfortable bench inside the plot, near the grave.

"When I arrived at the bank the next afternoon, he was already there, waiting. One of the managers, a friend, took us to a small room reserved for clients. BD waited while I went off with the manager. Our business took a time—bank business always does, doesn't it?—and by the time I rejoined BD, he was in a filthy temper. He snapped at me and I snapped back, although I should have understood it was caused by his desperation. I handed him an envelope that

260

contained a draft written on the bank's American branch and sat down. BD started out. I stopped him and told him to look at the draft. He asked why and I suggested he might have some question about it. He opened the envelope, dropped it onto the table and looked at the draft. Then *he* sat down, too.

"After a time, he said, 'Is this your idea of a joke?'

" 'It's not *my* idea at all,' I said. 'And by the way, it's not a loan. It's yours. It belongs to you. Tax-free.'

"He looked at it again and began to cry. Oh, did I tell you? No, I think not. The draft was for six hundred and forty-seven thousand dollars."

As the number hit me, I thought I might faint. Here, sitting with an old lady in a Parisian cemetery, had come—after long years—the simplest answer to one of the most tantalizing of questions. Thoughts and memories and faces raced through my head, bumping into one another crazily: BD's failure to reveal this—why? Whitman. The Old Actor and his loans. Freer—did his uncle invest it for T? If so, why wasn't there more? Tumulty scrimping along to the end, with a fortune at his fingertips. BD giving the same amount precisely to the kid . . .

She was still talking.

"—had known that he would. I must say, BD made the most brilliant use of the money. He stayed on in Europe for a year or so—although I never saw him again. He bought a great French film, for a song. When he remade it in English, it was a sensation. And in Italy, he found Rosella Giotto and signed her and made her a star."

"And married her."

"Yes. But making her a star was far more important to him, I'm sure."

"Then it was right after the remake that he did *Pocahontas* with her?"

"Yes," she said, and laughed. "Actually, it was our old stand-by, *The Captain and the Princess.*"

"You told me you smiled when BD asked you for the loan."

"Yes."

"And you said you'd tell me why."

I waited for her to continue, but her attention was fixed on a spot somewhere behind me. I turned. That pain-in-the-ass Pierre Saint-Blaise was standing there. Damn! Was it over? It was.

I cannot remember the words of our exchange but the atmosphere was unpleasant. There was a lot of hudga-budga about putting the matter into the hands of his lawyer. *What* matter? He is a real thrusting take-charge and was already arranging for his taxi to take me back while leading his aunt away.

She was able to stop him long enough to hand me a manila envelope. "This will interest you and explain the rest. Keep it."

She waved to me as Pierre drove her off. I felt like a character in a novel by Balzac.

I said to the ninety-year-old taxi driver, *"A l'Hôtel Raphaël, s'il vous plaît. Dix-sept Avenue Kléber. C'est au coin de la Rue Jean Giraudoux."* It is the one spill, because of endless repetition, that I say, apparently, without discernible accent. This gave the driver the idea that I was French and he began to talk and wouldn't stop. I grunted from time to time, which kept him talking and interfering with the only thing I wanted to do—study the contents of the envelope.

It turned out to be a letter to Rose from Tumulty. The old

262

taxi, the winding roads, the chattering driver, my attempt to read in motion, and the heady events of the morning combined to make me sick. I had to give up trying to read the letter.

I have read it now. It is written on large sheets of ornate stationery, from The Palace Hotel in San Francisco, in JJT's beautiful, flowing, steel-engraving penmanship:

> As from:
> 18 Hobhill Road
> c/o Jorgenson
> San Francisco, California
> 1 February 1930

Rose, my dear Rose:

I see you in my mind's eye as I write, and I thank you for the <u>joy</u> this vision brings. You have meant much to me throughout the strange course of these whirling years—<u>more</u> than you can possibly know. I daresay there has not been a day in my life in which the thought of you has not passed through my mind—and consider, if you will, what a VAST number of days that totals! Too many, I sometimes think—not often, only when the bothersome manifestations of age take hold—inexorable, incurable. For the most part, I am gay as a grig and mightily occupied. Some four weeks ago, at the invitation of Professor Roy Bascomb—the <u>grandson,</u> no less, of our old reliable prompter Roy—I mounted at Stanford University a production of "What Price Glory?" by Laurence Stallings and Maxfield Anderson. Do you know it? A stirring play of the new sort. The language is often rather "advanced" and since no one has yet devised a manner in which a player can effectively enunciate dashes or asterisks, it was necessary to be bold, and trust to understanding. The

263

audience, although it gasped now and again, responded well. How _frequently_ we _underestimate_ the public! You will be pleased to learn, I trust, that I no longer consider the audience "a thousand-headed monster."

I have given a series of readings at The Bohemian Club. (Do you recall the three recitals I did a thousand and one years ago with the assistance of Miss Rosamund Manders, that lovely and extraordinary English lady? Some of our ancients here _still_ speak of those occasions. Are we not _fortunate,_ you and I and others, to have been part of a profession which made it possible for us to pollinate our fellow-beings with pleasant memories?) One recent evening I even dared "Blow, winds, and crack your cheeks! etc." from Lear, and although it gave _me_ a splitting _headache,_ it brought down the house!

Enough of me, except for one piece of irksome intelligence. Dr. de Young, who does me the _honor_ of _candor,_ has informed me that on the basis of the results of his most recent tests and examinations of my person, the pace of the march of the _inevitable_ in my direction has been somewhat ACCELERATED. You are to be n_o more alarmed_ than I am. I am not ill. As you know, I have had but _little_ illness in the course of my long span, a circumstance for which I am _most grateful._ I am simply wearing out and SPARE PARTS for the 1849 model are exceedingly difficult to come by. No matter. I have few regrets. My life, for the most part, has been fulfilled. I have had my share of _joys_ and _GOOD ROLES._ Fourscore is a generous span.

Mind, the good doctor may be in error. It is wholly within the realm of possibility that _I_ may _outlive_ you _all!_ It is _not,_ I assure you, a prospect which attracts me.

What he was attempting to convey, I believe, was the _suggestion_ that I would be wise to have my affairs in order. Since my affairs are but few, the matter is reasonably simple.

In one aspect, however, I am in need of your assistance (as I have so _often_ been!). It concerns my son (I think of him thus, in spite of all) and I turn to you in view of the fact that he was once your husband.

Today—February 1—is <u>Johnny's birthday.</u> Did you remember it, I wonder? He is <u>41</u>. It boggles the mind. How on <u>earth</u> can a little boy be <u>41</u>?

I had <u>hoped</u> to go to Los Angeles and deliver his gift in person. I bought him a beautiful imported necktie at Gump's, but Dr. de Young advised against the arduous journey.

To business, then. My lawyer's name is Clark S. Crocker. My financial advisor is Frederick Freer. I shall provide each of them with a fair copy of this letter.

There is a <u>LAST WILL AND TESTAMENT,</u> needless to say, of which they (or their designates) are the <u>executors.</u> When it is probated, you will find that <u>you</u> are my sole heir. However, it is the purpose of this letter to explain the reason for this, and to request your most essential; nay, your indispensable <u>co-operation.</u>

By way of prologue, let us move backward in memory.

By the time our Johnny had tasted his first great SUCCESS as an actor in photoplays, I had come to know him well, although he <u>never</u> came to know me. (A continuing condition of children and parents, as tragic as it is common.) The pattern of his personality had become clear; his habits fixed; his virtues formed; his faults ingrained.

The world of which he became a part is a world of <u>questionable</u> values and hollow aims; where Success and Failure are the North and South Poles. As I saw Johnny take his place in that world, I began to fear for his future. There are those who rise, then fall, but go on living—even working—with philosophical equanimity. Knowing

Johnny, I know that no such course is possible for him. A descent from glory would, in his case, spell disaster, the more so since extravagance, imprudence, and profligacy have long commanded his existence. On several occasions, I attempted to IMPRESS upon him the necessity of planning and providing for the days to come. I could not achieve so much as his attention, let alone his agreement.

My concern grew with my observation of the direction his life was taking. At one time, my friend Whitman, who was close to him, informed me that Johnny was already deep in debt.

In the course of one LONG sleepless night, I devised a scheme: I would call upon him for loans and advances. I would then place the amounts in expert hands against the day when they might be needed by him. Affluent as he was, I did not anticipate the difficulty I encountered, nor the bitterness (later enmity) it would engender. It goes without saying that I could have desisted at any time; but curiously, when one becomes involved in a plan such as this, one becomes more TENACIOUS at each block, more determined with each hurdle.

The amount accrued with the passing years and is now considerable. The two splendid gentlemen previously identified have done their work admirably.

I do not wish to trouble you with boresome figures or details, but I am told that the total sum advanced to me by Johnny comes to $647,000. By prudent care and investment, this figure has more than TREBLED. (Imagine it! Clearly, Money makes Money. I believe I have proved that Actors do not!) I am told that the amount may indeed increase still further. There is no possibility that the original amount will be increased, since try as I might, I have not been able to "borrow" so much as a ten-spot from the lad in some months. We have no contact. He does NOT accept my telephone calls (even when they are not collect!); my letters go unanswered; and I have been unable to attempt a personal visit in a year and a half.

When the time comes (I shall explain presently) I ask you to turn over to Johnny the above-mentioned sum. The residue, whatever it may be by that time, is yours. You will displease my shade and my memory if you do anything more—or less—than I ask.

Many years ago, I placed in my safety deposit box (and a copy in Crocker's vaults) a sealed letter containing duplicate instructions to my executors. This was a precaution in the event of my sudden death or of yours. (Have you observed what a great number of people die suddenly? If only a like number could live suddenly!)

You have richly earned your part of this. Money cannot heal wounds. I was WRONG to force your marriage. I now confess that I was thinking more of him than of you and for this I shall be eternally regretful.

There are complex matters of taxes and expenses and the like, but the experts will deal with all that for you. At one time, we seriously considered adding a legal rate of interest to his sum, but in the past months, I have decided against it.

Now—as to the propitious time: I charge you, my dear, to keep an eye on him as I have done always. In addition, Whitman will keep you informed. Crocker and Fred Freer will do likewise. Among you, there will be no error.

Johnny is to have his money returned to him when he needs it, and NOT BEFORE.

You will do this for me, I know, because you know that I have always loved you, perhaps only you. I cannot be certain. The memory of even the deepest feeling fades with the years.

Time played us a cruel trick in separating our ages, else we might have ASTOUNDED the world with a life together. (I think of dear, gentle Maude. Did she ever guess

267

that I lived with her because she was your mother? I offend you. Forgive me. Old men tell the truth.)

This screed will be delivered into your hands at the <u>appropriate</u> time.

Meanwhile, I shall be writing to you; hoping even to see you in happy <u>reality</u> at least once again.

My last thought on earth will be of you and of the beauty not only of your being, but of your spirit—in which I found, as in my art, hope for humanity.

I thank you, my dearest, for ALL you have done for me: for all you YET will do. I love you, my lovely Rose, and I bid you a perhaps goodbye.

John.

I have now read the letter four times and each time it is more overwhelming.

Thousands of images and snatches of conversation and remembered documents fly up out of memory. Some of them fit the information contained in the letter, some are at variance with it.

I am tempted now to take it as the whole truth and discard everything that does not jibe with it.

In any case, what a development!

>>> <<<

Later. All my efforts to contact Rose have been frustrated.

I phone. The maid says that *Madame est partie.* Where? *Sais pas.* She seems to have been coached. Of course, I do not believe her.

Against my better judgment (and Ruth's) I go on over there. No answer at all to the doorbell. The house does, indeed, appear to be deserted.

I give up.

5.1.73   London.   The Connaught.   TMY.

This is going to be hard to set down in longhand because my hand is trembling. In an attempt to travel light, I left my typewriter behind this time. Mistake. Would it be any easier to do on the machine? I doubt it. Not only my hand, but the rest of me is pretty shaky, too.

From the beginning.

Lunch downstairs with Ruth and Binkie. I was having a fine time, savoring the kipper pâté on Hovis bread and listening to the London theatre dirt.

All at once I saw, across the room, Rosella! Her companion was turned away from me. I put on my distance glasses. After a time, I saw it was Ena.

I made my excuses and crossed the room. Rosella looked at me and frowned as I approached. She was having difficulty remembering who I was. I said my name. She took my hand and smiled.

Ena rose, as a man would, and remained standing the whole time I visited, although I said, "Please sit down," several times. (It occurs to me now that she did this purposely in order to cut down the length of my stay. She succeeded.)

Rosella and I talked. Ena glared, more or less—mostly more. Possessive. Jealous. Dyke?

They live in Italy, in Florence, come to London at this time every year for six weeks. Yes, we must meet. Lunch? Oh, how sad. Well, another time. And so on. And on.

I left and returned to my table. I rejoined the conversation, but my head had not left the other side of the room.

Forty minutes later, I am standing in front of the Connaught. Ruth and Binkie are gone, she to Elizabeth Arden's; he, back to his office.

I am waiting for a taxi to take me to the meeting at The National Film Theatre.

Rosella and Ena come out of the hotel. I move away because I don't feel like talking to them any more.

Presently, a Rolls is brought round. Small, but a beauty. Do they bring it from Florence, I wonder?

Ena tips the attendant, tips the doorman. Rosella gets into the front seat of the car. Now Ena slides in and takes the wheel and there is an explosion in my head and I think I may pass out because in a hundred-thousand-candlepower flash I know where I first saw her! She was the man who damn near ran me down on Doheny Drive. Yes. I know as I set it down it sounds impossible if not insane, but I know I am right. Her hair was shorter. (A wig?) She wore a false mustache. And men's clothes.

Didn't I once suspect Rosella of being the author of the pink notes? Why? Because of that last one. Dante. Italian. If I am right today about Ena, I was right then.

But remember Felix's caution: "Certainty is *not* certitude."

As the revelation struck me, I moved instinctively toward the car. Ena saw me, gave me an odd look (was it a smile?) and took off.

I came right up here, back to our rooms. I have phoned the NFT, told them I have been delayed. I need a few minutes.

Now what? I am calming down, slowly.

Should I call Rosella, arrange a meeting and face her with it? Why not? Why?

Trust your instinct, is the usual advice. But what if your instinct is wrong?

There are many things in the Tumulty story that will remain unknown to me always, and I am probably dead wrong about this bizarre speculation.

Still . . .

28.xi.76   Raphaël, Paris.

Here we are, for too brief a time. Movie business involving Ruth, not me.

Yesterday, she was tied up all afternoon, so I walked. Correction. I wandered. The older I grow, the more affected I am by the rich civilization of this surpassing city. I have never been able to live here as much as I wished; now I believe I would like to die here.

I find myself standing on the Ile St. Louis, looking up at Rose Adriance Saint-Blaise's apartment. Is she alive? I wonder. How can I find out? And can I get to see her if she is?

Early this morning, I ring her number. That male/female voice comes on.

"Oui, j'écoute."

"Madame Saint-Blaise, s'il vous plaît."

"De la part de qui?"

I take a deep breath and say, *"C'est l'ambassade des Etats-Unis."*

"Un moment."

And indeed, *un moment* later, her voice. *"Oui?"*

"It's me," I say, and repeat my name.

That merry, musical laugh.

"What a curious creature you are," she says.

"Did you ever get any of my letters?"

"No, I'm afraid not."

"No, I didn't think you would."

"Does it matter?"

"To me, yes. I wanted you to know that that Tumulty letter you gave me meant—well, everything to me."

"Good."

"And you're sure you don't want it back? I could have a Xerox made of it for myself. I don't leave here until tomorrow."

"A *what* made of it?"

"A photocopy."

"No, no. I have no further need for it. I'm certain you'll do with it what needs to be done. If you haven't already."

"Thank you, then."

There was a long pause.

I was framing a final, reluctant farewell, when she startled me by saying, "What time can you drop up here today?"

"What?"

"Didn't you say it was tomorrow that you depart?"

"Yes."

"Well, then. Wouldn't it be possible for you to call on me some time today?"

"*Any* time."

"I nap after lunch. Shall we say three?"

"Great."

"There are some loose ends I want to tie."

"I'll be there."

She must have heard the apprehension in my voice, because she said, "There will be no difficulty, I assure you.

However it has seemed, I am in charge here."

"I'll be there."

>>> <<<

. . . Later. I have just returned, and I feel a migraine coming on. The well-known jagged flash in my left eye has come and gone. I have loaded up on sugar, had coffee, and started the Cafergot tablets; but I have no confidence that any of it will work today. I cannot sort things out. I am rattled. My instinct for what is true and what is not has been badly blunted by a surfeit of impressions.

This afternoon, for example. Is this the on-the-level version or is it a corrected afterthought? She changed her story. Why? Did she regret telling the truth or did she regret lying? Are the versions all that different? Yes. What of it?

I arrive at three, punctually. I ring, then steel myself for the reception. She opens the door, wearing a provocative negligée, and looks recently awakened.

"How good of you to come," she says. She leads me into her bedroom, gets back into bed, and asks, "Do you mind this? I find my bed the place in which I feel most comfortable, most safe. I was reflecting only this morning that I regret the many years I spent in the upright position. Florence Nightingale, you know, returned from the Crimean War and took to her bed and remained in it—quite happily, I believe—for fifty years! Can I offer you something?"

"Nothing."

"Good. It would be a nuisance. Everyone is off today." She laughs. "My favorite day of the week."

Would there be trouble if someone turned up? That son-of-a-bitch Pierre?

"I can't tell you," she says, "how relieved I am to have this opportunity—to make a rectification."

I don't think I have ever heard the word spoken and it threw me for a moment.

She went on. "What I told you at the cemetery that day was substantially true, but foolishly edited. I had somehow forgotten—in that atmosphere—that BD is dead and so I omitted one or two things."

"Oh?"

"We did not part as I described it, after I had given him the bank draft. It's quite true he broke down, but he soon recovered. He then asked me if I would step over to the Crillon bar with him. I declined, but he became importunate and, rather than risk a scene, I went. It was only a few steps away. He ordered a drink for himself, and a *citron presse* for me. The place was deserted and quiet.

"After he had downed his drink and ordered another, he said, 'All right, now what is all this?'

"I explained again, as carefully as I could, that the sum was his; that it represented what he had given to John across the years; that John had guarded it for him to have in the event of an emergency or of reverses.

"He looked at me angrily and said, 'I don't believe you. It's a goddamn invention—some cockeyed idea you've got about making him a hero now that he's cooled.'

"The more I protested, the less he believed me. I thought of offering to show him the letter, but in his state, he'd have called it a forgery. It was a case of the truth being unbearable. He questioned me sharply about Crocker and Freer and succeeded in muddling me and confusing me until I contradicted myself and sounded devious. Finally, I said I had to leave.

"He held me back and said, 'How come the amount is

274

exact? Don't tell me those old pirates kept it in a box some-where without investing it!'

"Now that he had a finger, you see, he wanted the hand. He was reverting to his old self.

"Then he asked, 'Was there more?' And I told him that, yes, there had been. He shouted, 'I suppose *you* got something?'

"And I said, 'Yes.'

"He wanted to know how much and I wouldn't tell him. He pressed and wheedled and threatened lawsuits and all sorts of things, but I was firm.

"Finally he laughed and asked, 'More than me?'

"And out of my irritation, I'm afraid, I said, 'Yes! *Much more.*'

"At this—and I couldn't bear to tell it to you that day—he struck me; slapped me full in the face with all his strength. By the time I had recovered from the shock, the waiter and the manager had come over and remonstrated; he was shouting at them, and I knew there was going to be trouble. I ran out as fast as I could.

"He telephoned me later, but I would not—*could* not—speak to him. He telephoned again and again. He wrote apologies and conciliatory letters from everywhere: London, Cannes, Rome. He continued to telephone. His final letter was nasty. In it, he proclaimed that he had been in touch with both Freer and Crocker in San Francisco and was satisfied this was all a hoax; that what I had turned over to him was money I had appropriated during our marriage and was now, out of guilt, returning. He could not find it within himself to believe that John had come from the grave, as it were, to save him. I suppose admitting it would have made it impossible for him to have lived with himself and his recollections of John. I'm sure he believed—to the end of his

275

days—that there was more to the story than John and I had told him."

"*Was* there?" I asked in confusion.

There was a too-long pause.

"I think you'd better go," she said. "I'm beginning to dislike you."

"Please don't. I didn't mean anything."

She gave me her hand and we said goodbye.

In the slow, slow elevator down, I realized she had not answered my last question.

5.ii.77

No more.

So there they are, the notes on Tumulty, and I know that there are to be no more.

Taken all in all, do I regret the time and energy, the effort and emotion, that went into the pursuit of this obsession? I do not know.

I do know that out of it I came to understand a truly good man in all his complexity and contradiction; also, a great deal about bloodlines and heredity and environment, about the use and misuse of talent, about the importance and unimportance of money, about youth and age, about what matters most in the short span of life, as well as about several kinds of love.

The long journey is over—not only for now, but forever.

Goodbye, John.